MISS ROYAL'S MULES

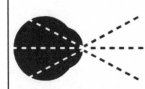

This Large Print Book carries the
Seal of Approval of N.A.V.H.

NICKEL HILL SERIES, BOOK 1

MISS ROYAL'S MULES

IRENE BENNETT BROWN

WHEELER PUBLISHING
A part of Gale, a Cengage Company

A Cengage Company

Farmington Hills, Mich • San Francisco • New York • Waterville, Maine
Meriden, Conn • Mason, Ohio • Chicago

GALE
A Cengage Company

Wheeler Publishing Large Print Western.
The text of this Large Print edition is unabridged.
Other aspects of the book may vary from the original edition.
Set in 16 pt. Plantin.

LIBRARY OF CONGRESS CIP DATA ON FILE.
CATALOGUING IN PUBLICATION FOR THIS BOOK
IS AVAILABLE FROM THE LIBRARY OF CONGRESS

ISBN-13: 978-1-4328-3858-4 (softcover alk. paper)

Published in 2019 by arrangement with Irene Bennett Brown

Printed in Mexico
1 2 3 4 5 6 7 23 22 21 20 19

In memory of my grandmother,
Pearl Pickering,
born in Skiddy, Kansas, in 1886.
And my mother,
Vestal Helberg Bennett,
who had her own adventure with mules.

ACKNOWLEDGEMENTS

To begin with, heartfelt gratitude goes to my husband, Bob. No author could ask for better help and support. At the Hell's Canyon Mule Days celebration, we enjoyed learning the wonderful character of mules — my first foray into research about them. The folks who put on that yearly event near Enterprise, Oregon, deserve a big thank-you.

My first readers, Mary Trimble and Carol Crigger, were gems providing helpful feedback, as well as praise for the story. I appreciate them so much.

I'm grateful to Bonnie Shields, known as the "Tennessee Mule Artist." Illustrator, judge, and owner of mules, she generously shared her time and expertise.

There are two stellar groups I'd find it hard to live without. They are Women Writing the West, of which I am a founding member, and Western Writers of America. I am eternally grateful to them for the inspiration, advice, and enjoyment they consistently provide.

CHAPTER ONE

Dusk was descending as Jocelyn Royal slipped into the darker interior of the Emporia livery stable. Moving through patchy shadows on the ground floor, she held her breath, worried that the liveryman might wake from his doze in his corner office chair. She gripped the weathered wood of the ladder to the loft and, hanging onto her bundle of possessions, climbed slowly, quietly. Below her, horses in their stalls snuffled and blew; some shifted restlessly, God willing covering any sounds she made.

Seconds later, nestled deep into the mounds of sweet smelling hay, hungry, tired, and exasperated beyond measure, tears burned behind her eyes. *She was not a child. How, in the name of old Hannah, had she plummeted into this predicament?*

For now, she'd bed down here in the hay, a safe place to hide. Come morning, she'd ask the stable owner for a job as hostler in the livery, feeding and watering the horses, mucking out stalls — a position no doubt uncommon to most young, unmarried women this year of nineteen hundred, even those who'd farmed like she had. Tears dampened her temples as her mind turned to her own animals she'd never see again: her old buggy horse, Napoleon, and her mules, Sadie and Blossom. Her pastures, her crops, the old barn, and the little house — all gone — unless somehow, some way, she could earn them back.

Taking a furious swipe at her eyes, ashamed of her tears, Jocelyn decided that whatever the liveryman might pay for the chores, given that he hired her, she'd accept. Until something better came along it'd have to do. At least she wouldn't have to take the saloon keeper's sordid offer. She would have had a room above the saloon and meals, but the rest of what he hinted at with a greasy smile brought her close to upchucking.

Jocelyn had barely drifted off, forearm across her eyes, when she awoke to the sound of male voices below the loft. She lay still and listened carefully for a moment, then crawled through the hay toward the edge of the loft and peeked. In the gloom beneath her, the liveryman was lighting a lantern at the same time his head tipped, listening to the soft drawl of a tall, broad-shouldered man in a wide-brimmed, black hat.

"You know of a cowhand I can hire to help trail a herd of mules up to around Skiddy?" the latter was asking. "Won't be a long drive, take just four or five days to my place."

The hostler, a weathered man of middling height, questioned in a raspy voice, "You asked at the saloon? Always some out-of-work drifters over there could need a riding job."

The stranger stood with hands on his hips, disgust in his tone. "They might be out of work, but they ain't exactly desperate. I got laughed right out the door. High-minded bunch," he growled, "they wanted nothing to do with a mule drive. Cattle or horses might interest them, they said, but not mules. That, they claimed, would be as sad as herding goats and chickens around a farmyard."

Jocelyn jerked to a sitting position and blinked sleep from her eyes, excitement building. She stuffed escaping tendrils of hair into her battered, navy-blue straw hat, wishing there was some way she might fool the rancher into thinking she was a man.

11

But she couldn't in her rose-colored, calico dress and ladies' scuffed, black brogans, not to mention her womanly figure. No men's clothes to change into. Grabbing her bundle, she flew down the ladder so fast she could have collected a hundred slivers — and wouldn't have minded. She strode purposefully into the circle of light from the lantern. "I can do that," she told the handsome stranger, who gaped at her. "I can herd your mules for you, sir."

"Where in the Billy Hill did you come from?" the hostler asked, holding the lantern high for a good look at her. "You're a woman, for Christ sakes."

"I came from up there." She nodded in the direction of the loft. "And, yes, I'm a woman. Doesn't matter a whit in this instance, though; I'm more than able." She waved the heat of the lantern away from her face and noted rejection in the stranger's otherwise soft, brown eyes. He eyed her head to toe with dismissal.

"You're a woman," he said bluntly. "I'm looking for a man for this job."

"We've already made it clear I'm a woman; now let's put that aside. Mister, I want this job, and I swear I can do it." She stood straight, chin up. Blessed if she would beg, but she had to make him understand.

"I'm sorry, Miss," he removed his hat. "Maybe you could. But it wouldn't be . . . proper — you, me, and my hired hand, Sam Birdwhistle, together trailing my mule herd — two men and a lady. You can see how wrong that'd be, can't you?"

"I can see it's not half as unfitting as the upstairs job at the saloon I was offered," she retorted, her face blazing. "And listen, please. I don't want to tell you any old sad story, but this is the way it is: when I was just a girl ten years or so back, I bundled my sick Gram into our old wagon pulled by our horse Napoleon, and I drove us all the way from Kansas City, Missouri, to a farm my papa had abandoned here in Kansas."

Neither he nor the hostler appeared particularly interested, but she wasn't finished. "I ran the farm by myself." Her hands gestured like wild butterflies. "I plowed, planted, cultivated, built a dam in the creek for more water. I did everything from turning ground to marketing what I grew, besides taking care of my gram until she got better and helped some. My father came home from fighting in one hostility or other down in Mexico. He used to be a school teacher, was never good at farming." She hesitated to gather her scrambling thoughts.

The stranger seized the opportunity to

shove in his two cents. "A woman like you needs to go back there, to the farm and to your father, so he can look after you." Under thick, dark brows his eyes were thoughtful, kindly. "Go on back to your pa, Miss. Find a man, get married, and have children." His expression said, *"Like a woman is supposed to do."*

"Well," Jocelyn told him, "I'd do what you say if I could. Our farm was lost to the bank, and my father has passed. I've got nowhere and nothing to go to if you don't hire me. Unless, of course, you think it's *proper* I accept work upstairs at the saloon." If she was making him feel responsible for sending her into the pits of hell, maybe he would change his mind. Alone in the world and with nobody to turn to, she'd never admit how verily terrified she was of being reduced to such a life.

He scowled, his fingers riddling his hair until the black waves practically stood on end. "Hell, no, I don't want anything like that happening. But, Miss, you really ain't my concern." Clamping his hat on, he turned and stomped toward the door, dust rising from the straw-strewn dirt floor. He hesitated for a second, then moved forward again before whipping around to face Jocelyn, standing stock still for a full minute glaring at her. He sighed, clearly not pleased with the decision he was arriving at. "Maybe, if I changed my plans some, I could hire you."

"Changed in what way?" She kept her voice calm and steady at the same time her heart thumped with hope.

"My cook normally drives the supply wagon, and I, with the help of a cowboy who had to leave us, drove the mules. Sam Birdwhistle, my cook, could take over the other riding chore, and you could drive the wagon and cook for us." He was shaking his head derisively against the plan even as he laid it out.

Jocelyn moved to take his hand in a firm handshake before he could backtrack and change his mind. "Thank you, sir, thank you so much. You won't be sorry, my word on it. My name is Jocelyn Belle Royal, or Jocey." Her childhood nickname didn't seem a good fit anymore, but that would be up to him.

"Whit Hanley," he grunted, "and I think it remains to be seen whether I'll be sorry or not, Miss Royal. I ain't giving up hiring a cowhand for the job, so you can consider this employment temporary."

She shrugged, and a grin tugged at her lips. "I wasn't thinking of it for a lifetime

15

occupation, Mr. Hanley. But I'll see your mules to where you're going." She didn't ask what the pay might be, but he seemed to read her mind, or maybe he was reading the questioning look on her face.

He grunted. "If this works out, I'll give you what I'd pay anybody I hired. Twenty-five dollars for the time of the drive; likely that'll be four or five days. I intended to add another five dollars per mule that's sold, if the person stays to help through the sales. However long that'll be, the pay's a dollar a day, but you'll likely want to be shut of the job before then."

"I'll stay on to the finish, Mr. Hanley," she said with quick seriousness, "and do my part to earn your fair offer." She hid the giddiness she felt inside. Fair? It was a godsend and a fortune toward what she needed to buy back her farm . . . to have a good life again, from her own hands.

His deep-brown eyes glinted frustration in the lantern light. "I reckon if I don't regain my good sense, I'll be back for you in the morning." He turned away, striding for the door.

"No, not in the morning, Mr. Hanley." She hurried after him and reached for his arm, then let her hand drop when he turned. "I'm going with you now." She tried not to sound as desperate as she felt. "Like I said, this opportunity you've given me is all I have. That and this." She held up her bundle, a red shawl holding her entire belongings: a few items of clothing, a favorite book from her past, a precious bar of Ivory soap and a towel, a pocket tobacco can of seeds, and Gram's crochet hooks with a bit of crochet work Gram had done.

He seemed to be weighing his options once again and disliking all of them. "Hell's fire, I'm rightly insane to even consider this!" He glared, taking her elbow. "All right. I left my team and wagon hitched at the mercantile."

Out front of the general store, he reached to assist her onto the seat of the supply wagon, but Jocelyn waved him away and, holding her skirts carefully, clambered up without aid. She wasn't helpless, was not going to be a burden in any way, if he was thinking that. A minute or so later their wagon rattled along the main street as Hanley goaded his mule team from town and Jocelyn breathed deep satisfaction.

A silvery spring moon was beginning to lighten the way as they moved along in a night that smelled of green grass, fresh air, and wildflowers. Whit Hanley spoke first. "Not my business, I reckon, but are you telling me you never had a place to stay, a home or family, since your pa passed?"

She drew a deep breath. "Not to speak of, although three days ago I had a job and a place to live. Waitress at the Sunrise Café back in town, and a room at Mrs. Lottie Williams's Boarding House." She braced herself, but, for the sake of propriety, she prayed he'd not ask any more.

"What happened you're not there now?" He shook the reins to quicken the team's step.

It was a minute or two before she could admit, "I turned a bowl of pickled beets over the bald head of a gentleman diner." She added, "Truth to tell, he wasn't a gentleman."

"How's that?"

Normally, she wouldn't repeat anything so personal to anyone, but if it would help her keep this job . . . Her face hot, she continued, "He — he sneaked a pinch at my backside, thinking it was funny, 'til I crowned him. He was mad as a snake that'd been stepped on, then. Cursed me like someone possessed, old coot." She stared straight ahead into the darkness. This stranger was probably like many fellows, who thought it was their right to touch a waitress or barmaid anytime and any way

18

they wanted. He surprised her with his next words.

"Somebody ought to've stood up for you and coldcocked him. Who was he? What's his name?"

"Doesn't matter now, but Deeter Williams is his name," she replied quietly. "He is a barber and Mrs. Lottie Williams's husband. You know, owner of the boarding house. I told the truth, but she claimed that I lied to the café owner about what happened, tarnished her husband's 'fine reputation.' I was fired for insulting one of the café's best customers, and, without money for rent, I was also forced from Mrs. Williams's boarding house."

She couldn't help thinking about Kansas women who, in the cause of suffrage, fought for equality. Why then, did there have to be women who turned a blind eye to their own kind and supported a male liar when they had to know better?

"Hardly fair." Whit Hanley echoed her conclusion in the matter. He chuckled softly. "I say good for you, what you did. He deserved a lot more. Anybody can see you're a nice young woman, Miss Royal. That's one reason I feel this is not a good idea, hiring you for the drive. It ain't seemly, is what I'm saying." He was quiet a moment. "But that saloon owner . . . I couldn't let that happen to you, neither."

"I appreciate that, Mr. Hanley, truthfully. Anyways, that's how I ended up sleeping in the livery loft. I was going to ask for a job at the stable tomorrow morning."

"Hmph," the man grunted to that, and Jocelyn smiled.

They rolled along, wagon wheels creaking. If campaigning for the suffrage cause was a paid job, Jocelyn thought, her mind wandering, she'd join without hesitation. But first she had to have work that'd provide food and shelter.

Unfortunately, from the time Kansas organized as a territory, the aim for women's equality was a thankless, unpaid, never-ending struggle for those women brave enough to battle scorn from folks who didn't see the matter their way. With one gratifying success in 1887, mostly due to women crusaders' tireless efforts, but with support from men, too, Kansas women won the right not only to vote but to run for office in civic elections. Jocelyn's chin went high, thinking about those determined women who would not give up.

State and federal voting rights were still being denied Kansas women, but the day would come, right soon possibly, when that would change — she felt sure. In the meantime, she had a job as cook on a mule drive, and from hat to socks she couldn't be more thankful.

They had traveled a mile or so out of town when Whit Hanley drew the team and wagon off the road into a large pasture. A dark grove of trees was outlined in the distance. The sound of a braying mule and another answering was unmistakable. Moonlight showed a patch of perhaps thirty or forty mules bedding down or grazing. The outline of a rider on a moose of a long-eared mule poked his way around them. When he came close, dismounting to unhitch the mule team from the wagon, Jocelyn saw that the drover was black as night.

"Sam Birdwhistle," Whit Hanley said, as she climbed from the wagon, "this lady is Miss Jocelyn Royal. I hired her tonight to cook for us and to drive the supply wagon the next few days. You'll cowboy these mules from here on, like you've been saying you'd rather do. And we both know your cooking ain't anything to brag about."

"Appreciate that, Whit," he replied in a deep, rich voice, as he removed the mules' harness. "Howdo, Miss Jocelyn." He lifted his hat and turned to tell her, "We got some beans and biscuits yonder by the fire" — he waved toward the red glow in the distance — "iffen y'all are hungry." He clapped his hat back on.

"Thank you." She stretched her shoulders back against her tiredness. At mention of food her stomach rumbled. "I could stand to eat." She walked toward the cook-fire. Now that she was here, she wondered if her decision was smart, or the most foolish thing she'd ever agreed to do. Here she was, with two strange men. Granted, both appeared nice enough, gentlemen, even. But she didn't know them from Adam's worst enemies, whoever Adam and his off ox were in the old saying. These men could be outlaws, thieves, rapists, murderers for all she knew. If she wasn't so tired she'd just slip away in the dark and start walking, like a tumbleweed in the wind but to better promise. She crossed her fingers and decided to trust them for now.

CHAPTER TWO

For the time being Jocelyn put frightening thoughts aside and accepted the steaming plate of beans and biscuit handed her. Seated on a supply keg, she forked food into her mouth far too gustily for a lady, as Whit Hanley had described her. "That was v-very good," she said numbly, later, as she began to nod over the empty plate in her lap.

Whit Hanley was asking her if she knew this country, the Flint Hills, well, since she'd be driving the wagon ahead of the mules that he and Birdwhistle would be herding. She was trying to answer, but the words were like cotton stuffed in her mouth. "I d-do," she stammered. She was telling the truth, but that was all she could say about it now.

Through a fog of exhaustion, she heard her new boss say, "You can sleep in the wagon, Miss Royal. There's an extra bedroll in there off to the left side that you're welcome to. We'll talk again in the morning."

"Um-Um," she replied and stumbled toward the wagon. She climbed inside on weighted limbs, untied her brogans, and pulled them off, the last possible thing she could accomplish this day, she was certain. Crawling around in the wagon bed, she tugged the bedroll away from the boxes and bags where Mr. Hanley said it would be, spread it, and plopped down amid the dusty smells of potatoes and onions. Already drifting off, she pulled the blanket around her.

One good meal, she told herself, one good night's sleep, and she'd part ways with these men and, when safely away, keep trying to find honest woman-work, if she could. Like teaching small school children — she felt smart enough, though she'd had no formal training. She'd applied to three different country schools and was convinced that it was her aloneness, a wandering young woman without roots, that suspicioned them into turning her down. If she had to, she'd try one more time. She yawned and fell asleep to the soft sounds of the Neosho River a few yards away, the singing of night-time insects in the tall grass and the trees, and the snuffling and nickering of mules.

Jocelyn woke in the half-dark before dawn,

thinking that she should be on her way, soon. Blinking sleep from her eyes, she saw that she was surrounded by a wealth of supplies: sacks labeled flour, sugar, beans. Crates of canned peaches and tomatoes. Arbuckles' coffee, lard, dried beef, salt pork, carrots, apples, and more. If she were staying on with the drive, it would be a plentitude of choices to cook from. In a far corner of the wagon bed there were stacks of wood and extra tack — halters, bridles, a spare saddle, tools. Supplies meant not just for the drive, she reasoned, but also for use at the destination. It made sense.

She sat up and yanked on her brogans, tying them with flying fingers. There was the pay Whit had offered. She'd be a ninny to walk away from a fortune like that before giving the two men a fair chance — a day, maybe two, to show the truth of their character. Over the side of the wagon she saw Sam Birdwhistle wound tight in his bedroll beneath a tree, still asleep, while Whit was up in the dim light and stirring the fire, putting on a pot of coffee. *Her job.* "Morning," she mumbled a response to his greeting of the same.

She hurried past him and zigzagged through the herd of grazing mules and their fragrant dung, careful not to come up suddenly behind any of them. A mule could kick for little or no reason, and a swift kick could break a person's leg or knock them senseless. In minutes, she was deep in bur oak and cottonwood trees by the river. She did her business in the shelter of thick bushes and then washed up in cool water at the river's edge, finger-combing and re-braiding her hair. Set to return to camp, from the corner of her eye, she saw a slight movement in the woods to her left. Heart pounding, she went slowly to her knees behind a hackberry tree. Staying low in the scratchy grass and weeds, plagued about possible rattlesnakes, she strained to see.

The outline of the man and horse were vague in the trees, now still as a statue. Cold shivers raced along her spine, for no clear, honest to goodness reason she could claim. There was movement again as the rider lifted a cigarette to his mouth. Was he watching their camp, keeping out of sight the way he appeared to be? If so, why? Or was he a drifter with his own camp there-abouts? Maybe a ranch hand or farmer who'd stopped to roll a cigarette, take a smoke while on a search for a stray cow?

She waited and watched, then felt a jolt of surprise when a second rider joined the first. They seemed to be talking, but no way to tell from where she watched. A huge grasshopper landed on her arm. She brushed it off and rubbed clean where the insect left tobacco-like spit. When she looked up the riders had vanished — as if they'd only been in her imagination. She waited while her heart tried for a reasonable rhythm and shakiness left her legs before hurrying to camp.

"Sorry." Jocelyn hesitated in front of Whit Hanley. "I'll have pancakes and bacon rustled up right off."

"No need for cooking this morning." He shook his head. He took a long draught of coffee from a blue granite cup. "Sam says there are leftover biscuits in the grub box, over to the wagon," he nodded in that direction. "We'll have cold biscuits, a couple cans of peaches, and coffee. Morning is warming up to be a hot day, for May. I'd like to hustle this outfit along the road."

While they ate, thoughts of the riders she'd seen in the woods wouldn't let go of Jocelyn's mind. She was about to tell Whit what she'd seen but concluded he'd think he'd been burdened with a trembling lily. She'd hate that, and it would do her little good. If the riders back there had trouble in mind, she was sure Hanley and Birdwhistle could settle it themselves, perhaps with no harm to anybody. At least, she hoped so. Anyway, the Flint Hills of Kansas weren't exactly uninhabited wasteland. Endless pastures of grazing cattle, an occasional windmill, and fences showed civilization, and of course they'd see other folks from time to time. Despite feeling less than positive about her decision to keep quiet, Jocelyn mentally closed the door to the subject; it was the men's lookout, not hers.

After the meal, the three of them set to breaking camp. While Jocelyn washed tin plates and utensils and stowed everything back in its place in the wagon, the two men fed the milling mules and watered them at the river. The boss himself would take the night watch this time. Jocelyn smiled, feeling almost affection for the long-eared creatures, nearly as beautiful as horses, which, of course, they partly were, being half donkey and half horse. Some of these mules were black; others were grey, sorrel, or bay. Fewer were white, buckskin, roan, or dun. Some were tall, others short, all of them sleek and healthy. Come down to it, she liked their company. When she asked Sam why he named his mule Rover, he said it was because the towering critter tended to wander, to rove until he trained it otherwise. And, no, he didn't name him after no dog, and it wasn't the first time he'd been asked.

Using patience, apples, and a bit of coddling talk, Jocelyn got her mule team, named Zenith and Alice, harnessed up and hooked to the supply wagon. She took another few minutes to talk quietly to them and stroke their necks, as she would have her mules Sadie and Blossom on her farm. Mules were more apt to do your bidding the better they were treated, in her experience. Whit Hanley looked on with seeming approval. Not for the first time, she recognized how little she knew about the man. Time would tell how big a fool she was or wasn't, throwing in with him and his friend.

Stowing the grub box earlier, she'd spied a sleek Winchester rifle and a beaten-up shotgun under the wagon seat. Nothing uncommon about that — most ranchers and cowboys had weapons with them. Besides using the guns for hunting, cattle rustlers still plagued the Flint Hills and needed to be dealt with. It seemed that anywhere in cattle country there'd always be the lawless stripe trying to make money off somebody else's hard work.

In their last ten years together, Papa had taught her to shoot both a shotgun and a rifle. As much as he wanted Jocelyn "to be a proper lady," he felt it no harm for her to know how to do two important things — climb a windmill and shoot a gun. It was a bonus to him that he didn't have to put aside whatever book he was reading, while she went rabbit hunting for their supper or greased the windmill's gear system.

According to the peddler who sold Papa the weapon, the rifle she used was a Springfield Model 1861 that had done impressive service in the Civil War. Both weapons were later traded for a cow and calf, not a bad thing. Killing rabbits, prairie chickens, and possum was far different than shooting a human being, but she little doubted she could do that, too, if matters came to it.

Jocelyn went over to where Whit Hanley saddled his roan that he referred to as "Ol' Blue." "Is there any chance you'd have reason to believe outlaws might be after your herd of mules, with intention to steal them, Mr. Hanley?" Her lips pressed tight as she waited.

He turned slowly, his eyes boring into her. "I don't figure any such. Why do you ask?"

Tilting her head back and putting a lid on the hammering under her breastbone, she told him about the pair of riders she'd spotted by the river.

A deep frown creased his forehead, although his eyes didn't reveal a lot. He looked toward the area in the woods she spoke of and shook his head, his frown slowly fading. "We'll keep an eye out, but I think you're right in figuring they were cowboys from nearby, just taking their ease, or farmers looking for a stray critter. I wouldn't worry, Miss Royal. Unless you'd be more comfortable not making this drive? You don't have to, you know. I could leave you off with some farm family along the way and maybe pick up an extra hand to help me with the drive at the same time. Give some serious thought to that, Miss Royal." He swung into the saddle and clicked his tongue. "Good Ol' Blue." He patted his horse's neck as they ambled off to round up the mules.

Thinking to get rid of her? "I thought I should warn you," she called after him, scuffing dirt on their fire. "I wasn't saying I didn't want to work on this drive." Hands on her hips, she hid her worry. "Just curious — where *did* you come by these mules, Mr. Hanley? This drive start in Oklahoma? Texas?"

She scooted more dirt onto the ashes with the side of her work shoe. The boss might consider her nosey, but she wasn't only curious; she needed to know a few things. Most of her life she'd found it hard to trust others, with good reason. It wasn't all that easy now, with these two strangers, as much as she was beginning to like them and that after only a few hours. Gullible as her nature tended to be at unfortunate times, Hanley and Birdwhistle could be *thieves who stole this herd.* In which case, she'd be part and parcel of the crime, if she continued with them.

"Begging your pardon if this is a bother, but I'm interested to know how you come by the mules?"

He'd reined the roan around to face her. A bit curtly, he told her, "I bought most of them in one bunch that included a belled mule before I started out. The others a few at a time on the way up from the Missouri Bootheel to Kansas. Missouri has more mules to the acre than anywhere else. Borrowed my stake from a bank in Willow Springs. Got the mules cheap so have a chance to sell them high. Anything else you have to know, Miss Royal?" he asked bluntly.

Her face heated. Oh, she had questions aplenty, like where was his actual home? Did he have a family, a wife, little children? Or was he a loner? Sam, a drifter, too? Were they good men as they seemed, or ruffians in disguise? Her mind buzzed with questions that would allow her to know him better, but they would keep for the time being. "No. Thank you. That's all." She gave him a half smile, in exchange for having riled him. "We can go now."

They set off on a wagon trail that paralleled the Neosho River in a northwesterly direction. Jocelyn led, driving the supply wagon behind Alice, the sorrel belled mule that Sam referred to as "an old maid know-it-all mule." Whit said that in Spanish, Alice would be called "Madrina" meaning "godmother" and she was that, too. Teamed with her was Zenith, a good-sized grey mule. Both were well-trained and dependable as sunrise, according to Sam and Whit. The rest of the herd would follow Alice and Zenith, and a couple of other lead mules, with only occasional trouble. That looked to be true as the mule herd plodded along a quarter mile behind her wagon, dust rising into the blue sky.

Jocelyn glanced over her shoulder. The boss and Sam Birdwhistle pushed the herd along from behind; now and then one of them riding ahead, and out, to bring a wayward mule back where it belonged.

Facing forward again, Jocelyn smiled to herself, feeling a fair amount of contentment. It was a beautiful morning. She loved these Flint Hills stretched out in front of her as far as the eye could see. She likened the hills to immense grass-covered ocean waves, save where they were broken by rim-rock or tree-choked draws. Wildflowers dotted the green. On both sides of the wagon road, bluestem grass grew most as high as the wagon sides.

Before the white man came, the Flints were home to the Osage Indians. Flint rock under the rich soil was sharp as steel. Below layers of flint was ancient limestone, fine material for building homes and corrals, farm outbuildings, and fence posts.

Whit had said they would stay to the wagon trail along the Neosho River as long as possible. When fenced pastures, or a herd of cattle they ought not to disrupt, presented a problem in their path, they would take to the common road, or ask permission to cross a rancher's property, opening gates and closing them once the herd passed through. He hoped to make fifteen miles a day, or more, if possible.

As her wagon team and the following herd plodded along at a slow walk, she continued to take an occasional look back. At times, when the mule herd fell farther behind in the rising dust, it was harder to see Sam Birdwhistle and Whit Hanley on their mounts. Other times she could make out the mules being pushed to move faster. The drive was a slow, tedious effort, mile after mile, in any event. But each mile would add up to a nice sum for her at the end.

With little else to do except keep her team moving on the road and being entertained by the funny flopping of their tall ears, Jocelyn took the opportunity to consider her future. For certain she could use the money Whit Hanley said would be her pay. Maybe this job would lead to others paying as well, or better. It'd nearly killed her when she'd been evicted from the farm she loved to her very core. She loved her father, had missed him for the years of absence from her life. When they found one another, he insisted on taking over running the farm. It embarrassed him that his young daughter drudged like a farmhand. Papa wanted her to be the lady her mother had been before she died. He probably felt guilty, too, for being away so many years.

The truth was, the farm was her everything; she didn't mind the work, but she let him have his way. Because he was Papa, head of the house, after all.

Papa was a good man, but over their years together he'd proved to be not worth shucks at farming. He'd been a school teacher in earlier times, before her mother's death, and he went off drifting in his grief. He was a lover of reading books and tended to be lazy when it came to hard work. He was rash with money and borrowed from the bank with each losing crop, until they owed so much the farm belonged to the bank and not to them. Illness caught up with Papa, infection from an old gunshot wound he'd got down in Mexico during the time he'd fought with Indian oil workers against the dictator, Diaz. Applying all manner of medical treatment, from hot kerosene cloth packs to whiskey, she had frantically tried to save him, but he was gone in a matter of days.

Alone, Jocelyn buried him on the farm under his favorite shady elm tree. With her heart too broken even for tears, she had tied her few personal belongings in the red shawl that had belonged to her mother. How much she would have liked to have more than wisps of memories. But she was just a tot when her mama died of consumption.

With her shoulders pushed back, an awful fluttering pain in her chest, Jocelyn walked away from the farm and her father's grave, setting out with a single, determined aim: to find a way to earn back her farm. Or else.

Jocelyn was jerked from her reverie by the sudden shout in a harsh female voice, "You there in the chuck wagon, you take yourself offen my land, hear?" Jocelyn stiffened when she spotted the grey-haired woman in men's overalls and faded, brown shirt, her face a fierce map of wrinkles circled by her sunbonnet. She held a shotgun icily steady, aimed straight at Jocelyn. Somewhere in the distance a cow bawled.

Too stunned to react for a minute, Jocelyn found her voice, "Y-yes, of course, I will." She drew Zenith and Alice to a stop under a canopy of trees. "I'll wait here for my boss so that I can explain to him . . ."

The shotgun boomed, scattering dirt a mere foot from her wagon's wheel. Startled, her team flinched and began to bolt. "Whoa, there, whoa, mules." Jocelyn pulled up on the lines as the mules skittered. With pounding heart, she spoke in a calming but firm voice. "Whoa, Zenith, easy there, Alice. We're fine here, easy mules, easy." At the same time her blood churned in anger. She was hot, covered with dust, and growing short on patience. What on earth was the woman thinking? She turned and glared. "I plan to do your bidding," she said tightly, "but first I have to talk with my boss before I change our route."

"Ain't no talkin' necessary." She motioned with her arm and barked, "Keep movin' off yonder to the main road. Them that's followin' will be treated to some buckshot direct if they don't pay me mind and get offen my land."

Jocelyn began to perspire heavily despite the cool shade of the trees. "I'll go, as you ask," she continued to maintain, "but I'd like to talk first to my —"

The shotgun raised again, Jocelyn looked down the barrel while her heart climbed to her throat. She stared at the woman in complete disbelief, frozen.

CHAPTER THREE

The old woman snorted and with a grimace said, "No confounded talkin'. I already told you! Too many herds been pushin' through without a by-your-leave, grazin' to the ground the grass I need for my cattle. Now git on, like I said. If your herdsmen back there got good sense, they'll follow your grub wagon."

"All right." Jocelyn dropped brief thought of the two guns underneath the wagon seat. This crazy person could blow her brains out before she could even bring one of them up. She gathered her nerve and said through gritted teeth, meaning every word, "But if you fire that shotgun again, I'm reporting you to the county sheriff, and I'll press charges." She might anyway, if she lived through this maniacal nonsense.

The woman cackled with laughter, "You talkin' about my brother, George. He's county sheriff and part owner of this land

I'm protectin'. Now move along outta here."
She waved the shotgun, then steadied it a
third time against her shoulder.

Head high and nervous chills traveling her
spine, Jocelyn clicked her tongue. "Haw, get
up mules." She flicked the lines over their
backs and wheeled them off the river trail.
Blind with anger mixed with fear, she failed
to see a low-hanging branch until it whacked
hard into her shoulder and chest. She
gulped back the pain and took a quick look
behind her.

Etched against the blue sky, the mule herd
was a small crawling mass circled by dust.
Could her companions have heard the
shotgun blast? Did they make out any of
this kerfuffle with this dangerous woman, at
this distance? Sam Birdwhistle was a tiny
figure on his mule, too far away for her to
warn him, or have his help if the old woman
took a notion to shoot her *and* the mule
team after all. The old thing looked and
sounded crazy enough. Jocelyn saw no sign
of Hanley.

As she drove toward open pastures in the
direction of the country road the woman
ordered her to, the air filled with the angry
buzz of bees. She realized too late the
branch she'd struck had held a bee hive,
and she'd jarred it a'kilter. She swatted to

40

no avail. Bees zeroed in, stinging the backs of her hands holding the reins, her neck and face. Zenith and Alice began to fight their bits, braying, leaping, and dancing, then breaking into a hard run to escape the bees droning and stinging in their tall ears. All Jocelyn could do was hold on tight for what seemed like passing years. After a half mile or so the team slowed, and she drew them to a halt, letting them blow.

She hopped from the wagon and stroked the mules' necks. "Good Alice, good Zenith. I'm so, so sorry. I didn't like those bees any more than you did. I'm glad you got us away from those stinging son-of-a-guns — and that ornery old woman! We'll be fine," she said, despite the fact her face and hands felt like they were on fire. "We can go on soon as you're ready." Maybe her team was used to loud noises, had been raised around such as the shotgun blast, otherwise they'd have more than flinched — bees stinging their sensitive ears was a whole other thing.

In truth, Jocelyn didn't know whether to curse or cry. When the bees attacked, the old woman cackled with laughter so hard she gasped for breath. *Cursed old woman,* Jocelyn thought, looking over her shoulder. *She could have asked nicely. I'd have removed from her land just the same.*

God willing, Hanley and Birdwhistle would be all-of-a-piece and not bleeding from buckshot when they caught up with her at the camp she'd set up. If they did.

An hour passed before the men slowly hazed the mules into a circle outside the camp area and her wagon. The mules clearly welcomed the stop, some beginning to graze and one or two rolling in the grass to scratch sweat-itchy hides or for pure relaxation. Jocelyn had already unhitched and staked out Zenith and Alice, knowing with satisfaction that the other mules would then stay close by, most of the herd seeming to revere Alice and her tinkling bell.

Whit unsaddled his blue roan and, with a long rope to allow for plenty of grazing, staked out his mount. Sam did the same with his tall, rusty-colored mule, Rover.

"We saw you change direction," Whit said, striding over to the campfire, where Jocelyn had steaks sizzling in a skillet. He scrubbed a hand down over his face. "Sorry we weren't on hand when you needed us. We thought we heard a shot. Saw a woman who admitted she fired her shotgun in your direction. For trespassing." He stared at her bite-pimpled face in puzzled concern.

"Bees," she said by way of explanation. "Yes, the blamed old thing sure enough

turned her shotgun on me." She tamped down anger and gingerly wiped her perspiring forehead that was knotted from bee stings. Her eyelids were so swollen she could barely see Whit's face. "She threatened you, too?" Her tone was biting, despite her efforts not to explode.

He shrugged. "No, not exactly. She was still there, sitting in the shade under a tree, shotgun across her lap, watching us and no doubt ready to make a fuss if we didn't turn off and follow you." At Jocelyn's scowl, he continued, "I think she took ornery pleasure plaguing you. Some folks can be like that even when it ain't necessary. Like I said, I'm right sorry."

As Jocelyn turned the steaks in the skillet she recited the ordeal in steaming detail. "I ever see her again I'll want to wring her scrawny neck!"

"We gave her an earful." As if that was punishment enough, Jocelyn thought, rolling her eyes. He pulled plates and eating utensils from the grub box. "She didn't apologize, but she did sell us a jar of milk with cream to the top. I'll fetch it from my saddlebag."

Sam had mixed dirt with water, and he handed Jocelyn a large handful, kindness shining in his brown eyes. "Mud for the bee stings, Miss Jocelyn. Smear it on, and it'll take the fire out of them places you got stung." His expression turned grim. "Ain't right, what happened to you back there. You might'a been kilt."

Jocelyn nodded. "Yes, I might've, the way that old woman carried on, firing that shotgun." She thanked him for the mud and put it to work. Likely she looked a fright, but the mud began to deliciously cool the burning. With her face covered with mud she probably looked like she could be Sam's sister, she thought with wry humor. How she looked didn't matter. Different circumstances she might fret her appearance, but here with these strangers she had more important things to worry about.

A short while later she loaded steak, potatoes, and gravy onto the plates the men held out to her. While they ate, apple cobbler baked in a Dutch oven nestled in coals from the fire, sending a heavenly aroma into the evening air. "The old witch's cream is going to taste awfully good poured on cobbler," Jocelyn told the men.

"You're a fine cook," Whit said bluntly as he cut his steak and took a huge forkful.

"A mighty fine cook, Miss Royal," Sam agreed, his eyes gleaming with pleasure as he chewed.

She nodded, feeling a trifle better. She'd been tiredly wondering what was different about Whit's appearance and noted that he wore a holstered gun on his hip when he hadn't before. He caught her staring, and she waved her fork and asked, "If you don't mind, were you wearing that sidearm when you had the discussion with the old woman?"

He nodded but said nothing.

Jocelyn's lip twitched. "I see."

"It ain't what you're thinking, Miss Royal. I don't wear this .44 to shoot old ladies. Or to scare them."

"But you are wearing it of a sudden." She drained the last swallows of coffee from her cup. The sun was going down, the song of crickets beginning to fill the hot silence as she waited patiently for him to say more.

He sat on his heels, slowly chewing his steak, making no effort to explain. He stared absently into the red, smoking coals of the campfire, as though he were someplace far from camp. Or would like to be?

"You are expecting trouble of some kind, though?" she persisted, dying for an honest answer. He knew why he wore the gun. Why'd he not be forthright and tell her? She pushed her hair back from where it itched bee stings on the side of her face.

"Maybe," he agreed. The dismissive look he gave her put an end to the conversation. As he stood to help himself to more potatoes, he added a sketchy smile, possibly meant to placate her. It didn't.

Later, preparing to dish up the cobbler in the flickering light from the campfire, she studied his profile, her mind churning. An ordinary worker couldn't expect her boss to share every thought and plan — things none of her lookout. But if there was a matter that'd put her in trouble as well as him, or danger, she blamed well deserved to know and be warned.

Trouble maybe, he'd said . . . What was that supposed to mean? She scooped a pile of fruity cobbler with flaky brown crust onto a plate. If it wasn't to persuade the old woman to behave herself, did it have something to do with the men she'd seen in the woods? She gave the steaming apple-fragrant plate of cobbler to Sam and another to Whit. She brought them the jar of cream for pouring. Did he expect a pack of wolves to attack his mule herd, something of that nature? What trouble, to his mind, required his sidearm? In irritation, she realized that he'd allow her to wear her tongue to a thread and still not answer her question.

As she washed and dried the dishes and

put them away in the grub box, Jocelyn faced a thought she'd had earlier: was it simply Whit Hanley's way to be so close-mouthed? Or was he hiding something — something that she ought to know about? He didn't seem like a man who'd knowingly put a woman, herself, in danger. So . . . was her mind concocting imaginary troubles where a sparsity existed? And did he think of her as no more than a pestering fly with unnecessary questions?

Too tired to study the matter further tonight, she headed for her bedroll in the wagon. As she lay curled under the blanket, staring out at a star-filled sky, Sam's low voice sang to the mules, a comforting old song, *Some Folks Do,* a lullaby to her as well.

Next day, hour after hour, they continued to follow the long, dusty road over gentle swells of grass-rich country under a dome of blue sky. Mostly Jocelyn felt alone in the great emptiness, having been passed once beyond the town of Americus by a man in a horse-drawn buggy, clipping right along with rooster tails of dust following. An hour or two later, a buckboard carrying a ranch couple passed from the other direction. She waved, and they waved back, a pleasant exchange that broke the tedium.

Late that second day, a heaviness settled in her chest as she realized that as the crow flies — just directly west on the other side of the Neosho River — was her farm. Correctly, the farm she *used* to own, in the Neosho Valley. As she drove on, remembering times good and bad on that little farm, tears leaked unwanted from her eyes. She supposed it was childish to feel that the bank blood-sucked the farm from her. Papa was partly the cause, as was the depression a few years back in the late 1800s, which hurt the whole country. It wasn't only the banker's greed. She brushed the tears away, breathed deep, and flicked the lines over the mules' backs. She had fought and worked so hard to make the land provide a living for her and Gram. The Neosho Valley farm had to be hers again — it had to be! She drove on, her spine stiffened, the ache in her heart gradually easing.

They had eaten their evening meal of stew and biscuits. Jocelyn was finishing cleanup by the last light of day, feeling content that they were that much closer to their destination. A mule nickered, one or two others stomped and snorted nervously. *They're aware of something, or someone coming,* Jocelyn thought and raised her head to look.

Sure enough, minutes later a stranger on a bay horse rode into their camp. She went still, curious. Whit's hand rested close to his gun. Sam faded into the shadows.

"Good evenin'." Cheery and plump, their visitor astride a shuffling horse removed his bowler hat. He tipped his bald head in Jocelyn's direction, before directing his words to Whit Hanley. "I'm Duane Rawlins, circuit judge. I was in that little town of Dunlap yonder," he nodded in that direction, "ruling on a case of a stolen calf, when I saw from the town hall window you folks passing through town with your mule herd." His smile was broad as he put his hat back on. "Here to tell you I purely admire these critters, beautiful animals, sure enough. Once things settled in Dunlap I was able to catch up with you." He pulled a handkerchief from his pocket and wiped his brow. "Lordy but that's a nice lookin' animal" — he pointed — "that dark-brown mule yonder that's got a black nose. Yeah, and that brown one right there, with the white nose. You mind if I ask where you're goin' with them?"

Whit answered, "Trailing them up to near Skiddy, where I intend to hold 'em until I can arrange a sale."

The judge smiled. "Hopin' to hear that,

that you'd have them for sale. I need me a good team of mules and wonder if we could palaver a bit on a price?"

Standing aside, observing the ensuing conversation, Jocelyn's jaw dropped when Whit said the judge could have the pair for two hundred dollars. Whit added, "In some mule markets they'd be costing twice that, each."

"I know." The judge chuckled with pleasure, while reaching inside his vest pocket. "I've seen them sell for a lot more in Kansas City." While the men discussed delivery of the mules to Judge Rawlins's ranch, Jocelyn's mind spun.

Two hundred dollars for two mules out of a herd of forty or fifty? The shock was too much, and she plopped down to sit in the grass, her skirts tucked around her ankles, arms around her knees. Heavenly days — if Whit sold them all this easy, it'd be a blessed fortune! She looked at him in wonder, followed by a deep frown. He planned to pay her just five dollars from the sale of each mule? That had seemed like a gold mine when he'd first told her; now it sounded downright paltry. Her chin lifted. If she stayed with Mr. Hanley's outfit through the sale, she'd do a good job for him and, by Hannah, would ask more. On the other hand, if he turned her down, five dollars for each mule sold — possibly the entire herd — would be more than she'd have otherwise, and it'd still go a ways to recovering her farm. Live a normal life. She got to her feet and brushed her skirts, deciding that she'd handle the situation carefully, when it arrived.

She had no idea what Papa paid for Sadie and Blossom, but if he paid anything close to what Whit was pocketing for a pair, it was no wonder they lost the farm!

Jocelyn thought she might see a difference in Whit following the sale — that he'd be happy about it and maybe boast some. But he was as quiet as a barber pole, not voicing an opinion. She'd give a lot to read his mind. Without that, she instead observed his behavior as they took up the drive again.

He was more and more dissatisfied with the pace of the herd, and he pushed them ever harder to cover distance dawn to dark. Luckily, on two occasions a rancher rode out to see where they were headed and allowed them to shortcut across his land, cutting considerable miles off the trip.

Hanley was unnaturally watchful, to her mind. He often looked back along the road they'd covered, his jaw tight and his eyes in a thoughtful squint, his slow study seeming to penetrate the shadowy groves of trees or rocky areas along the way. There was still that sidearm on his hip. He was particularly restless when they made camp the third evening outside the town of Council Grove. He paced. When he rested on his heels by the fire he studied the flames like his destiny might be written there.

Jocelyn shrugged, knowing Whit Hanley wouldn't tell her even half of what he was thinking, and moved in front of his destiny to place a fresh pot of beans on the fire to simmer a few hours into the night, be cooked by morning. She'd only have to reheat them for dinner, heap them steaming on the plate with hot, buttered cornbread from the Dutch oven, a pitcher of honey on the side.

She wasn't aware what late hour her boss turned in, but he was still by the fire long after she had. Once she saw him with his head in his hands, only to let his hands drop.

To her thinking, mule drover didn't exactly fit Whit Hanley, as this job no doubt would if he were a rancher or cowboy. She sensed he was neither. What might his usual occupation be? Tinker, tailor, lawyer . . . thief? She couldn't totally discount that he and his partner could be thieves and the mules stolen. Sam, too, seemed edgy and worried when she could see no obvious reason for him to be. Were they concerned that the true owner was catching up? Had Whit, for a lot of money, sold a team of mules not fairly his? Only time would tell, and if they turned out to be outlaws, she'd better be long gone from their company.

CHAPTER FOUR

She'd like to think Whit Hanley was honest, not a thief, but what proof was there? Nice eyes and good manners were a start but hardly enough. Neither was being handsome from black hat to flat-heeled boots.

Tossing in her blanket in the middle of the night, drugged with the need for sleep but tormented from wild imagination, Jocelyn conjured a bloody shootout like happened in earlier days on cattle drives and in cow towns like Dodge City and Abilene — and her in the middle! Silliness, surely, but something deadly was ahead; she could sense it to her bones' marrow.

If she used common sense, she'd quit stalling. Cut and run. Have no more to do with these two, practically strangers. But she desperately needed pay from the drive. Being near her old farm's location today fortified her determination to have what rightfully belonged to her.

If it came to it, would she side with thieves, Whit Hanley and Sam Birdwhistle, or the rightful owner, should that be the facts? She really wasn't sure. Whit, her boss, if they could keep the mules, would likely be the most apt to pay her when they sold. The true owner wouldn't owe her anything. Unless she sided with him, helped him recover his mules, and he appreciated that to the point of paying for the trouble she'd gone to, to help him. She considered getting up, getting dressed, gathering her things, and crawling from the wagon. Instead, she turned restlessly to her other side and tugged her blanket to her chin. One more day, she thought, and she'd decide for sure.

Awakened by the braying "E-e-e-e-onk! E-e-e-e-onk, onk onk!" of a mule, Jocelyn climbed from her blankets the next morning. She saw no sign of Whit Hanley anywhere about their camp. Another mule or two joined the braying, like they were singing a terribly off-tune chorus. Sam was seeing that they were watered, and each got a bait of oats. She soon had a heaping platter of pancakes whipped up, and syrup heated, but the boss was still nowhere to be seen. She went to Sam as he finished chores and handed him a plate of pancakes drowned with syrup and a side of six slices of bacon. "Where's Mr. Hanley? I haven't seen him this morning."

Sam frowned, his mouth twisting with reluctance to speak as he took the plate and fork. His expression turned to anticipation as he eyed the food.

"Sam? Where is Whit Hanley?"

"Mr. Hanley done gone, Miss Jocelyn."

"Gone?" She clutched her skirts in her hands, dismayed. "He can't be *gone;* we still have to see these mules to Skiddy." She gaped at him, shoulders rigid.

"Rode out just 'afore dawn." He motioned with his head toward the road and forked a large chunk of pancakes followed by a well-cooked slice of bacon. "I barely woke up, myownself, but I heard him go." He began to eat, chewing with gusto.

"Where did he go? Do you know?" She crossed her arms and gripped her elbows.

"No'm." Sam licked syrup from his lips, shook his head, and continued to eat as he found a place to sit on the ground. She slumped down beside him. "Sam, what are we supposed to do? Did he say? Will he be gone long, and are we supposed to wait here until he returns?" How could the man just take off and not a word to them!

"We got to keep movin', take the herd on to Mr. Hanley's place up around Skiddy. I know that much; don't know no more." He swirled a chunk of pancake on his fork through the last of the syrup on his plate.

"How do you know we're supposed to keep on with the drive?" she demanded, her face heating with the start of a real conniption she might not be able to control.

"He tole me hisself, 'Anything happen that I ain't around to tell you what to do, you keep right on takin' the mules to Skiddy an' keep 'em there on my land.' Them's his orders, Miss Jocelyn." He blew on his coffee and took a swallow.

"When did he tell you that? Last night? Yesterday? When?" She jumped to her feet and strode back and forth.

"He give me them orders when we left Missouri, Miss Jocelyn, 'bout the time we crossed the border into Kansas — from right about the town of Joplin. That's when he tole me, and that's what I be doin'."

"All right," she said with a nervous laugh. "I suppose that's what I'll be doing, too." She stopped pacing and waved an arm. "On to Skiddy, on with the mules." The fact that Hanley would leave as he did, without a word to them as to *why* and *where* he was going seemed too peculiar to swallow. Did he just figure on Sam to remember what he'd told him, and do what he asked? That seemed probable. But he might have told her *something* about his plans, how and if she was included. Because she direly needed the money he'd promised, he likely considered that was enough to keep her on with the drive — as *she'd* promised.

So be it. Despite feeling anxious and worried, Jocelyn found herself looking forward to this ranch where they were taking the mules, and especially her forthcoming pay. Maybe Whit Hanley would be there primed for their arrival. They could hope. She and Sam would move right along, bypass the town of Council Grove today, keep the mules cracking.

Sam had a different plan. "Go right on by?" He gaped, his shoulders slumped forward in disbelief. He took his empty plate and coffee cup to the dishpan. "No-siree, I want to see the town, Miss Jocelyn. Whit tole me plenty about the post office tree where wagon trains passin' through left messages for other folks comin' that way. He also tole me about a kinda powwow in a grove of trees there, between some Osage Indian chiefs and important white folks from Washington, the guv'ment. The men from Washington give the Indians money for signing a paper saying that the white folks could survey and mark a trail from the Missouri River plumb to Santa Fe, in New Mexico Territory. I want to see that place that gave the town its name *Council* and *Grove*. You been there, Miss Jocelyn?"

"I was there a time or two with my father." Sam followed as she went about busily breaking camp, anxious to be on their way. "The treaty you spoke of took place about seventy-five years ago. It was very important to overland trade — taking clothes, cutlery, hardware, and the like to Santa Fe. Even before the town sprang up in the grove, travelers often gathered their wagons in that spot, hoping for safety by traveling with a larger group. Papa was a teacher, and he wanted me to know all about Council Grove, the city born in a grove of beautiful trees and with a lot of interesting history." She nodded in the direction of the mule herd, bringing to Sam's attention that they had begun to separate and drift, Alice braying as though to call them back.

"Then we be goin' for a bit to Council Grove, so's I can see it, too?" he asked over his shoulder as he headed for Rover, his riding mule grazing a few yards away.

Jocelyn shook her head. "It's not my job to tell you what to do, Sam, but I really think we need to be on our way to Skiddy. I'm sorry." She watched him climb on Rover and drive a stray mule back to the bunch.

"Well, I be sorry, too," he called over to her. "I won't never have me another chance this good to see the town of Council Grove on the Santa Fe Trail. I ain't your boss, neither, but please, Miss Jocelyn, let's go for a look-see."

She was close to giving in — he was so enthused about going — and she hated being responsible for his disappointment. To be truthful, she wouldn't mind a spell in town, for a change. She tried one last argument. "I don't think Mr. Hanley would favor it. We'll be a longer stretch to Skiddy, and the only way we can spend time in Council Grove is to take the mules with us. I don't see that working well."

"That be all right, I tell ya'! Whit tole me about cattle drives, an' long mule trains on the Santa Fe Trail, come right down the main street of Council Grove." Sam illustrated, throwing his arm. "He said some a' that's still happenin' nowadays."

Jocelyn heaved a sigh and gave in. "Fine. We'll go, but we can't tarry long. Our boss could be on the Skiddy ranch, waiting for us."

"He ain't there."

"How would you know that?" She whirled on him, dumbfounded.

"I don't know 'zactly, Miss Jocelyn. I just know he ain't there."

Exasperated, she asked him, brows lifted, "Where, then, do you think he is, Sam?"

"Tendin' to business, some'eres, I trust." He didn't look at her. "Don't know 'zactly where, or what might be the business he's tendin' to, but that's where he is and that be what he's a'doin."

"All right." She threw up her hands. "Enough. I need to get ready." She rushed to splash water on her face from a pan she'd already prepared for that purpose, redid her hair, and ran to the wagon for her red shawl of belongings. In a clump of bushes several yards from their camp, she quickly changed into a clean, lacy, white shirtwaist and a navy skirt.

They were making a mistake, she was positive, but she couldn't help feeling excited. There was even a possibility she might find the next job to go to, in Council Grove.

Their outfit, wagon and mule herd, crawled slowly down main street, Jocelyn marking the sights of town as she remembered each one. Checking over her shoulder, she could see that Sam was having a bit of trouble with a mule that drifted over to nose the window of Hays House Restaurant; another mule cropped grass out front of the courthouse; still another was rubbing its itchy hide against the Post Office Oak. Two were braying loudly as though they enjoyed each other's echo.

Jocelyn clamped a hand over her mouth in horror. They'd be lucky not to be arrested, the mules taken possession of and sold, with the money going to the city for damages. With effort, and Alice's tinkling bell, Sam got the strayed mules back into the herd and moving again. Jocelyn rotated her shoulders to ease the tension in her neck. *If the blamed boss was here they'd not have half the trouble, but heaven only knew where Whit Hanley might be.* He'd started out with another drover, he'd told her, a man who left before she hired on. She had to remember to ask Sam why the rider quit, or was fired . . . the whole situation now being left to just the two of them.

Coming hurriedly out of a place of business, a stout storekeeper with a bushy beard yelled at Jocelyn and Sam, "Lady, and you, black feller, run these mules off away from my store, and on out of town. Shoo!" He flapped the grey apron that covered his enormous stomach at a pair of mules that barred the way for two fluttery women trying to squirm past them into his store. "Git, now, you consarned critters. Come on in, ladies. Sorry, sorry."

Jocelyn was pulling on the lines to halt her wagon on the side of the street and go help Sam, when a familiar figure in a wrinkled, grey suit and derby hat came from the courthouse and strode swiftly her way. It was the judge who'd bought a pair of mules from Whit Hanley. "Miss, Miss, hold up there," he signaled to Jocelyn, his round face wreathed in smiles. He doffed his hat to her.

"Hello, Judge Rawlins." She jumped down from the wagon and tied the lines to a post. She talked to her team a moment and fed them a handful of oats.

The judge questioned as he joined her, "Are you here for a sale? Where is Mr. Hanley, your boss? I'd be happy to help him arrange a sale here in Council Grove."

"We were just passing through, Judge . . . well, and trying to do a little sightseeing, but that, as you can see, isn't working out. Mr. Hanley is tending to some business elsewhere and is not with us just now."

A handful of people had come out of shops to gawk. As if the mules, Sam, and she were a parade. Jocelyn's face grew hot.

The judge was saying, "Sorry to hear that.

I looked forward to speaking with Mr. Hanley again. You're here for a little sightseeing, too? I can help you with that, Miss Royal. Let's take these mules on yonder to the stock pens, next to the railroad. That'll hold them while you see the town. I'd like to treat you and your drover friend to dinner, if you'd like."

"Thanks, Judge. I'd like to give the mules a rest somewhere, but I'm not sure we can take you up on your kind offer of dinner."

While they were hazing the mules in the direction of the stock pens, a reedy, red-haired fellow came rushing from the newspaper office with a pad of paper and a pencil. Another man, short and with thin flyaway hair, followed, fumbling with a tripod and other photography equipment he was about to lose. "A story, please, Miss," the first man addressed Jocelyn. "We don't often see a lady herding this many mules along main street."

"No, thank you." She held him off with her hand, scooted around him, and quickened her pace.

The pair of newspapermen trotted down the street after Jocelyn, Sam, the judge, and the mules. The mules were gathered and locked inside the corral with a little hay to keep them happy. Jocelyn leaned back against the corral fence for a breather. Her previously clean, lacy shirtwaist was wilted against her skin. She fanned her warm face.

"Tell us about your mule herd, Miss — where you're going and what you plan for them." The red-haired editor's pen hovered. "This is going to be a wonderful story for our paper." With a raised eyebrow and pleased expression, he built his headline: " 'Mule Herd Driven Through Council Grove by Lady Drover and Her Servant.' Just like in the old days. Readers are going to love it." He held his arms wide as if to hug the whole county, doubtless envisioning customers for his news stories, endless buyers choosing from the ads inked in on the sides of the pages.

Jocelyn brushed her hair back, her jaw set. She was more than a little put out with his carrying on. "I don't own the mules; they aren't mine, sir." She nodded to where Sam circled the corral, making a last check of the mules. "Sam Birdwhistle is my friend and fellow worker, *not* my servant. We're taking the mules up near Skiddy for our boss. Simple as that."

"Oh." The newspaperman's smile faded, and his shoulders drooped. "Well, we'd still like a photograph of you and your — the black drover for the paper." His face brightened again. "I'm sure I can build a story around the picture."

Whoa. "Build" a story? What kind of story? He'd make something up to go with the picture? "No, no pictures," she said quickly, but it was too late. There was a loud pop and a flash, and a few seconds later the photographer popped out from the black cloth covering his head, where the camera sat on a tripod. "Got it!"

That was the trouble with some papers and the folks printing them, Jocelyn thought with disgust; they loved a dramatic story whether it was true, or not. Shaking her head, she gave the pair a hostile look and stomped off.

For the next hour, Jocelyn and Sam took their time seeing the town with Judge Rawlins as their guide. Crisscrossing dusty streets and dodging wagon and buggy traffic at times, they saw it all. A few folks coming and going on the sidewalks stared briefly at the trio; others nodded a friendly greeting, no doubt due to their acquaintance with the judge. Without the mules to worry over, every bit of the experience was highly enjoyable to Jocelyn.

"Thank you ever so much, Judge Rawlins, for your invitation to dinner," she told him later, "but we can't tarry; we really need to push our mules on to Skiddy." They'd already spent more time in Council Grove than they should have; she'd planned just a quick look-see.

The judge nodded and clasped his hands over his stomach. "I understand, Miss Royal, but I am disappointed." His face brightened. "But tell you what, you must have an ice cream sundae at the soda fountain, quick refreshment to top off your day."

"Do you mean a soda?" Jocelyn frowned. She knew nothing of an "ice cream sundae," whatever it might be.

"A sundae. You'll see!" Below his derby his happy face glistened with perspiration. "Come along. Ice cream sundaes are all the rage these days, and quite tasty and cold on a hot afternoon."

As they passed the busy saloon, with tinkling music and the odor of beer floating from the open door, Jocelyn saw Sam eye the establishment with longing. He caught her smiling before she could hide it. He put his hands in the air with a return grin of defeat and shrugged. Ice cream it was.

The judge explained as they neared the drugstore, "I believe it was in Illinois where a small boy asked for a dish of vanilla ice cream. Seeing the many bottled syrups on the shelves behind the counter, normally for making sodas, he asked the druggist to please pour some chocolate on his ice cream. The ice cream sundae was born. Yours will have chocolate syrup, marshmallow sauce, and a cherry on top!"

Chocolate syrup, marshmallow sauce, a cherry! Once more, Jocelyn weakened. But this had to be enough, or the next thing there'd be one of those noisy automobiles coming down the street, and the judge bartering a ride for them all!

It was Sam Birdwhistle's idea for taking their sundaes to eat in a clump of trees near the Post Office Oak. Sam leaned against a tree while eating his ice cream, the judge found a stump to sit on, and Jocelyn sat on a grungy blanket she'd retrieved from the wagon. She knew it was because Sam didn't want to cause a ruckus, should blacks not be allowed in the drugstore. It had been okayed that the sundae dishes be taken out and returned, but she didn't like it all the same.

Later, as they headed back to the stockyards to collect their mules, Jocelyn and Sam couldn't stop talking about the delicious treat. "It was so good," Jocelyn kept saying. "Ice cream sundae," she repeated. "Judge Rawlins says it got its name because serving ice cream 'sundays' on Sunday was outlawed in many towns. Changing the spelling made it acceptable. People sure have strange ideas about some things."

"That they do." Sam's long legs took giant strides along the walk. "But that ice cream doodaddie be the best thing this ol' mouth ever tasted!" And he began to whistle a cheery tune she recognized as *Buffalo Gals.*

"Sam Birdwhistle, is that how you got your name?" Jocelyn asked. "That was beautiful whistling."

"I dunno for positive, but I think I was born to the name. My Papa was named the same. Whistlin' just come natural as I growed."

They both laughed and hurried on to the precious herd. It occurred to Jocelyn that they had missed seeing the Kaw or *Kansa* Mission in the southeast part of town, opened in 1849 by Thomas Huffaker. He'd been sent by the Methodist Episcopal Church to teach local Indians. When the plan turned out to be less successful than hoped for, the mission, five years later, became a school for the first white children. She didn't mention the Kaw Mission to Sam for fear he'd want to see it, too, and they'd never reach Skiddy with the mules.

69

CHAPTER FIVE

It would be another day and a half before they reached their destination. Fighting boredom as she drove the wagon, Jocelyn patted her mouth in a yawn, spoke coaxingly to her mule team, then turned her thoughts to Skiddy. From what she'd heard and read in the papers, Skiddy was a small town that had sprung up some thirty years back beside the Missouri, Kansas, and Texas railroad built through northwest Morris County. Most folks called it the KATY railroad. Francis Skiddy, an official with the New York company that furnished the money to build the railroad, asked that the town be named for him, promising Skiddy a town hall and other structures. Folks were enthralled with the chance to do his bidding even if his name was a touch different.

The town was never awarded the town hall, but Skiddy flourished even so. It wasn't so far off the Santa Fe Trail that settlers looking for land to homestead couldn't find it and help the town to grow. The grain elevator and railroad station for the shipping of grain and livestock were said to be the heart of the town, although it had all the usual places of business: a couple of general stores, a drugstore, a harness shop and livery, a lumberyard, and a hotel with seventeen rooms. Jocelyn had never been to Skiddy, but she looked forward to seeing the town.

A while later she scolded herself for practically forgetting Sam herding the mules alone behind her. The day previous, she had offered to take a turn at night watch of the herd, but Sam had protested vigorously. "Ain't a job for you, Miss Jocelyn!" He'd added, "Don't tell the mules, but off and on I take me a little shuteye in the saddle."

Now, when she turned to look, a rider appeared out of the dust made by the mules, passing them at a lope and onto the open road. Her spirits lifted, thinking it might be Whit Hanley here to give them a hand and take over. The horse and rider loomed larger, moving right along as though trying to catch up with her. Then she saw that the horse was a dun in color, not Whit's blue roan, nor did the man in the saddle have Whit's solid, broad-shouldered build. He was skinny as a snake and slovenly garbed. Her hopes sagged.

He rode up alongside her wagon and reined his horse to a slow walk. Dust settled around them as he removed his battered, wide-brim hat and let it rest on his knee. "Howdy, Miss." He stood in the stirrups and leaned around to look her over with cold, gooseberry-grey eyes above a dry-rot grin. "Fine day, ain't it?"

She nodded with a curt, "I s'pose." Disappointment that he wasn't Hanley could've made her chew a horseshoe and spit it at this person. Besides, he was behaving right nervy.

"You with that nigra back there with them mules?" His horse clopped alongside her wagon while he continued to leer at her.

It was none of his never-mind, but Jocelyn answered, giving him a cutting stare, "I might be." She pursed her lips nervously as warning bells clanged in her reasoning, all her senses alert. This man smelled and looked trouble.

He continued his claptrap. "Just wonderin'. I think you're the one I saw talkin' to him back in Council Grove. A pretty thing like you can do better than him, Missy. He your husband? If he ain't, I'm available." His grin grew, exposing darkened, scummy teeth.

Her heart slowed at the word "pretty." There was a time no one would have called her that, even such as this filthy louse eyeing her all over. She stared straight ahead, speaking loud, although her voice shook. "Why don't you take yourself on up the road and leave me be? And stop asking fool questions that aren't your concern."

He laughed, rode closer, and grabbed the side of her wagon. "An' why don't you be a little friendly? You ain't better'n me or anybody else, with that nigra sidekick, ya' know."

She looked down at his dirty wrist that was near the same size as her own. If he tried anything, it'd be a sorry day for him. Even so, her knuckles on the reins were white, and her heart raced, wishing that this wasn't happening.

"That gentleman back there with the mules could beat you six ways to Sunday for manners, I can tell you that!" She slapped the lines hard, trying to hurry Zenith's and Alice's plodding. Tired as they were, they paid her little mind.

The scalawag grew silent, turned loose of her wagon, and fell back. She was about to believe she was rid of him when she realized he'd tied his horse to the steel rod that held the end gate of her wagon. He was in the wagon crawling towards where she sat. Her mind raced, frantic. There was no way to escape him without jumping out, abandoning her team and wagon. Nor could she grab a gun from under the seat in time. She'd have to handle him some other way. But, in the name of Hannah, how? She dragged a moist palm over her skirt while her stomach roiled.

When he swung his legs over the bench seat and pushed close beside her, she could smell the stench of him. Fear gripped her to the point she couldn't speak, could scarcely breathe. Seconds later, a torrent of fury replaced her fear. She raged at him, shoving his shoulder with hers as hard as she could. "Get your sorry, good-for-nothing carcass off my wagon, this minute!"

He laughed and put his hand on her knee, fingering the fabric of her long skirt. His slaty eyes were half-lidded like a frog's. "I could sure have me a good time tamin' you. But what I really want to talk about is that mule herd back there." He motioned with his head, greasy hair swinging. "Them mules is valuable as gold to whoever has 'em, but mebbe you know that."

She threw his clutching fingers from her knee. Being present at Whit Hanley's recent dealings for a pair of mules, she darn well had a good idea of their value. In a few states, on gigantic farms steam tractors were starting to be used, but thousands upon thousands of average farmers in the Midwest — and other parts of the country like Texas and the Northwest — were partial to mules, for pulling plows, harrows, hay rakes, and harvesters through the fields, as well as to ride or pull a wagon on trips to town. She knew of mule-drawn streetcars ambling the streets of Arkansas City in southwestern Cowley County, Kansas, and was sure other towns had them, too.

"I reckon if I aimed to shoot the darkey, you'd let me have them mules an' come along with me to boot."

"And I reckon you're crazy as a barn full of bats!" She jerked further away from him until she was on the far edge of the bench seat. A chill worked along her spine.

"Now then, now then, settle down. You headin' for White City, or Skiddy, mebbe? Or are you takin' off on one of them side roads?" He put his arm around her and attempted to kiss her. As much as she hated it, she took advantage of his closeness to sink her teeth into his neck, hard. He howled from pain, and, when he lifted his hand to strike her, she rammed her elbow

75

into his chest. He made strangling sounds fighting for breath, his head back, eyes on her thunderous. As he grabbed for her, she swung a broganed foot around and kicked him hard enough to rattle his teeth. A second hard kick sent him off the wagon. He hit the ground hard, cursing her as he staggered to his feet, hand to his neck. He looked in amazement at blood on his fingers.

"You had it coming, you fool!" Jocelyn spat the filth of him from her mouth, spat again, and slapped the lines over Zenith and Alice. "Git up there! Go, mules!" Maybe the mules sensed her desperation, or were rested, as Zenith and Alice threw themselves into the harness and ran like racehorses.

Feeling deep satisfaction, but still shaky, Jocelyn waited until they'd covered six or seven miles before she drew the team to a gradual halt. She climbed to the back of the wagon and freed the dun horse that had galloped along with them. It'd serve that no-good filthy scum right if she kept his horse. She hoped the gink was laying back there realizing the wrong he'd done. Afoot and unarmed, he'd not be much of a threat to Sam and the mules coming along behind. If he never saw his horse again, which was now wandering ahead in a westerly direction, he deserved that, too.

She worried, though, that he could be a thief in cahoots with others and would try again to steal the herd. If he came alone, hating her now, she and Sam could handle the skinny snake, but if he brought help with him, who knew what might happen.

As soon as Sam and the mules caught up to where she'd made their last camp of the trip that night, Jocelyn wanted to know if he'd seen the culprit she'd left afoot on the road and whether he'd given Sam trouble.

"Like you'd 'spect, he tried to steal a mule to ride. Jumped out of the ditch onto one an' was bucked off. Tried another one, and same thing happen. I said I had a pistol in my boot, and I'd shoot him 'tween the eyes he tried again."

"Do you pack a pistol in your boot?"

"Used to, years back."

"Was that the end of it, then, with the rat?"

"No, Miss Jocelyn, 'twasn't. I was chousing our mules right proper, and 'fore long they stampeded, wouldn't ya know. That fella was a hop toad here, like a flyin' bird there, all over the road to keep from dyin' under they's hooves." He laughed. "Left him cussin' and squawlin' on the side of the road."

She sighed mightily. "I hope to heaven we

never see him again."

"Don't think we will, Miss Jocelyn. Them mules put the fear in him, they sure did."

After they'd had supper, Jocelyn double-checked to make sure the guns below the wagon seat were loaded and ready.

Sam didn't like that she worried. "Miss Jocelyn, you can't shoot folks just for what they be sayin'. We see that good-for-nothin' goat dung again, I be takin' care of him, not you, iffen he tries anything. He ain't touchin' you, and he ain't touchin' our mules; I guarantee you that."

When she looked at him without saying anything, he continued, "Men like that feller is mostly cowards. They like to give women trouble when they ain't nobody close around to put a stop to it. He got a good lesson from your boots, an' I figger for him it was plenty enough. Some other innocent lady, alone, that's who he'll be botherin' next. Time or two more a' that, somebody'll be blowin' his brains out. But not you, Miss Jocelyn, not you. Blood on your hands, rest of your life behind bars — that ain't for you."

His words brought tears to Jocelyn's eyes. "Sam," she choked, "I don't know what I'd do without you. Lord-a-mighty, I'll be so thankful to reach Skiddy and turn these mules over to the boss." Sam frowned, and she knew he was thinking again that Whit Hanley wouldn't be there waiting for them. She refused to believe it; Sam had to be wrong.

On the afternoon of the fifth day, they reached the Skiddy ranch following directions Whit had drawn on a piece of paper for Sam. In her whole life, Jocelyn had never seen a more desolate looking place; even the windmill creaked tiredly in the breeze. Taking it all in, one thing was clear: Whit Hanley wasn't there waiting and, from the looks of things, maybe had never been there.

The house, an unpainted, rundown, story-and-a-half clapboard, was situated at the foot of a grassy knoll in a grove of cottonwood trees. The abode looked like it had been empty for years and was sad enough to sink into the earth. The old barn, sheds, and corrals at the top of the gentle rise appeared to be in slightly better shape than the house, though not by much.

On closer examination, the layout of the old stone-fenced corrals and pasture impressed Jocelyn and Sam both. Two and a half feet at the bottom and one and a half feet at the top, the stone fencing was on average five feet high, in some places higher.

"These stone fences have been here a very long time," Jocelyn mused, "probably built by one of the first settlers to these parts. Rock fences didn't just keep a rancher's stock in and wild animals out; they saved homes, crops, and even lives by stopping prairie fires blown by the wind."

Inside the main corral were empty hayracks — they'd have to cut and dry hay if they were there for any length of time. There was an empty, dirty water tank. The gears of the windmill needed oiling for sure, and the flow pipe to the tank checked. With a handful of oats for Zenith, who had been making a nervous sound in his nose, and a taste of salt for Alice, Jocelyn coaxed the pair into the unfamiliar corral. Once they were accustomed, gates into other pastures could be opened. The rest of the milling mules followed with some urging from Sam. Jocelyn, despite uneasy feelings about the look of the property and Whit Hanley's absence, was relieved when the mules, to the last, were inside the corral and the gate was secure.

They'd done it. She straightened her tired, aching back and let the south wind blow over her, exhilarated. She and Sam had brought the mules to Skiddy as they were hired to do. What was next, how and when they were to be paid in this sad, lonely place, was anybody's guess. And where, in the name of Hannah, was Whit Hanley?

She couldn't believe he would just abandon these valuable mules. Or would he, if he was in serious trouble with the law, or had personal enemies after him? Were she and Sam scapegoats in some unlawful scheme? Was Hanley even alive? She'd know one way or the other, if Whit Hanley ever showed up and spelled things out for her!

Chapter Six

Jocelyn wasn't sure what she expected to find when she was first told they were taking the mules to Skiddy, but it wasn't a rundown, abandoned ranch with no boss present. The house was built in a T shape; the top of the T faced the road — two stories in front, and one story, the kitchen, in back. She wandered through the house, taking inventory. The kitchen had a pump and sink, an old cast-iron stove, a table, and two chairs. Dust-laden shelves lined the wall to the right of the stove. On the opposite side of the room was a window with square panes, one of them cracked and another missing. Thick dust, along with rat and mice droppings, was everywhere.

The kitchen led to a small, screened back porch that she liked, as did a resident wren that had made a nest on a rafter above and flew in and out of a hole in the screen. A creek not far from the porch and green hills rolling away under a cloudless, blue sky brought a smile to her face.

Back inside, upstairs over the front room was a bedroom containing a rope bed with a thin, worn mattress. Next to the bed was a dusty, battered trunk, empty. She walked across the creaking floor to the two bleary windows looking out over the overgrown front yard and the lane to the main road. Jocelyn tried to open the windows, to air the hot, musty room, but they wouldn't budge. She wanted so much to sleep in a real bed, under a roof.

No matter; she wasn't leaving until she was paid. Did that mean this was her home until Whit Hanley came, however long that might be? With a heavy sigh, she took the narrow steps down into the front room again. The room was empty except for a three-year-old calendar on the wall. Peeling pink and yellow wallpaper was so faded it was hard to make out the flower and vine design. On either side of the front door were windows, so dirty she could barely see out of them. But Sam was out there unloading the wagon, and she had to find out if he knew anything about the situation facing them. Good guesses would do, if he truly didn't know.

Sam had driven the wagon up past the

ramshackle outbuildings on the left of the house, to the barn. He was hefting a bag of grain and then a saddle from the wagon by the time she caught up to him. He continued to maintain that Whit was "tendin' to business." "Right important or he'd be here." He did add one clue about the ranch, "Whit didn't care much for his daddy, who left him this property. Little bit I heard about it, his daddy was a high auger, but awful mean to his wife and his boy."

" 'High auger'? Do you mean a great talker, important, and a boss?"

"Yep. An' might be that's why young Mr. Hanley ain't lived here or tried to make a livin' off the place."

"Inherited from a father he hated, it was hard to care about the ranch — until he's needed it for the mules," she mused, chewing her lip and nodding.

"I seed it that way, Miss Jocelyn."

"All right, then. As soon as you've unloaded what's to be stored in the barn, drive the wagon down, and we'll tote the food, dishes, utensils, and bedding into the house. Right now, I'm grabbing one of the goodly yellow bars of soap I've been using in camp to wash dishes. It'll be a trial, but I want to clean as much of the kitchen as I can, before we store anything." She climbed into the wagon to hunt for the soap and dishrags and prayed that she'd be able to prime the kitchen pump with water from the creek. Looking down on Sam, she said, "And thank you for telling me why you think Hanley hasn't already taken possession of this property. It makes sense. In a way."

On her return to the house, Jocelyn stopped to use the outhouse. She added the small building with the half-moon cutout in the door to her mental list of things needing attention. Sam could eliminate the buzzing hornets' nest in the overhead corner. She'd had enough of bees.

Jocelyn tackled cleaning and fixing the house and outbuildings with dedication, even though their stay would be temporary. Sam got the windmill running more efficiently so that the mules had water. He had found a broken axe in the barn, repaired it, and chopped wood for the kitchen stove, a chore that also cleaned up old cottonwood limbs blown to the ground by the wind. With each day of work on the house, Jocelyn found it more livable than it first had seemed.

She hung her few items of clothing on two nails in the wall of the upstairs bedroom. Then, cleaning the empty trunk and moving it closer to the bed, she removed the remaining items from her red shawl and placed them on top of the trunk: soap, towel, book, a bit of Gram's crocheting, a tobacco tin of seeds. She folded the red shawl carefully and, remembering her mother and father, held it to her cheek for a moment. Hearing it from her papa, theirs was a sweet love story. He was in his second year of teaching school in Kansas City, Missouri, when he met Mama in a downtown library. She was only sixteen, beautiful, but frail. They fell in love and soon married. Jocelyn arrived about a year later.

When she was still a baby, Papa decided he'd never become rich as a teacher, and he wanted to provide well for his family. He'd heard about a gold strike in South Dakota and went there, leaving Jocelyn and her mother with Gram. He didn't find gold, himself, but earned money from selling hardware goods to the miners, enough to buy the Kansas farm. Papa was readying the farm for them when Mama, in Kansas City, died in her sleep.

Jocelyn sat on the edge of the bed, holding the wadded shawl close, fighting the pain in her throat and wondering what she could truly expect from the future. A crystal ball would be handy, but no matter — wasn't the present as important, if not more so? She swallowed her tears and, after a few quiet moments, returned to her tasks.

Sam arranged his living quarters in the barn in a small, empty storage room with a window where, he said, he'd be handy to look out for the mules and for other chores, like dispensing with the ancient pyramid of manure behind the barn.

Hard work was a distraction from wondering when Whit Hanley might arrive. Sam found an old buggy seat, which Jocelyn cleaned and Sam moved into the front room for additional seating. It was seldom used since she and Sam were constantly busy indoors and out. Most days, Jocelyn was tired like a sinking ship by day's end, with cooking and washing their clothes added to the rest of her chores. It did her no good to rant at Sam Birdwhistle about Hanley's leaving them in a state of unknowing — Sam continued to defend his partner.

Somehow, Zenith had located a lower place in the lengthy stone wall where he could jump over into greener pastures. Jocelyn was sure that Alice didn't really approve, but she nevertheless followed him from the corral, with most of the rest of the herd following her.

They had finally gotten the mule herd

back into the corral. Sam, in dirty overalls, with sweat running in trails down his dusty face, returned to the chore of building up the low place in the stone fence. Jocelyn helped as much as possible, selecting and toting rocks from a pile behind one of the outbuildings.

A distant rattling sound made them both turn to look down the hill. A buggy with a woman driving was pulling up in front of the house, dust settling behind the rig.

Jocelyn stared for a moment with the sun in her eyes, wiped an arm across her brow, and told Sam, "I'll go see what this is about." He nodded and grabbed another flat chunk of limestone. On her way to meet the visitor, Jocelyn was thinking how she would have reacted in this instance as a child — she would have run to hide. She still felt a bit of trepidation, left over from those days when she was taunted and shunned because of her facial disfigurement. But that was long ago, before her face changed with the miracle of surgery, in the hospital on the hill in Kansas City.

She pushed those thoughts aside and rushed to aid the stout woman alighting from the buggy. "May I help you, ma'am?"

The woman laughed and grasped the handle of her maroon, floral reticule. "You sure can; I'm obliged. These old bones take to aching when I least want them to, you know what I mean? Well, of course you don't, young woman like you. But I've been wanting to meet you, pay a neighborly visit. Wait just a minute; fetch that basket there in the buggy, please. I brought you a half-dozen little fried peach pies."

"Oh, my, and they smell so good!" Jocelyn said as the fragrance of peaches and warm crust drifted from the dishtowel-covered basket. "By the way, my name is Jocelyn Royal."

"Mable Goody." The woman's rosy face crinkled in a warm smile. "I'm your closest neighbor. You can see our place — Well, from here just a clump of trees and teensy buildings if you look hard along the west road. Our farm — me and my husband, Lyman's, hundred and sixty acres — touches on a west portion of your Nickel Hill ranch. Just a little bitty farm compared to your two thousand or so acres here at Nickel Hill."

Jocelyn gulped in surprise at the size of Hanley's ranch, having no positive knowledge where the property lines were, nor that it had a name, Nickel Hill Ranch. An explanation was necessary as to who the actual owner was, but first she needed to make her guest comfortable in the clean but near empty house. She called to Sam up by the corrals to take care of Mrs. Goody's horse and buggy. He looked up from the mule's hoof he was examining, nodded, and waved agreement.

As they walked to the house, Jocelyn guessed her visitor to be about twice her age. Her helmet style hat was bedecked with varying shades of lavender silk flowers with a cluster of rosebuds on top, revealing light-brown hair threaded with grey and worn with a tight bun in back. Her high-necked, plum, calico dress swept over her ample form to the toes of her laced, black shoes.

"Please come in." Jocelyn opened the front door and stood aside for her guest to enter.

Mrs. Goody pursed her lips in surprise and stared around at the front room, empty except for the blanket-covered buggy seat. "Oh."

"It's a long story." Jocelyn's face heated. "Please make yourself comfortable." She motioned to the buggy seat serving as a sofa. She lifted the basket held in her other hand. "I'll take these to the kitchen and make us some tea." Thank goodness tea had been among the supplies Hanley had stocked in Emporia, but they had rarely used it on the drive. The men preferred coffee — which she and Sam would be out of soon.

While the tea brewed, Jocelyn returned to the front room with a chair from the kitchen and explained the empty house and how she and Sam came to be there, he a drover, she the cook. All they had with them were the mules and a wagon and some supplies. "Our boss, Whit Hanley, is the owner of the ranch. He's not here right now, but we expect him any time."

"Nickel Hill used to belong to the sweetest old lady, Matilda Scott," Mrs. Goody said. "She used to say that she and her husband, Emmett, hardly had two coins to rub together after they got the place, which is why they named it what they did." She bit her bottom lip and shook her head. "Mrs. Scott was a widow when she died. You can't imagine how quick her children got rid of the cattle and horses she'd kept, her milk cow, and her hens. They sold the ranch and skedaddled to California, or maybe it was Oregon. Emmett wouldn't have liked the way they treated their mother, not a bit, but he'd been dead a long time. Rumor was, a money man in Topeka bought Nickel Hill as an investment, but nobody come around to occupy it, or keep the place up. Strangest thing. Another rumor said the investor fellow died and left the ranch to his heirs. Maybe that's your Mr. Whit Hanley?"

The boss and his father, likely.

Her guest reached to take Jocelyn's hands in her own. "Now don't look so worried, dear; everything will be fine. I'm delighted to meet you, Miss Royal . . . Jocelyn. Seeing life around the place, I expected to find the owner, but you'll do. My husband, Lyman, and I have wanted to make things right with whoever owned the place — for the longest time." She shook her head. "Lyman would've come today, but he's getting our sickles, rakes, and horse tack cleaned up and repaired before full summer. Chores he mostly took care of last winter, but Lyman can't stand anything not being in prime condition."

Her forehead wrinkled, and she sighed. "If there *is* a hay crop and grain. This time of year, you know, we could get pouring rain, sleet, or even hail that would pound into the ground every bit of the hay crop, and oats. Leaving no way to feed our animals."

Jocelyn nodded, knowing that problem well.

Mrs. Goody waved a hand. "But back to today. It was so sunny and pretty I decided to take a drive. Lyman agreed with me that I should come here and," she chewed her lip, "take care of the — an embarrassing situation."

Embarrassing? "I'll bring the tea, and a couple of the little peach pies," Jocelyn said quickly, "and then you can tell me?"

"Not the pies, dear; those are for you."

Minutes later, frowning in apology, Jocelyn handed a blue enamel cup of steaming tea to her guest. "Sorry, there are no real dishes in this place."

Mrs. Goody accepted the tea with a smile. "That's quite all right, dear. I don't expect trail-driving cowboys to stock the chuck wagon with china teacups."

Jocelyn smiled back. "No, they don't." She took her chair again and waited for Mrs. Goody to finish what she'd come to say.

"I'm here to purge a guilty conscience, mine and Lyman's, too. Like I said, our farm is smaller than Nickel Hill. Lyman and I ran some of our cows on eighty acres of this ranch that's right next to our place. That grazing land had been going to waste, not being used. Don't you know," she said quickly, leaning toward Jocelyn, her expression serious, "we would have asked permission had there been anybody to ask. We're honest people." Her burden of guilt lifted, her shoulders eased in relief, and she smiled proudly. "I've come to pay rent on the time we used the pasture. We were hoping to make an offer to buy those eighty acres, too, thinking maybe the rent could go toward the price." Her brow furrowed in a righteous frown. "Such a shame, the land not being used for cattle, crops, or something."

"You're right, but —" Jocelyn tried to break in, but Mrs. Goody wasn't finished.

"I'm going to leave the pasture rent money with you to give to Mr. Hanley, the owner, when he comes." She opened her reticule and fingered inside. "And perhaps you'll mention to him that, if it's agreeable, we'd like to buy that same parcel."

Jocelyn hesitated. "I work for him, but I'm only sort of in charge. If you'd rather wait until Mr. Hanley is here . . ." *Which could be until doomsday . . . or sooner.*

"I trust you, dear." With a warm smile, Mable Goody placed a sheaf of bills in Jocelyn's hand and added sympathetically, "And if you need to use some of the money while you're here taking care of the ranch, I'm sure Mr. Hanley would understand. He has left you in quite a pickle, it looks to me."

You have no idea. "Thank you. I'll keep the money for him, and I'll see that he knows you and Mr. Goody would like to

94

buy the eighty acres you're renting now. Please go ahead and let your cows graze there, until we hear otherwise." She sighed. "I wish I could tell you exactly when Mr. Hanley is expected to show up here, but I honestly don't know. There is a chance it could be longer than we hope for, and in that case I'll have to use some of the money for salt and grain for the mules, and other needs on the ranch." She hesitated. "I could sell one of the mules to buy what's needed, but I'd rather not since I don't have Mr. Hanley's permission."

"If it comes to that, I'm sure in my bones you'd find a buyer for a mule; more than one, likely, so don't you worry. You've got good neighbors hereabouts, though they can be a bit suspicious about newcomers until they're used to you. Summer's a busy time for all us Rolling Prairie folks, but we now and then have a picnic by the creek, a dance at somebody's house, or a box supper and speechifying at the schoolhouse — the only school in quite a distance. You'll want to be there and meet your neighbors."

"That sounds very nice, and maybe, while I'm here, I can come. But I really don't think I'll be here long."

"Pshaw. You never know." Mrs. Goody fluttered a plump hand at Jocelyn.

They talked a while longer, and then Mrs. Goody struggled to her feet from the makeshift sofa. "This has been a most pleasant visit, Miss Royal, but I must be going on home. Lyman will be coming in from the fields for his supper."

Jocelyn excused herself to ask Sam to bring Mrs. Goody's horse and buggy. As he approached down the slope, leading the horse, Mrs. Goody whispered to Jocelyn, "He's a colored man."

Leaning close, Jocelyn answered, "I know."

Mrs. Goody's face furrowed in confusion. She looked at Jocelyn, embarrassed, then, with the handle of her reticule looped over an elbow, she held her cheeks, laughing. "You got me, Miss Royal."

"I like you, Mrs. Goody." Jocelyn smiled.

"I like you, too, dear, very much."

Jocelyn introduced her to Sam Birdwhistle, who grinned, doffed his hat, and returned to work. Taking her new friend's arm, Jocelyn helped her into the buggy.

Mrs. Goody lifted the reins and clicked to her horse, then as suddenly drew her rig to a stop. "I remind you again, Jocelyn, that nobody lived here in a dog's age, an' we couldn't find a soul to contact. What I near forgot to tell you is that Mr. Clem Kittredge, your neighbor to the south about six miles, borrowed two rocking chairs and a little table off the screen porch here. I'll tell Clem it's time to bring them back."

Surprised at the announcement, Jocelyn caught her bottom lip in her teeth to suppress a smile, not knowing for a second or two how to reply. "My goodness — well, yes," she said, her spirits dancing. "That'd be fine. Thank you, Mrs. Goody. I've enjoyed our visit today; please come again, any time."

Mr. Kittredge, a reedy old man with squinty eyes and a protruding nose below a ten-gallon hat, gruffly returned the porch table and wicker rockers three days later. In return, she invited Mr. Kittredge to stay for a supper of fried potatoes, wilted greens, and beans cooked with smoked pork. After they'd eaten, he asked to see the mules. He looked them over for some time, stood back with his thumbs hooked in his overall suspenders, and said, "Sure would like to buy me one of them. What you askin' for one?"

"I'm sorry," she said, "they aren't mine to sell. My boss would sell you a mule, I'm sure, when he shows up."

"When'd that be?"

"Umm, I'm not really sure."

"Well, how far does he have to come, an' I can probably tell you, Miss."

"I'm not sure where he is."

He nodded, like he'd just bet on a horse race and won a full purse. "Dadgummit! I thought it looked mighty peculiar, a young woman showin' up outta nowhere with a large herd'a mules. This ain't some crooked business, is it? If you stole these mules, Miss, I can guarantee you're in for a right smart of trouble with the law. They might not hang you, but you'll be spendin' many a year in prison. Life, probably."

She stiffened, heart racing, and hugged herself. "I promise you, Mr. Kittredge, everything about this ranch, the mules, and me is on the up and up." It was only a little lie that could turn out to be true in time. When she knew more. "I helped drive them here from when I joined Mr. Hanley and his mule herd in Emporia. I'm responsible for them here at . . . Nickel Hill, that's all."

CHAPTER SEVEN

Clem Kittredge didn't seem ready to leave, so Jocelyn asked him if he'd like to sit a while. They took their coffee to the rocking chairs he'd placed on the porch. "You or your folks from around here?" the old fellow asked, tilting his head and squinting.

"Only in the last few years. I was born in Kansas City, Missouri." They sat quietly for a few moments, sipping coffee. Jocelyn asked, "How about you, Mr. Kittredge, have you always lived here, in this part of Kansas?"

"Wouldn't live anywhere else!" he retorted. "Born right here in Morris County." He waved a hand, and his voice cracked. "Life . . . everything keeps changin' on me, though, some good ways, some not." He said it almost as a question, then continued, "When I was your age, I rode with the Morris County Rangers. Nobody remembers them anymore, don't believe."

Her eyebrows rose. "I've heard of Texas Rangers. Kansas had rangers, too?"

"I just said so, didn't I?" he growled. "Afore that I was a soldier in the army, fighting for the Union and liberty. Not a lot of folks living in Morris County then, only 'bout eight hundred total in 1861, and of them a hundred and fifty or so was voters. As the war went on, one hundred and twenty-five men had enlisted. You hear what I'm sayin'? That's near every loyal man in Morris County at the time, taking up their rifles for the Union. And that weren't enough. Morris County also sent a company of eighty Kaw Indians to serve with the Union army. How about that?"

"I think it's fascinating." She rocked, turning his way to listen.

"When I come home from the rebellion between the states, there was trouble right here, guerrillas and bushwhackers, thievin', takin' over, and in general makin' folks fear for their lives. That was when the Rangers got organized. We took care of them problems, right enough! Proud days, but a good thing they're over." His sad old eyes looked off toward the creek, more than likely seeing beyond it to the past.

"You've had a very interesting life, and I'm glad you told me. Come visit, anytime, please." She reached over and wrapped her fingers around his.

"I will, but you've kept me long enough." He pulled his fingers loose, his face under his moustache and whiskers crimson. "I have to be headed home."

After that, more neighbors returned things they had "borrowed" from the vacant house and barn, assuring Jocelyn that they were good people and wanted nothing more than to be good neighbors. With diplomacy and delight, Jocelyn accepted crockery, a lovely old dresser, and a lamp that had been taken from the house; a pitchfork, a whiffletree, grindstone, and sheep shears from the barn and outbuildings. Luckily, she had just baked a large batch of ginger cookies when Jess and Emma Hunter came with "borrowed" farm tools.

Like Mr. Kittredge, they acted suspicious. She overheard the husband saying to the wife that *"no man in his right mind would put a woman in charge of a valuable herd of mules. Somebody somewhere has went plumb loco."*

It required a whole lot of neighborliness to stay silent and not argue the matter!

Unfortunately, all she could offer was tea in the blue granite cups when the young Webbers, Tarsy and Gordon, visited, but they were too embarrassed seeing their faces in the framed mirror they had "borrowed" to stay long, anyway. Or, she thought later, did they see her as too peculiar to mingle with? Was a woman mule keeper that much of an oddity? Tarsy and Gordon looked to be near her age. She would have liked to know them better, if she were staying any time at all.

Darn Hanley, for putting her in this position of being an outsider and probable liar. All she'd wanted was a simple job.

By mid-June, weeks had passed, and Whit had still not shown up. Jocelyn was stunned when Sam Birdwhistle came to where she was washing clothes under a cottonwood by the creek and haltingly, avoiding her eyes, informed her that he'd be leaving soon. She stood up straight from the washboard, shook soapsuds from her hands back into the tin tub, and stared hard at him.

"Good grief, Sam, you can't go!" From the nearby creek bank, frogs croaked in the silence while she waited in rising panic for Sam's response. A breeze through the cottonwoods seemed to moan a warning. "Why're *you* doing this?" she asked him.

"It be best, Miss Jocelyn." Sam looked at her shamefaced as she stepped away from her washtubs. "Mebbe I can fine' out what happened to Whit. An' there be other reasons I can't stay on here. 'Sides, we got a lot of fixin' done. You're a good hand with the mules. I got a lotta fences fixed so you can open the corral gates wide and let them mules graze the pasture. More room for them to roll around on the ground when they wants to itch they's hide. When you need to corral them, wait'll they'll come in for water, or a bit a grain. An' iffen you need anything, they's neighbors who'll hep you. Look out for you."

"I didn't bargain for this, Sam!" she said with her wet soapy hands on her hips. She shook a finger at him. "Unless Whit Hanley has a good excuse for the fix he's left us in, as far as I care, he can go to hades and stay there. I want my pay; I don't want to be left without a nickel to my name and responsible for forty-two mules. Don't go, Sam, please." She put a hand on his arm, and his hand covered hers, patting it.

"There's a full bushel of reasons for me to go, Miss Jocelyn, sorry as my heart is to do it. I'm black, and you be a nice, white young lady. I seed how the neighbors look at me, all down in the mouth and they's eyes clouded with unfriendly. What they be thinkin' ain't fair to you, or right." He took a deep breath and shook his head. "An' there's more, Miss Jocelyn, that I wisht I didn't have to tell you."

"More?" Wasn't it plenty that he had to leave? She turned away, her gaze bouncing from the creek to the mules, the barn, and back to Sam. "What do you mean?"

"Whit could be in a right smart of trouble and need my hep. Could be they's mean-minded ruffians after both our scalps — an' mebbe caught up with him a'ready an' lookin' for me next." He opened his mouth to say more, then stopped short. There was tension in the cords of his neck.

Jocelyn went suddenly cold. "After you and Whit Hanley? For what? Why?"

He sighed and looked away for minute, then his brown eyes came back to her. "For a fix we got into on the wrong side of the law." His jaw set stubbornly. "Was a long time ago. I still think he be tendin' to business, not kilt or throwed back in jail, but I needs to make sure a'that."

Maybe killed, or in jail? "Good grief, Sam," she groaned, shoulders dropping, "why haven't you said something about this before? Why didn't he tell me? I've had suspicions of wrongdoing from the time the three of us met. I made myself believe *each* time that I was allowing my imagination to run off with itself." She could scarcely choke out her next words. "Whit might be dead? Tell me everything, Sam. I need to know." Should have been told long before this day. Finding it suddenly hard to stand, she sat down in the grass away from the sawhorse holding her washtub. She breathed deep and rubbed her arms.

"When Whit was hardly more than a button," he said, following and looking down at her, " 'bout twelve or fourteen and bein' constant at cross purposes with his mean papa, he run away from home. He took to wild behavior for a while — not serious trouble, but not good, neither. Later he — me an' him — fell in with a bunch of Missouri outlaws, bad'uns, not really knowin' what we be mixin' into. We was young and not smart, is what. A plan to rob a train didn't work out too good. I warn't exactly part of that, but Whit was. He paid for it, though, Miss Jocelyn."

A look of sadness crossed his face and disappeared. He told her earnestly, "My good friend spent two years in a Missouri prison; it wasn't no play party, neither." He pounded a fist into his other palm, making his point. "Whit, he stayed strong an' paid his debt to society, come out of prison all growed up an' not carin' to follow the wild road no more atall. Last few years he had his own blacksmith shop down in south Missouri, honest and respectable, Miss Jocelyn."

She climbed slowly to her feet and crossed her arms over her chest. This was the real reason, or at least part of the reason, why there was no sign of Whit Hanley's ever being here at this ranch his father had left him. *He was tied up in outlawry.* She was stunned by what Sam was telling her and yet not really surprised. After taking the job with the drive, not knowing a thimble's worth about either man, she'd begun to have suspicions but hadn't done a thing about it. If she'd just known for sure sooner, though . . . would she have done differently? She asked accusingly, "How come you've not mentioned a word of this before, Sam?"

"It warn't for me to be tellin' you. That was for Whit, when the time was right."

"Well, to my mind the right time was before we got so far into this awful fix."

"You likely be kareck, Miss Jocelyn, but it's done now. I need to see if I can find him, and iffen I can't, I won't be back noway. I could be in danger my ownself, and my family needs me. I have to be back to take care of my wife and chil'rens in Missouri."

More details she hadn't known, but good ones. She stood back, head tilted, half smiling. "There are little Birdwhistles, Sam? You have a wife?"

His brow smoothed. A smile broke across his face, showing his white teeth. "Two boys, two girls, an' my wife was expectin' another chile when I agreed to help Whit drive these mules to Kansas. Warn't supposed to be away from home this long."

"And you think Whit Hanley is worth the trouble of you looking for him? You're going to help him?" Her lips tightened, and she shook her head.

"He's a good man, Miss Jocelyn. No matter what you thinks about it, Whit Hanley is a good man. One of the best there is, to my way of thinkin'."

For a moment or two she was silent, considering his opinion. She heaved a heavy sigh. "I agree you should go to your family, Sam. But for all the aggravation Hanley has caused us, there will be icicles hanging in hades before I change my mind about him." She got to her feet and snatched a towel from the soapy water, wringing it with all her strength.

"You be hurtin' that towel, Missy," he said softly.

Catching the gentle humor in his voice,

she laughed, too. "I suppose I am. You've been a good friend, Sam, and a great worker. I'll miss you like fire."

A few hours later, with tears in her eyes, she watched Sam leave on his mule, Rover, his bedroll and "war bag" behind the cantle, and a bag of food she'd fixed for him dangling from the saddle horn, his voice faintly singing his favorite song, Stephen Foster's *Some Folks Do.*

"Good luck, Sam," she whispered as he disappeared from sight, "but I'm blamed if I know what's going to happen around here, now."

She doubted very much that she'd ever see him again. Sam was a good person, and despite what she'd said, she hoped he was right about Whit Hanley. In that moment, she remembered that she'd forgotten to ask Sam about the third rider with the mule drive, the one she'd replaced. A member of that youthful outlaw gang he spoke of, she supposed, and the law had been hunting him and Sam, too?

Lonely days followed, more than Jocelyn could count. At least, she told herself, she didn't have to worry about Indian outbreaks or raids of bushwhackers such as Mr. Kittredge had told her about.

Two or three times, with chores taken care of, she rode Zenith or Alice bareback, the other following, as they didn't like to be separated. For two or three hours she explored the far reaches of the Nickel Hill Ranch. If Hanley didn't return soon, she believed she'd know every rattlesnake den in the stony ridges, every black-tailed jackrabbit hole in the brush and grassy areas. Like much of the Flint Hills, the soil was thin, with rich big bluestem and little bluestem grass poking up through grey drifts of limestone. Not a good place for raising crops but ideal for grazing cattle, or mules.

As far back as 1870, settlers poured into the country she looked out on, driving large herds of cattle to fatten on its rich, abundant grass. From what she'd heard, it was a time of happy prosperity. If she didn't have a plan to go back to her farm on the Neosho, she wouldn't mind staying where she was.

She was surprised to find a second windmill in distant pastures, with an open pipe that would drain into a man-made pond. There was little water. Sam's help could have had the windmill operating properly, drawing water from deep in the earth. About three miles from the house and corrals, she'd also discovered a small building beside a grassy overgrown trail — a line shack or ranch-hand's cabin, she first assumed. But closer examination showed windows on both sides of the small structure and a fallen flag pole rotting in the grass. Her heart lifted in surprise. This was a schoolhouse, probably for the first settlers in the area. Her mind conjured images of Mr. and Mrs. Goody, and Clem Kittredge, as youngsters attending this school. The image made her smile, then laugh out loud.

From the highest point, she sat on her mule and took it all in: sapphire sky and puffy clouds over cascading green hills dotted with purple prairie clover, orange butterfly milkweed, and white poppy mallow, the quiet broken by the occasional song of a sparrow, or meadowlark. Some would consider the view she soaked in as *nothing,* but for her, these Flint Hills were so beautiful they took her breath away.

Sometimes in the evening, she would sit in the shadow of the windmill and sing sad sweet songs to the mules that'd come into the stone corral to drink or sleep. *Oh, Shenandoah, Swannee River, My Old Kentucky Home.* The mules stayed calm and seemed to like her company. And she could let her mind roam far from where she was.

After her disfigured mouth was repaired, a

favorite discovery was that she could sing — at least better than she could before. Back then it'd been hard for some people to even understand her speech. Papa, when he came home again, taught her song after song, sitting out on their porch of an evening. How she loved those song evenings, singing with Papa, sometimes dancing with fireflies in the yard as she sang.

It chafed that regardless how fond she was of the critters, responsibility for the mule herd and this blasted ranch was now heavily on her shoulders. Alone. Her fault as much as anyone's — she hadn't shown good sense when she hired on in the first place. Now that it was done, it wasn't in her to abandon the mules, as she'd been abandoned. It helped to remember that for now she had a roof over her head, food, and friendly neighbors — far more than she'd had that night she'd crawled into the hayloft in the Emporia livery.

Come morning, she decided, she'd go to town and shop for the things she was running out of on the ranch. For the time being she'd quit her fretting so much about Whit Hanley's absence and make do as much as possible . . . without a parcel of an idea what was next, blame his hide.

CHAPTER EIGHT

As she approached Skiddy, Jocelyn watched the impressive grain elevator grow larger and larger against June's blue sky. The dusty, sleepy town of a half-dozen blocks or so turned out to be not much different from others she'd seen: business establishments with false fronts that declared their name and wares, old men dozing on benches outside the barber shop, the ring of hammer on iron from the livery, homes with window boxes of flowers fronted by picket fences, buggy and wagon traffic, and an occasional horseback rider moving slowly along the street. All of it calm and welcoming.

Feeling a happy flutter of anticipation, at the corner of Main and Front Streets, she left her team and wagon tied to the hitch rail and entered the Skiddy General Store. She was met by a medley of pleasant aromas — apples, coffee, hams, spices, pickles, and yeasty baked goods. Moving into the cooler interior of the store and the dry-goods area she noted the storekeeper, a robust woman in a yellow, polka-dot dress with ballooning leg-o-mutton sleeves. She was offering effusive encouragement as she showed a bolt of fabric — violet cotton with tiny cream and navy dots and swirls — to a blonde young woman Jocelyn recognized. She'd met Tarsy Webber a few weeks past when the Webbers came to the ranch to return the "borrowed" mirror. Tarsy's blue eyes in her heart-shaped face reflected her desire for the dress goods.

Jocelyn looked on in envy. She would love to have a new dress to wear in the hot days of the coming summer, but until she had money strictly her own, she couldn't think of it. Even if she did have her own money, she reconsidered, she'd be saving her earnings toward buying back her farm.

"Hello, Tarsy. That violet color would be so pretty on you," she said. The young woman turned with a smile, but, recognizing Jocelyn, she flushed a deep pink, and her smile faded. She looked like she might turn and run from the store. Embarrassment ought not to bar a possible friendship, Jocelyn decided, and she reached to touch the other young woman's arm. "Truly, I mean it. You'd be positively beautiful in a dress made from that cloth." The female storekeeper beamed at Jocelyn, who continued, "Next time I come to town, I hope to buy something in a rose or pale-green print. A cool cotton." She smiled again, encouragingly, and moved away. "So nice to see you; now I'd better give mind to my own shopping."

After a few moments, Tarsy Webber came over to where Jocelyn was examining a pair of jet earrings and said, "It is nice to see you, too, Jocelyn." She seemed to struggle for her next words, then she plunged ahead. "I feel terrible about tak— borrowing the mirror from the Nickel Hill ranch house even though it was vacant and . . . I'd like to show you that I'm a normal, law-abiding person. I'm having lunch today in the hotel's dining room in about a half hour. Would you care to join me, please?"

Jocelyn laughed. "You gave the mirror back, and I'd judge you to be an honest person regardless. All is well. Thank you for inviting me. I'd like nothing better than for us to have lunch and to know one another better."

Tarsy heaved a sigh. "I'll look forward to it. See you in a bit."

Jocelyn nodded and smiled. She moved

on, exploring the many tempting goods like the earrings, settling only on the most needed to go into her basket — thread and needle, hair pins, and candles. Two iced tea glasses were a luxury, but she put them in her basket as well. Tarsy Webber purchased several yards of the violet cotton, plus ribbon and buttons to match, and left the store saying she needed to complete an errand at the drugstore.

"Would you have block salt for sale?" Jocelyn asked the storekeeper, after she'd placed her basket of items on the counter next to the cash register.

"We do. We're 'general merchandise,' meaning everything from groceries to clothing, boots, shoes, feed and seed, salt blocks, and, in the spring, baby chicks. The salt blocks are in the back of the store, along with my husband's work room. I'll have him bring the salt block for you."

"Thank you, ma'am. Besides these," she nodded at her selections on the counter, "I will need flour, sugar, beans, lard . . . and oh, yes, a bottle of lemon extract, please. I won't be leaving town for an hour or so; would you keep my purchases here until I'm ready for them?"

"Don't mind at all, Miss. They'll be here. You're new around here, aren't you? I don't think I've seen you in the store before. I'm the store owner's wife, Mrs. Noack, but you may call me Elsa." She brushed the front of her lace trimmed apron and waited, eyebrows raised.

"Jocelyn Royal." She offered her hand. "Nice to meet you, Mrs. Noack . . . Elsa."

"Are you a neighbor of Tarsy and Gordon Webber? They both grew up in the Skiddy area; fine young folks. I thank you for helping make the sale to young Tarsy, by the way."

Jocelyn shrugged. "The violet print is so fitting for her, but you're welcome. I am new, but I don't know how long I'll be here." She paid for her purchases from the pasture rental money. "I'm staying on the Nickel Hill Ranch west of Skiddy; maybe you know of it? I'm in charge of things until the owner comes to take over." *Me and the mules,* but she didn't say it aloud.

"I do know of the Nickel Hill place. Matilda Scott, who used to own it, was a dear friend of mine. Who did you say bought it?"

She hadn't said, but she told Mrs. Noack, "My boss, Whit Hanley, inherited the property, as I understand it, from his father, who bought it from Mrs. Scott's children after she passed on."

116

"Poor soul. Those addleheads' eagerness to be shed of the place she loved so much pesters my mind, still. But nothing can be done about that now." Her nimble fingers quickly righted a display of canned cherries on the counter. "Glad to have you here, Miss Royal."

"I appreciate that, Mrs. Noack, but I can't imagine I'll be in this part of the country much longer."

"Well, if you are, I'll look forward to seeing you again here at the store, or a community affair." She smiled. "Seems like something is going on all the time, and you'd be most welcome." Mrs. Noack pointed to a homemade sign tacked to the wall behind her, scrawled letters announcing an upcoming Fourth of July celebration, with cowboy riding and roping contests, a picnic, and speeches.

Jocelyn thanked her, thought longingly again about the jet earrings and necklace, then mentally scolded herself for even thinking of buying such folderol. Maybe someday that would change, and she'd no longer be a pauper looking after somebody else's mules! For now, she'd stick to the barest necessities, and even so, she was spending Whit Hanley's money, not a cent of it hers.

Leaving the store, she checked on her

team, gave Zenith and Alice each a bit of oats, and stroked them for a few minutes. She couldn't tarry long at lunch with Tarsy Webber. She needed to be back at the ranch making sure all was well there, and in time for the evening feeding and watering. But lunch with her new friend beckoned, and she walked in long happy strides to the D. J. Shore Hotel.

The dining room was just off the lobby, spare but tasteful. She spotted Tarsy at a table by the window and hurried that way. After a few moments of chitchat, becoming more comfortable in each other's company, they ordered. The special was fried chicken, new potatoes and gravy, warm bread, and greens with sliced egg and vinegar. Jocelyn's mouth watered so much she had to blot her lips with her napkin. She had not had fried chicken since she'd been forced to give up her farm. Regardless of the price out of Whit Hanley's money, she was having it now! "Iced tea, too, please," she said, spending more of Hanley's cache.

Tarsy ordered salmon cakes with coleslaw, new potatoes, and peas. For a few minutes, they ate in silence, then Tarsy spoke. "May I ask if you are married, Jocelyn?"

She shook her head and blotted greasy lips. "No husband, no conquests. I'm sure at my age of twenty-four years I fit the bill of spinster." She looked Tarsy in the eye. "Not that I'm pleased to be stamped as such. I'd not mind to be married. I'd like to have children; it just hasn't happened." She hesitated, brushing off a twinge of sadness. "If marriage never comes to pass, I'm sure I'll have a fair life." She smiled. "How about you? Do you and Gordon have little ones?"

Tarsy flushed, a small grin playing at her lips. "Not yet." She leaned forward to whisper, "But we're trying. We'd love to have five or six children, at least. Gordon wouldn't mind having all boys, to work with him on the farm, and to hunt with him, but I'd like one or two girls."

"Pretty dresses . . . sugar and spice; I don't blame you."

The Webbers owned an established farm, six hundred and forty acres in a valley of the Flints, inherited from her family. In answer to Jocelyn's questions, Tarsy answered, "We raise wheat, which we ship mostly to Texas from the Skiddy railroad station. We have chickens, milk cows, pigs. A huge garden, and I put up a lot of it for winter but enjoy it fresh, too. We're experimenting with an orchard, apples, plums, and peaches — which reminds me, we have fruit to share when it ripens. You must come for a visit, so I can send some garden sass home with you."

Jocelyn hesitated to reveal her own situation by comparison, but she believed in being truthful when making new friends. She told Tarsy the facts, that she and her father had lost their farm, a small one across the river from the town of Dunlap, near Bushong. She'd tried waitressing in an Emporia restaurant, but that ended badly. Tarsy's eyes grew wide when Jocelyn told how she'd hired on with Whit Hanley and Sam Birdwhistle as cook, one woman with two men, on their drive of mules to the Skiddy ranch.

"You're so brave!" she said in a near whisper. "Mules. And men . . ."

"Both men have gone off," Jocelyn finished quietly, "about their own affairs. Mr. Hanley surely intends to be back. Nickel Hill is his ranch, his mules, but something has happened to keep him away, and I have no idea what that is. I'm not even sure he can return. I could be fettered heaven knows how long, waiting. I am determined, though," her voice grew strong, "to see these mules sold and to be paid my share. I'm going to have my farm again."

Tarsy reached across the table to take Jocelyn's hand, her blue eyes understanding. "I'll pray for you, Jocelyn, that that happens. I believe it will. You seem to be a very strong person."

"Thank you." Jocelyn sipped her iced tea. "I apologize for my sad story, but I wanted you to know who I am, why I'm here. I am strong, most of the time. But brave — I'm not as sure about that." She laughed to herself, then went on to tell about a time in school when she was a little girl, and she stuck her finger into a pencil sharpener while the scamp who urged her on turned the crank. "Whittled my pride down to size, as well as cutting my finger near to pieces."

"You poor thing!" Tarsy gasped, her hands to her face. "Whyever did you listen to him? Why'd you do that?"

"I wanted a friend, and he said it wouldn't hurt. I believed him, and I wanted to show I could be brave. My finger healed fine," Jocelyn showed her, "and I'd had a good lesson — you can't trust just anybody." She smiled and pushed back her chair. "But right now, I must be going along. I've enjoyed our lunch together, very much. I'm obliged that you invited me, Tarsy. Say hello to your husband, Gordon, for me, too, please." *And good luck having those babies,* she thought enviously.

As they were saying good-bye outside the hotel, Tarsy told Jocelyn, "There's going to

121

be a *rodeo,* as some folks are starting to call cowboy contests, and a picnic here at Skiddy to celebrate Independence Day, on a ranch east of town. Gordon wouldn't miss it. He's like a little boy, riding broncs and roping steers, getting dirty, bruised up, and hardly able to walk afterward, but happy. I'd be pleased if you'd come and watch the cowboys show off their skills with me, Jocelyn. Everyone brings a picnic basket lunch, too. We all have a good time and look forward to it all year." She shrugged and said with a laugh, "Like we do any of the holidays."

"I saw the sign about the celebration when I was in the Noacks' store. I might come, if I can be sure the mules will be there on the ranch when I return," she said with a frown. "They've broken out once and would have been scattered to Timbuktu if we hadn't noticed right away. I like to keep the usual time feeding and watering them. I think it would be fine if I'd be away only a few hours. We'll see, and I'm obliged."

They parted, and Jocelyn headed toward her team and wagon out front of the mercantile. She took sudden note of a man going into the saloon across the way. Her heart nearly stopped. In the glare from the sun it was hard to be sure, but the man looked like the no-good scalawag who'd forced his way into her wagon, attacked her, and threatened to kill Sam Birdwhistle so that he could steal the mules. A chill crept along her spine.

Did he know she was in town? If he'd seen her team and wagon, he'd surely recognize them and come looking for *her.* Clutching her skirts, she took off at a run. She burst into the store and asked for her order. The owner, Mr. Noack, who was now minding the store, carried out her bundles and bags and stowed them in the wagon.

"Is there anything wrong, Miss?" He rubbed his hands down the front of his apron and made a better adjustment of her purchases in the wagon.

"I . . . No, I don't think so." She nervously brushed her hair from her eyes. "But I have to be going." Her heart thudded in her ears as her mind replayed the awful incident on the road to the ranch. She'd come so close to unbelievable trouble — losing the mules, losing Sam, losing her life. If she hadn't acted in time and booted the louse off her wagon, leaving him afoot and without his horse for miles, the situation could have turned out so much worse.

Even as she trembled inside, she told herself that the man going into the saloon could have been someone else, and she was making a mistake. But no matter, she would be back to the ranch all the sooner in any regard. Make sure the mules were all right. She shouldn't have left them this long. Undoing the lines from the post, she climbed into the wagon and backed her team from the hitch rail. "Thank you, Mr. Noack." He looked perplexed but waved as she turned her team to leave town. She snapped the lines, urging them into a high trot. "Git up, Zenith. Go, Alice. Git mules."

As she passed the corner where the saloon was located, the door was open in the hot afternoon. Laughter, music, and loud male voices spilled out into the street. In her swift examination, she didn't spot the lowlife she feared among the male figures at the bar, or at tables close to the front. Not that she'd had a good look, or wanted one.

On this first leave-taking from the ranch, was she spoiling a good time seeing ghosts where there weren't any? She couldn't help hoping that her imagination was the culprit.

All the way home, she kept looking back, only to see a long empty road from town. She began to relax and breathe easier. Her poor team, on the other hand, was blowing hard, heads drooping, their sides covered with sweat when they arrived at the ranch.

She babied them with words, stroking their necks as she unhooked them from the wagon and led them into the corral where they could drink from the tank and she could rub them down.

She sighed in relief. She was back among her ranging mules; all was right with her world. The wheel atop the tall wooden windmill tower turned in the gentle wind, the sucker rod in the pipe clanked its steady, almost musical rhythm, a sound she'd always liked. Water. Cool, clean water drawn from deep in the earth for animal and human. Thank heaven for it. She unloaded her groceries and other household items, put them away in the house, and took the salt block to the corral for her mules.

A week passed. The calm and quiet of the ranch continued. She was wrong about the man she'd seen in Skiddy, who would have surely followed her from town that day if he'd recognized her team and wagon.

On a bright morning a few days after that, she was in the corral just finished seeing to her daily chore of freshening the mules' water and shoveling manure over the fence into a pile, when hands grabbed her hard from behind and a male voice grunted. She screamed and fought to be free. Fear exploded inside her. It was him! The thin wrists, the stringy body, the smell of him — the devil was still after her. She twisted, turned, and fought, stabbing with her elbows, but he hung on with an iron grip, grunting from her blows.

"He'll kill you, you know," she lied through chattering teeth, "*him,* my neighbor over there by the barn with the gun on you. Go ahead, shoot!" He turned to look, and for the briefest second his grip loosened. She jerked free and ran from the corral on legs that suddenly wanted to go weak and fail her.

He caught up and grabbed her, brutally clutching her against him. "You'll be sorry as hell you try foolin' me again! Where's Whit Hanley?" he snarled in her ear, breathing hard. "I ain't seen him here, but you know where he is. Damn you, girl, tell me now!" He twisted her arms up behind her back. "An' mebbe, after we have a little romp, I won't kill you. You keep fightin' though, and I'll hafta." He whipped her around and slapped her so hard her head rocked, and her hair came loose from its pins.

Feeling woozy, Jocelyn staggered, barely staying on her feet. Her face stung; her cheekbone felt broken from his blow. He caught her up tightly again, holding both her arms in a painful grip. She sobbed in anger and fought, stomping his booted feet. She wrenched hard from one side to the other to break his hold. Nothing worked.

"I don't know anybody named Whit Hanley," she screamed at him. "Why are you here? Let me go!"

CHAPTER NINE

"You know damned well who I'm talkin' about!" her attacker yelled and jerked her around, leaving her dizzy and in pain. With her arms pinned down by his and being held tightly back against him, with his leg wrapped around hers, she couldn't escape.

He grunted in her ear with a nasty laugh. "I saw your rig in town. I only went to the saloon for a nip or two of celebration whiskey, then I'd come after you. Little ol' fuss sprung up in the saloon, and I had to knife a feller. I was throwed in jail on a drunk and disorderly charge. But it gave me time to figger all I want to do to you. Soon's I was free I asked around and found out that this is Whit Hanley's place, an' you been right here with the mules!" He laughed again, his breath making her gag.

His voice turned hard. "Now tell me: where's that son of a bitch Hanley at? We want him." He gave her a slobbery kiss on her neck and tightened his hold until the pain was nearly unbearable and she couldn't breathe.

A few mules had begun to trot out of the corral, agitated by the commotion. Regaining her equilibrium, Jocelyn fought with freshly fueled anger. This hoodlum was not going to kill her and take the mules! She slammed her head backward into his nose. He yelped and cursed, his arms loosening just enough for her to hurtle out of his reach. A small cinnamon colored mule colt she'd tagged with the name Rusty let fly and viciously kicked her attacker. The man screamed and, holding his middle, dropped to the ground. The mule kicked again, a lightning movement that caught her attacker again, this time in the head.

When the ruffian didn't move, Jocelyn crept back. Rubbing her aching arms, her head solid pain from using it as a weapon, unsteady on her feet, she looked down through bleary eyes at her attacker. If he wasn't dead, he was close; blood trickled from the side of his head, and he didn't move. His face, under blood and dirt, was sickly white. His clothes were torn where Rusty's first kick had struck him in the side.

She backed away, her hand to her mouth, not sure what to do. She drove the mules back into the corral and locked the gate so they couldn't do any more damage or wander away. In her aching head, Sam's voice was telling her over and over, *"Blood on your hands, the rest of your life behind bars, ain't for you."*

The thing to do was to move her attacker down to the house, where she might save his life — his good-for-nothing life — Jocelyn decided. But she couldn't lift him; she would have to drag him, or roll him down, and that alone would kill him if he were still alive. He could be hurt inside as well as his head. Rusty, the little mule, had done a good job of saving her.

She needed help. She needed the Skiddy marshal and a doctor, if she didn't want to go to jail for murder. She went into the corral with a halter, swiftly brought Alice out, and locked the gate. Minutes later, she was astride, her heels urging speed from Alice toward the Goodys' farm, the closest neighbor.

Mr. Goody was cultivating a cornfield near their house and heard her yelling in panic as she pulled up hard into their yard. He came running. "What is it, Miss? What's wrong?" He stared at her torn dress, the welts on her arms, her battered face. "What in God's name happened to you?"

She told him what had taken place. "He was attacking me, threatened to kill me. I got loose of him for just a bit, and one of our mules kicked him, twice. He may be dead. I need somebody to go for the marshal and a doctor if there's anything can be done."

Mr. Goody's nimble fingers unhooked his horse from the plow in seconds. He leaped astride and rode out fast ahead of Jocelyn to the ranch. As hard as she pounded Alice's sides with her heels, following, it seemed to Jocelyn that it was taking years to reach where she'd left the man bleeding into the corral dust.

They sent their mounts flying up the slope to the barn and corrals. Jocelyn leaped off her mule. "He's over here," she cried and led the way in a painful lope. Except that he wasn't. There was nothing where he had lain except blood-soaked soil. She looked around, frantic, wondering if he might have crawled away to a spot close by. For the next hour, she and Mr. Goody searched the barnyard, pastures, in the barn and all around, the house included. The devil was gone, like he'd never been there, except for his blood.

Jocelyn rubbed her forehead. Her mind was clouded, and her whole body ached.

"He — he couldn't have gone by himself, I'm s-sure of it," she mumbled mostly to herself. "Somebody else must have been c-close, put him on his horse, took him away. That's the only thing could have happened, Mr. Goody." She looked at him, fighting dizziness. "H-his hair is long, and it's hard to be sure, but I'm almost positive the mule's hoof broke his skull on the side, by his temple.

"Here." Her hand shook as she touched her head. "He was bleeding bad. I couldn't tell for sure that he was breathing, but I think he was." She prattled on, unable to stop. "I don't know where he's gone to, but he was here." She looked around as though she might have missed seeing him earlier. "The man was very badly hurt — if not dead. Someone might have taken him away, his body. To go to the marshal? To the doctor if there was a chance? I don't understand this, Mr. Goody, I purely don't." She was shaking hard.

"I'll go looking for him, Miss Royal. I saw some tracks might be his, riding off. You go on into the house and take care of yourself."

Jocelyn nodded, looked to double-check that all the mules were where they belonged, and stumbled toward the house. Feeling numb throughout mind and body, she washed up and changed her dress. Hearing Mr. Goody's return to the yard an hour so later, she went out to the porch and, though half expecting it, was stunned to see that he led the outlaw's horse, the body across the saddle.

She leaned against the porch post for support, shivering despite the hot sun, while Mr. Goody explained. "Appears to me like your attacker got one foot in the stirrup but either died right then or was too bad off to make it into the saddle. His horse dragged him a long way. Found the body in a draw, cold as a wagon wheel, then the horse wandering. I don't think anybody else had anything to do with it. Only saw one set of horse tracks."

"Thank you, Mr. Goody."

"No thanks needed, Miss Royal; you been through a lot. I'm going to take the body on into Skiddy to the marshal's office. They'll know what to do."

She nodded. "All right. I'm obliged, Mr. Goody. If the marshal wants to talk to me, I'll be here." She turned and went into the house. For long miserable moments she sat at the table staring blindly at the wall, feeling sick inside. Why was this nightmare happening? Why wasn't Whit Hanley here to take care of his own obligations, such as this killer who'd been looking for him? At least it was almost over, surely. Needing something to steady her quaking body, she put on a pot of coffee.

The marshal had no problem believing Jocelyn's story, or Mr. Goody's explanation of what he'd seen and found. Jocelyn was innocent of any wrongdoing. The dead man's name was Rufe Tuttle; he'd been hanging around Skiddy recently, causing trouble — picking fights, bullying old men to buy him drinks, beating up saloon girls. He'd been released from jail the day Jocelyn first spotted him going into the saloon, then thrown back in the same day for drunk and disorderly conduct after knifing another man in a brawl. "He was a bad'un," the marshal said. Both he and Mr. Goody believed Tuttle worked alone. Jocelyn wished she could be sure of that.

In the days that followed Jocelyn was seldom alone. Neighbors came bearing sympathy gifts of food — a quart jar of milk, a dozen eggs, a loaf of fresh bread, jam, vegetables from their gardens — and stayed to visit. All wanted to hear the story of what happened, far more often than she wanted to be reminded of what took place. It was a relief when the visits lessened.

A few days before the Fourth of July, dear grumpy old Mr. Kittredge came to inform her that he would be staying to keep watch on the ranch and the mules, while she attended the Independence Day picnic with the Webbers. She turned him down gently, telling him she'd rather stay and take care of the mule herd, that they were her responsibility. Within hours, word of her refusal made the rounds of neighbors. One and all insisted she go to the celebration and have a good time for a change. Tiring of the argument, she agreed. The Webbers would stop by for her in their buggy.

Once she'd made the decision, to Jocelyn's surprise she began to look forward to the day.

The morning sun was already beating down when they arrived at their destination. "We'll try to find some shade," Gordon said. Tarsy's husband was a short, well-built man with a friendly grin. "Can't make no promises, though." He drove their rig across an enormous grassy field dotted with clots of trees and toward the main arena. Deftly, he maneuvered the buggy between groups of farmers and their wives talking to friends, cowboys and young women chatting and flirting, snow-haired old ranchers leaning

135

on their canes and obviously swapping stories of other days like this. Laughter and good-natured shouts occurred in irregular bursts. Broncs and wild steers stirred dust in a variety of makeshift pens and added a stringent odors to the air.

The arena was a large fenced pasture surrounded by wagons, buggies, and tethered horses. Finding a good spot between other rigs under a large sycamore tree, Gordon kissed his wife's cheek, nodded and tipped his hat to Jocelyn, and left them to join a group of other cowboys clustered near the gate into the pasture where events would take place.

Jocelyn and Tarsy sat high in the Webbers' buggy and for the first half hour, under Tarsy's baby-blue parasol, watched cowboys take their turns riding bucking broncs and mules. A few times, an animal hardly bucked at all, leaving the rider to dismount in red-faced embarrassment and onlookers laughing. More often, the two young women cringed and sometimes cried out when a rider was tossed furiously about on the mount's back, only to be thrown like a bag of grain into the dust.

"Don't you worry that a time will come when Gordon might not move after being thrown like that?" Jocelyn asked.

"Yes, I worry," Tarsy turned to say. Her fingers nervously crumpled her bonnet strings. "But it does little good. He was a cowboy before he married me and became a rancher. He's broken his left ankle, three ribs, and his collarbone in riding competitions. These 'bucking shows' go back years, and I'm afraid it is in his blood. Cowboys like to take a break on holidays to try and prove they are better than cowboys from the next ranch, the next county, at riding, roping, and taking steers down, all normally part of their everyday work. It's disgusting to consider, but according to Gordon, there is a cowhand known to bite a steer's lip to help bring the animal down. Using his teeth, like a bulldog. Ugh."

Jocelyn wore a half smile and shook her head. "Tough, reckless, prideful men, I take it."

"Yes," Tarsy agreed, nodding, "and a cowboy can be the most hardheaded human you'll ever meet." Hesitating, she added with a quiet smile, "Many, though, have an enormous heart and are very cordial to women."

Their attention was soon taken by the next bronc ride. The red roan bucked high into the air, then twisted a full turn and back again, coming down so hard on its front hooves that it had to have jarred the rider's spine painfully. Jocelyn gasped but kept her eyes admiringly on the cowboy in the saddle, one hand on the buck rein and the other fanning the horse with his hat while raking his spurs along the horse's side. The horse continued to pitch and contort unbelievably in an attempt to throw the rider. After an interminable time, a shot was fired into the air signaling "a ride to the finish." Another cowboy charged his mount into the arena and grabbed the bucking horse's reins while the rider leaped off into the dust, brushed off his denim pants, and lifted his black hat to a crowd roaring approval of his winning ride.

Jocelyn sat frozen as she took a better look at the cowboy. Her heart began to pound in surprise and happy recognition. "I know him," she whispered under her breath. "I know him!" He was medium height, broad-shouldered, his collar-length hair the color of sunlit wheat. His Norwegian ancestry was evident in his longish face and high cheek-bones. She recalled his blue eyes, a teenage boy's eyes during the time she remembered.

"Know who?" Tarsy wanted to know, gazing right and left and breaking into Jocelyn's fond remembering. "You recognize some-one?"

"The rider who just won the bucking horse event," Jocelyn answered, "and if he's who I think he is, he was part of a family that lived near our farm." Her heart returned to a normal beat. "We were youngsters." He was a man now, heading from the arena in the easy rolling walk of a cowboy. She might be wrong, but, just in case, she planted in her mind what he wore — the black hat, dark-blue shirt, red bandana, denim pants, and black boots. "Do you know him, Tarsy?"

"He looks familiar, but I'm not sure who he is. Some of these cowboys come from miles around, from Chase and Geary Counties and from here in Morris County and even further away. A few of them are first-timers, although many have competed for years. You're looking kind of strange, Jocelyn. Was he special to you or something?"

"Yes," she spoke quietly. "He was special."

She was twelve and had just taken over Papa's abandoned farm, with Gram to guide her in working the place. The neighbor boy's mother had sent him with a cow, on loan, to repay for quite a bit of damage his family's sheep had done to her vegetable garden. But it was the gift he brought her from himself that sent her heart soaring in surprise, a moment forever engraved in her soul. He'd grinned. "These are from me because I was supposed to watch the sheep," he'd told her. From behind his back he brought out a nosegay of blue and pink Sweet William. And her life was changed.

Tarsy was studying her face. "You should talk to him, Jocelyn. Here, I'll go with you. Maybe Gordon already knows that cowboy." Tarsy started to rise, taking Jocelyn's arm.

"Not — not right now." She took a deep breath, holding back. "After a while, maybe." She wasn't sure why she hesitated, unless it was that she enjoyed thinking that he was the boy she remembered, and he might not be. She moistened her lips. "It's been years; he probably wouldn't remember me." Even with those thoughts, throughout the following events — steer roping, a wild horse race, and bull riding — Jocelyn couldn't take her eyes from him, couldn't help clapping wildly when he was a contestant. *Tosten. Tosten Pladson was his name.*

Midday, Tarsy and Jocelyn spread a blanket under nearby trees and brought out the picnic lunches they'd packed. Fried fish with bones removed, coleslaw, bread and butter, and apple cake from Jocelyn's basket; ham sandwiches, boiled eggs, and fat sugar cookies from Tarsy's. Lemonade in burlap-wrapped jars to keep the drink cool. Jocelyn hadn't spied Tosten for some time; possibly he'd left the grounds. It was hard to put him from her thoughts and pay more mind to the good food. She was idly forking her cake when Tarsy grabbed her elbow, almost spilling the cake into Jocelyn's lap. "There he is, Jocelyn! You go talk to him, right now! Hurry!"

"All right, if you're going to keep pestering." Jocelyn stood slowly, rubbing her hands down her sides from nerves. He was walking away, leading an impressive black horse with white blaze face and stockings, to where several other horses were tethered. She felt stiff, like she walked in deep mud, when she wanted to feel confident. "Tosten!" she called in a husky voice. "Tosten?"

In the same second another cowboy grabbed his shoulder and, with a wide grin, said, "Good goin', Pete. Nice ridin'. I hear most of the bettin' is on you today."

Pete? The man wasn't Tosten, then? She halted, feeling foolish. He could have been Tosten's twin! Her disappointment drove deep, her shoulders slumped, and she turned back the way she'd come.

"Jocey, that you?" a male voice hollered. "Where you goin'? Wait! C'mere, don't leave."

"Tosten?" she turned around and stared

141

at him, a wide smile creeping across her face.

CHAPTER TEN

The other cowboy clapped him on the back. "Ya' don't have to be that lucky, Pete! But g'wan, I'm headin' yonder for a drink."

She walked to him slowly. "He called you Pete. Twice. But you are Tosten, aren't you? Tosten Pladson?"

"Sure am. My lord it's good to see you, Jocey. You've gotten plumb beautiful." He lifted his hat to her, stood and stared and grinned while his horse nudged his shoulder for attention.

She hadn't been beautiful then, and she wasn't now, but she wasn't going to argue. She felt nicer looking when he said it. She smiled. "Thank you. Why did he call you Pete?" she motioned toward the cowboy who'd joined a group who were passing a bottle.

"Tell you in a minute." He spoke with the slightest of accents, and if she remembered correctly his parents were the only ones in the family born in the Old Country; in fact, he had more of a Kansas twang now. "Don't go away," he said. "In fact, come with me while I take care of Raven, here." He patted his horse. As they walked along, him leading the black gelding, and Jocelyn feeling like she was in a dream occurring out of nowhere, he said, "Where've you been? I haven't seen you since I took off from home. I heard a couple years ago," he hesitated, "that your Pa passed on, and you'd lost the farm?"

"That's a long story that can wait." She steadied her voice. "How about you, Tosten? You left home kind of early. I heard about you, for a while, from your sisters and your mother, but not a lot. I haven't seen them for quite a while." After her father died and the farm was gone, she had moved around, seeking odd jobs for her keep.

"Well," he drawled, "I work on a Geary County ranch, the 7Cs. Skiddy being on the county line between Morris and Geary, the ranch isn't a far piece north of here. I've been a cowhand pretty much since I left home." He was still staring at her, grinning.

"The Seven Seas, a ranch on the Kansas prairie — hardly an ocean?"

He laughed, a warm sound from deep in

his throat. "Not 'sea' — the letter *C* for the family Carman. Seven brothers owned it. I work for the last of them, Daniel and his wife, Adella. I'm Pete to everybody who knows me, except family. My whole name is Tosten *Peder* Pladson. Peder is Norwegian for Peter. So . . . Pete."

A tall gangly cowboy strode to meet them, taking off his hat and revealing a full head of red hair. He grinned. "See you found yourself a pretty girl, huh, Pete? How about introducing her in case she has a change of mind about you?"

Pete tipped his head toward the new-comer. "Jocey, that ugly cowboy there is Red Miller, good friend, stinkin' poor rider. Red, Jocey is way too good for you. Don't bother for a minute to think you've got a chance. Besides, Jocey Royal and me are friends from way back."

"Figures," Red groaned sorrowfully, bely-ing the glimmer in his eyes. "You always was a lucky cuss." He bowed to Jocelyn, holding his hat to his chest. "In case you do change your mind, Miss Royal, remember the name, handsome Red Miller, top hand at rodeo, if ugly old Pete finds the courage to tell you the truth."

"I'll try to remember that," Jocelyn re-plied, laughing. After Red Miller left, she said, "I suppose I can call you Pete." She brushed back a tendril of hair that blew into her eyes. "And hardly anybody calls me Jocey, anymore. My given name is Jocelyn. I'm called that, now."

"Shoot, I don't know if I can call you, uh, Jocelyn. You've always been Jocey to me, but I'll try."

She waited while he penned and curried his horse and made sure there was hay and water. Finished, he said, "I'm starving. Shall we look for something to eat in town at the café? Or maybe at the hotel's dining room; that'd be better. Something fancy to celebrate our meeting again."

"We could, but I've eaten. I do have food left over in my basket, though. Fresh baked bread and butter, coleslaw and fish, apple cake with burnt-sugar icing. Come meet my friends, and I'll fix you a plate." She turned to lead the way, her heart thumping with pleasure. She'd had very few friends as a youngster; Tosten — Pete — was the best.

Tarsy and Gordon had vanished, but Jocelyn's blanket was carefully spread, centered with her food basket, which had two sugar cookies on top — likely put there by Tarsy.

Jocelyn sat quietly by and watched Tosten — *Pete* — take a large bite from his fish and bread, a cup of lemonade in his other hand. When he'd remarked that he was starved he was clearly truthful, she thought with a private smile, as he dug into his coleslaw. She compared *the man* to the nice, golden-haired boy who'd been so kind to her and concluded, from the look of him, he was the same decent human being; surely married by now, and a father. When he was finished except for the bits of icing he was fingering from his plate, she asked him, curiosity claiming the better of her, "Have you married . . . Pete? Do you have a wife? Children?"

His eyebrows rose in surprise. "*Me?* Lord-a-mighty, no!" He rubbed the back of his neck and put on a wide grin. "Nope, not cut out for that kind of harness. Just a jinglebob cowboy, and I aim to stay that way. How about you, Jocey . . . I mean Jocelyn?"

"No, not married." *Had never even been close.* She smiled at him and nibbled her cookie. "So, just a cowhand, hmm? No plans to someday have your own ranch? Or a farm?"

He shuddered at the word *farm,* and humor flickered in his eyes. "Never a farm." His Adam's apple bobbed. "That might suit Far, my father, the hard-hearted old son-of-gun, but farming's not for me. Now a small cow outfit . . . yep, I'd like that. Especially if ranching allowed me a little spare time now and then, for something else I'm interested in."

"Oh, what's that?" She poured herself a glass of lemonade and waited.

"Well, it isn't something I could make a livin' at, so that puts the whoa on it right quick. Jocey," he hesitated, "Jocelyn, have you heard the name Frederic Remington? Know who he is and what he does?"

"Isn't he an artist who paints pictures of western things — horses, cowboys, scenery?" She sipped her lemonade and made a face; the lemonade could have used more sugar. She turned her attention back to Tosten — Pete.

His glass clinked against hers, and he looked pleased. "You're right; he's a western artist, quite well known, actually. I want to be an artist, like him. Okay, not totally like him . . . I want to do art in my own style. Is this laughable for a cowpoke, do you think? I'd really like your opinion, Jocey." He waited, broad shoulders back, his blue-eyed gaze fastened on her face.

She felt suddenly more at ease, meeting Pete after all this time, gratified that he wanted her opinion. "Why shouldn't you be

148

an artist, if that's what you want? Wasn't Remington a cowhand here in Kansas for a time?"

A very bowlegged cowboy walked by them, and Pete nodded and waved. "That was a good ride, Mac." The rider, chewing on a straw, grinned and answered, "I reckon it was."

"Yep, about Remington," Pete said when the other rider had passed, "although he was an easterner, hailing from New York, I believe. He spent quite a bit of time here in Kansas, working as a cowhand with the Plum Creek outfit, so he'd be close up to the life he wanted to paint."

She nodded. "Here in the Flint Hills, near Strong City in Chase County, I remember hearing."

"I wouldn't mind working for the same outfit, might have learned a thing or two from him about art." He rubbed his eyebrow with the ball of his thumb. "When I think about it, Frederic Remington also raised sheep here in Kansas on a ranch in Butler County, south of Peabody, for a while. Me, being a cowhand through and through, would likely have butted heads with him over raising sheep in cow country." He winked, and Jocelyn smiled.

"When we were still back home," she said,

"I didn't know that you liked to draw. Did you then?" She finished her cookie and wiped her fingers over her mouth.

"I did but kept it secret. Far would have killed me if he'd found out I was giving time to anything but hard farm work. Do you remember the book of your father's that you loaned our family, *The Dog of Flanders?*" He ate his cookie in two bites.

"I do, and I still have it."

"You've kept it . . . that's good, Jocelyn. When we borrowed that book is when I started to draw. I drew dogs, lots of them. Then farm animals, horses, cowboys at work. People at their trades. Western scenes. Okay, I'm busting to tell you more, so I might as well do it."

She smiled and waited expectantly, with her hands folded in her lap, for him to tell her what he was arriving at.

"A drawing of mine, cowboys in their long johns, washing up and watering their horses in a pond, was published in a magazine, *The Kansas Ruralist.* They've asked for more. It's not exactly *Harper's Weekly,* but maybe, someday . . ."

"*The Kansas Ruralist* is a good start, Pete!" She leaned toward him and put her hand on his arm. "It could happen, your drawings, or paintings being in *Harper's*

150

Weekly. And other places as fine, for folks to enjoy. It's a wonderful dream! I had no idea, back when we were neighbors. But, I wasn't very friendly, then, was I?"

He looked at her for a long moment, brows knitted in thought. "You had your reasons, Jocey. I'm glad you don't have them anymore. As far as I'm concerned, those reasons didn't hold water even back then. You've always looked good to me. Beautiful eyes, beautiful hair, spunky as a young mare, hard working as all get out. You've always been special, whether you knew it or not. My family saw it; I saw it, too."

"Your family was always good to me. Well, your father got pretty grumpy at me when I dammed the creek without knowing it was stopping water to your farm."

They laughed, their gazes locked in enjoyment of the memory.

"Far has been grumpy about a lot of things. I doubt he knows about my drawings to this day, and that's fine with me."

"What about the rest of your family — all healthy and happy, I suppose?" She got to her feet, and he followed.

"I believe they are; I don't see them as often as I should. Anne got married and has two little kids. Haven't seen the latest one. My brother's and sisters' farms are a few miles apart, and they look out for one another, and the folks."

As they were putting away the empty food dishes, Pete said, "There's a dance after the rest of the show tonight, over to the Z Bar O's barn. Jocey . . ." he grinned and corrected himself, "*Jocelyn, Miss Royal,* I'd be mighty favored if you'd come with me."

She looked down at the ground, to hide her disappointment, and then back up at him. "I'd like to, very much, but I came here with friends, and they'll likely be leaving soon, with chores waiting for them at home. I'll need to go for the same reason. I'm sorry."

Just then Tarsy walked up behind her and put an arm around Jocelyn's waist. "We're staying. Our hired man will see to our chores."

Jocelyn started to introduce Tarsy and Gordon to Pete, but, as it turned out, they'd met at other "bucking shows" and soon were laughing and congratulating one another on today's rides.

A minute or two later Jocelyn told the others, "I would like to go to the dance, but I can't. I'd best head back to the ranch and the mules. I'm sure I can find someone else going my way, and they'll take me home. I saw the Goodys watching the show earlier; I can ride with them."

"Stop worrying, Jocelyn," Tarsy said, giving her waist a squeeze. "Gordon talked to Mr. Kittredge, and he knows about the dance. Clem wants to do this; he's already there, and he told us he'll spend the night, sleep in the barn. His orders are that you're to have a good time and come home when the sun comes up, if the dance lasts that long, and it usually does." She added, "Clem Kittredge can be gruff at times, but inside he's as soft as melted butter."

She thought it over, looked at Pete, and concluded that spending a little more time in her old friend's company was blessed hard to resist. She grinned. "I guess I'm staying with you-all then for the dance."

A lot of clowning took place in most of the events the rest of the day, possibly due to the flasks trading hands during the earlier break. A cowboy named Pickering rode a mule backward, laughing and waving at the crowd until the mule began to buck and threw him into the dust. The cowboy went limping and swearing from the corral, but Jocelyn thought he had it coming for insulting the mule. *Try making a fool out a mule, and the mule will make a fool out of you.* He was lucky not to have his brains kicked out.

She noted that Tosten — Pete — was the

first cowboy to clap the rider on the shoulder and with a grin give him a look that asked if he was okay. Her friend from the past hadn't changed; inside he was still the kind Tosten she remembered.

The rodeo ended with the crowd's rowdy, full-throated rendition of *America – My Country 'tis of Thee,* followed by a patriotic speech by Skiddy's mayor, who also invited everyone to the Z Bar O dance.

A caravan of wagons, buggies, and riders on horseback made their way through the lowering dark to the other side of Skiddy and the cavernous lantern-lit barn where the dance was being held.

Jocelyn had been to barn dances in recent years with her father, but none so apparently popular and crowded as this one. The musicians — a fiddler, guitar player, and a tall, string-bean fellow with an accordion — were tuning up on a platform at the far end of the room. Folks of every age churned to find a place to sit on the benches at the sides of the room, or to choose a dance partner, or pull a friend aside for a chat.

At a large table in the corner, women were setting out food: fried chicken, deviled eggs, pickled peaches, cakes, and pies. Mrs. Noack, the storekeeper's wife, was among them, and Jocelyn returned her wave. Had she known she was coming to the dance following the "rodeo," Jocelyn would have brought another dish of some kind, but she hadn't known, and Pete had finished what was in her basket. She mentioned it to Tarsy, who told her these were town women who always provided the fixings for the Fourth of July dance.

She saw Pete come inside after putting up his horse. A young woman in orange calico, with braids flying, scuttled his way, arms out as though for a dance. He grinned, shook his head, and motioned in Jocelyn's direction. The girl didn't seem to mind and in the next instant trotted toward another good-looking cowboy. He seemed more than glad to take her up on the offer, and they were soon jigging and stomping as the musicians played a fast rendition of *Arkansas Traveler.*

Jocelyn and Pete headed with the rest to the dance floor, moving smoothly and happily to the old-time fiddle song. "You're a good dancer, Jocelyn," he told her.

"Thank you. You step lively yourself. It appears you've had a lot of practice." He led so well she could be a terrible dancer and still follow the steps with little blunder.

"Cowboys like to dance. I reckon I'm no different from most of them; we like to dance, and we think we're blamed good even if we're stompin' like we have two left feet."

She laughed. "You definitely have a right and a left."

The next dance was to *Turkey in the Straw,* which left them both fanning their faces when it ended. More fast tunes followed, feet stomping to the *Nightingale Polka* and *The Gal I Left Behind Me,* accompanied now and then by a loud whoop. It was a relief, in the hot barn with so many dancers and fresh air nonexistent, that a series of slow waltzes followed: *The Beautiful Blue Danube, When You and I Were Young, Maggie,* and *Green Grow the Lilacs.*

Showing good manners as the evening wore on, both Pete and Jocelyn danced with other partners, but Pete wasted no time reclaiming Jocelyn after each dance, and she didn't hide how happy she was that he did. It'd been such an enjoyable day, thanks to Tarsy's inviting her and Clem Kitteridge keeping watch on the mules. Then there was Pete . . . Maybe she'd see him again sometime, and maybe she wouldn't. Messy as her life was, it was hard to tell about anything.

CHAPTER ELEVEN

Around midnight at the dance, Jocelyn was plagued with a growing tightness in her chest from guilt that she'd stayed. She really should be at Nickel Hill. If something bad happened to the mules, she didn't know what she'd do. She would be in so much trouble with Whit Hanley. Her chance for earnings from the work she'd done would be gone as well as opportunity to buy back her farm. Clem was an old man, who might sleep through trouble and never know. Fear and pain connected with the Rufe Tuttle incident were always at the back of her mind, hard to forget.

Pete sensed that her mood had changed drastically when her feet stopped moving to a dance. "What's wrong?"

"Nothing's wrong. I'm sorry."

He took a good look at her and frowned. "That's bull, Jocey. Something's troubling you. We can talk about it, you know. Maybe

I can help?"

"I have to get back to Nickel Hill and the mules, that's all!" She sounded crankier than she'd meant to.

"Right this minute you came to that conclusion — you gotta leave, now? You've got something on your mind that needs airing. C'mon outside where it's quiet and we can talk." He tucked her hand in the crook of his arm. Out front of the barn, boards laid across squat kegs formed benches. They sat down side by side in the moonlight. His voice was stone quiet. "Tell me, Jocelyn, what's got you scared this way?"

"I'm not true scared," she protested, "just . . . a little uneasy is all. I don't want to pile my troubles on you like . . . like a pot of beans spilling all over. There's no need; we can go back inside." She started to rise.

Pete pulled her back. "Tell me what's going on, Jocelyn. I'm your friend."

She didn't want to tell him, didn't want him to know one word of it, but her voice wouldn't stop, and she spilled everything — from how she'd come to take a job cooking for Whit Hanley on the mule drive, to his disappearance, leaving her unexpectedly responsible for a herd of mules worth a lot of money. About the scoundrel Rufe Tuttle,

158

who intended to steal the mules, had assaulted her, and was killed on the place she was staying, when one of the mules kicked him to death. Not that he didn't deserve it. "I didn't mean to bring all this up and spoil the evening. Just forget it, Pete; my troubles are my own."

They'd only just met again; he didn't need to know every detail of her life. She might as well tell him her nightgown was raggedy blue flannel she'd worn since she was sixteen. Her face burned with embarrassment.

"Not now, they're not just *your* problems," his voice rasped. "Damn, Jocelyn, honey, you might've been killed. You're still in danger; you can't be sure this rotter, Tuttle, was working alone to steal the mules. He might still have a partner out there waiting for the next chance." He stood and pulled her up. "Is there someone you can stay with, until this is over? Your friend Tarsy Webber, maybe. Or move to town where the sheriff would be close."

"You don't understand. *I am responsible for the mules;* there's no one else. I agreed to the job in good faith. I want my share of the money they'll bring when they sell. I can take care of myself, Pete. I just got a little shaken tonight because I'm here and not on the ranch where I belong. And listen: I have weapons, and I know how to use them. Nobody is going to bother me, or the mules. But I do need to be at Nickel Hill."

From his growl of disagreement, she knew he didn't like it, but he said, "I'll take you home then. We can go now."

"But how? You rode here on your horse. We'd ride double on Raven?" Calming down, she could even make a small joke.

"We could, but it's not necessary. I'll leave Raven at the livery and hire a rig. Go back inside and stay with Tarsy and Gordon until I come for you."

She shook her head. "Please, there's no need for you to do that." She had to admit she felt better after telling her story to Pete, but he needn't feel obligated beyond that, and she told him so.

He caught her arm. "I had a good time tonight, and I know you did, too." He was silent a moment, considering. He cleared his throat, his voice deeply serious, "Now I've met you again I can't — *won't* — turn my back on your predicament, Jocey. Until I know that you're safe from ruffians like the one you were telling me about. That's my word, and I ain't changing it."

She shrugged and shook her head, not knowing what to reply to that. Heaven knew her list of friends was grievously short.

They were about to enter the barn, where the dancing continued at a noisy din, when Tarsy and Gordon came out. "There you two are," Tarsy said. "We wore ourselves out and are ready to go home, if you are, Jocelyn."

"I'm ready. We can go." When Pete started to protest, she thanked him and told him firmly, "I'll go with them, and I guarantee that I'll be fine."

"I sure as hell hope so. I would've liked to see you home, myself. Have Gordon make sure there's nobody suspicious hanging around when you get there."

She nodded. "We'll make sure. I'll ask Mr. Kittredge if he wants to stay on until morning, which won't be long after I get there." She fell in step with the Webbers, strolling a moon-washed path to their buggy.

"Be seeing you, Jocey," Pete called after her.

She smiled at the old nickname, turned, and called to his shadowy figure, "All right."

"I figure this Hanley gent you're mixed up with could be an outlaw still," Pete said to Jocelyn when he came to Nickel Hill a few evenings later. They sat in the porch rocking chairs after supper. The blistering temperature during the day had cooled some, but it was still hot. A frown creased Pete's forehead, and his expression and tone of his voice were solemn. "I'd bet my last cent that those mules out there are stolen, and Hanley is laying low, afraid to come around here because the law is after him. All of which puts you right in the middle of a peck of trouble, Jocelyn."

She took a deep breath and set her rocker in motion. "Holding stolen goods, the mules, puts me in the same light as him, you're saying? I don't know, Pete. I've believed a time or two what you say. But Mr. Hanley swore he bought the mules legally, and, for the most part, I think he did. His friend Sam Birdwhistle says Whit Hanley's honest and fair, his wild days long over."

"If they were in this together, he'd naturally defend Hanley, the way I see it. Lie if he had to, don't you think?" The porch floor creaked under their rocking chairs.

"No. I can't believe that of Sam. They were — are — friends, who made mistakes when they were years younger. People do, you know. I'm sure Sam Birdwhistle is reformed. He's a family man with children who hired on to help Hanley's mule drive. He was very good to me, a decent man."

Pete's rocker stilled. He was quiet for a long time, then he leaned toward her, eyes leveled on her face, "Jocey — er Jocelyn, you were such a loner as a kid, what I know about you. I don't reckon you've been around the company of different folks enough that you'd learn the foolish, mixed up ways of human nature; recognize trouble and see the lawless stripe for what it is."

Even if he was sincere and not far off the truth, his words were a jab of insult, and it riled her. "I'm not an empty-headed fool, Pete, and I don't appreciate your seeing me as if I am one. I'm a grown woman." He looked surprised at her sharp tone, but she couldn't stop. "Yes, in the past, I stayed away from other people as much as possible, for the way they treated me. Which was badly, by the way, for something that was no fault of my own, but a freak of nature I had nothing to do with. If you don't think I learned a lot about people then, you would be wrong!"

She was close to tears and hated it, refusing to break down. "All the time I was growing up I read book after book, and I learned a thing or two from reading — but I don't suppose you'd credit that." She gulped and continued, "I believe that Whit Hanley may be dealing with trouble of some kind, yes;

I'll admit it. And when he's taken care of whatever that problem is, there'll be no worrying. He could show up any minute with an explanation to prove nothing unlawful is going on." *Providing she was right and that he was still alive and able.*

Why she was now defending her boss this way, she had no idea, but now that she'd begun she had to have her say. "Aren't I supposed to trust? That's what people told me after my mouth was fixed. I had to learn how to be who I really am, natural, with other folks. It wasn't easy, but every day that's what I'm trying to do, and I think I'm doing fair. You think Whit Hanley and Sam are outlaws out to do harm. I *don't* think so, but if it turns out I'm wrong, I still had nothing to do with any crime. Nobody would leave a corral full of defenseless animals on their own to starve, and I won't, either." She pressed her lips tightly together. Her brogans sent the rocker into swift motion.

Pete leaned forward, elbows on his knees, looking at the porch floor. He ran his hands through his golden hair, and his eyes met hers. "I'm sorry, Jocelyn. I didn't mean to upset you. I've been thinking about what's happening to you a lot since that day we met again at the 4th of July celebration. I won't lie to you. I gauge the situation you're in as probably not lawful, and for plumb sure unfair and not safe." He threw his hands in the air. "I don't think I'm wrong, but I'd sure like to be."

He continued more calmly on a different tack. "A blind man could see that you aren't the same little girl I remember; that you're as capable as any woman — providing the stakes are even." He stressed the last point as his eyes roamed her face. "If you need me, please send word by a neighbor to the 7Cs, and me and my old horse will be here."

"Thank you, Pete." She conceded, "I hope I'm not the one who is blind!"

The temperature had grown tolerable as they sat, sharing the quiet, eyes on the beauty of an orange and purple sunset filling the western sky. Having reached an unspoken but shaky truce, they talked quietly of everyday things: the hot weather and wouldn't it be nice to have all the ice one wanted for making ice cream or tea during a Kansas summer like this. They talked about his drawings, about her dreams of having her farm again.

She said, as light began to fade, "It's late, Pete, and I suppose you have a long ride ahead of you."

"Yep, I'd better be going," he said, worry

returning to his voice. He shifted in his chair and got to his feet slowly.

"Thank you for coming. It's been nice, seeing you again. How far do you have to ride, to the 7Cs?" She stood and led the way to the edge of the porch.

He shrugged and grinned. "If I didn't get back 'til sunup to do my work it'd be all right. As it is, it's not a full hour's ride. S'long, Jocelyn, you take care now." His boot heels went thumping down the steps.

She watched him ride away into the dark on the black gelding. If he took any of her words tonight as turning him away, and she never saw her good friend again, she'd hate herself for the rest of her life.

Another week passed before Pete rode up the knoll to where Jocelyn was stacking hay late one dusky evening. With little else to do, she'd taken to scything hay in small amounts, having no mowing machine. Unprepared for company, she worked barefoot, her dress soaked with perspiration, and her hair streaming from its pins, rough pitchfork handle in hand. "I look a sight, heaven knows," she told him, trying to hide her dirt-blackened toes behind the hem of her dress. "If you'll go wait on the porch, I'll make myself presentable and then bring us some cool tea I keep in a jar deep in the well." She waved away a droning fly.

He looked around, shaking his head in disgust, a look that would scorch a rock. He removed his hat, ran his hand through his hair, and slapped his hat back on. "I was counting on seeing this fella, Whit Hanley, back and taking over. You'd be packing up to move on, and I'd come just in time to say good-bye, hear your plans."

"Nope. I'm here, but the boss isn't. Yet."

"Give me the pitchfork," he growled as he dismounted. He handed her the reins, and as she took them Raven nickered softly in greeting. "Tie him by the corral. I'll finish stacking for you. Go tackle that dust an' straw you're wearing, unsightly stuff that it is," he said. Humor flickered in his eyes. She was glad to see his slanted grin.

She couldn't help but smile at him, before taking off at a fast clip for the house and the pump in the kitchen. While she washed with Ivory soap, a rag, and cool water, she kept an eye on the window, making sure he stayed where he was so she could take her "spit" bath without him seeing. She brushed her hair and worked it into a loose coronet pinned high on her head and changed into clothes fresh off her clothesline, happy that she now smelled clean and not of sweaty work under a hot sun.

Placing tea and lemon cookies on the small table between their rockers, Jocelyn said, "I thought you might not be coming back, Pete. I couldn't have been good company, carrying on so when you were here. You don't ride down this far to hear me steam like a teakettle." She waited as he threw his head back and downed half a glassful of tea.

"I'd come more often, if I could." He licked the moisture from his lips. "Like you, here on this place, we've been making hay, but we're finished 'til it's dry and ready to haul to the barns. Been riding pastures, checking windmills and water holes, doctoring cattle that need it, but I wish I could be closer, keeping watch against more trouble. Anything suspicious been happening?"

"Not a thing." She took her chair. "Neighbors stop in now and then, and most of them are such busybodies I don't think anything could happen without every one of them knowing." She sipped her tea, in the back of her mind wishing as usual that she'd added more sugar, a habit she'd developed having read about the "sweet tea" common in the South. "Other than that, it's quiet, just me and the mules — keeping them fed and watered and tending to a couple instances of mules' sores from horseflies. Spend a lot of time in the hayfield. I miss Sam's help, but I'm doing all right. Of course, I expect Mr. Hanley to show up and relieve me of this pesky conundrum, but no sign of him yet."

He rubbed a hand down his face, his expression dead serious as he told her, with caution, "I'd still be careful if I was you, keep my eyes open and not let my guard down. A lot could be going on that you don't know about. This whole setup is plenty fishy. I know you don't like me telling you what to do, and that you believe you got everything in hand, and I reckon in a way I don't blame you. But things could blow up in a trifle — with no warning." He took another long draught of tea and most of a cookie in one bite. "It ain't right how you've been treated, and with no change in sight." He brushed cookie crumbs from his shirtfront.

Jocelyn nodded. "I understand what you're saying, and I appreciate your caring what happens to me, Pete. I am on guard, I really am. To be honest, I like having your company when you can be here. I like talking about when we were neighbors as kids. How things were back then. My Gram, the farm . . . You brought me flowers one time."

It was a bald-faced effort to steer conversation away from argument, and she could tell by his face that he wasn't fooled and might not go along.

Her spirits lifted when he complied with a smile. "Sure did — flowers and the loan of a milk cow. I'd got into a lot of trouble for our sheep ruining your garden. I didn't mind; it was a chance to come over and see you."

"You wanted to?" She couldn't hide her surprise. She'd been so different then.

"I'd've brought you a frog, not flowers, if I didn't." His grin widened. "Your Grandma Letty was funny, and special. I can't think of her without laughing. You must miss her a bunch."

Jocelyn sighed. "I loved my Gram, but nobody knows what a trial she was for me back then. I doubt you know that, before we came to the farm, she was a washerwoman in Kansas City. She got sick, and she wanted me to learn the trade, be a washerwoman to survive when she was gone." Jocelyn wrinkled her nose. "I was doing the work in her place already and wanted shut of it as soon as I could. It was a blessing when a letter came from a Council Grove lawyer. What welcome news it was!" she emphasized.

Pete's eyebrows rose, and she explained. "Papa owned that farm near Council Grove," she waved a hand, "well, closer to Bushong, but he took off and abandoned it after my mother died. The lawyer had written to say that people were interested in buying the farm. My father couldn't be located to make the deal. That wasn't the happy part, of course. I was included in the written agreement; the farm was mine in trust." She gave a slight head shake and pursed her lips. "All Gram could talk about was the 'grand funeral' she could have with the money if we sold the farm to the folks who wanted the place. 'Banks of lilies around her coffin, a preacher in a cutaway suit saying fine words over her.' " She lifted a hand. "Pete, I tell you, she was a handful for a young girl to handle. Gram was nowhere close to dying. I had the word of a doctor on that." She added quietly after a moment, "She lived another three years, happy as a kitten in a basket of yarn, before she died peacefully in her sleep."

"She'd been against the move to Kansas?"

"Purely so, to the bone, and she argued against it in no uncertain terms. But I knew the fresh air and food on the farm would help recover her health, and it did, although she pretended to be sicker than she was for a long time."

"I kinda remember that. To a boy that was not only funny, it was plenty smart. I'd've tried it if I'd thought I wouldn't be found out and punished."

"It was funny and smart to me, later," Jocelyn admitted with a small laugh. "Gram had always worked hard, and now she enjoyed being a *lay-about.* It took me a while to catch on. I was all the time on the run," she defended herself, hands in the air, "with farm work, cleaning house, washing our clothes, doing the cooking, *and* waiting on Gram. I let her know she could take on a few household chores." Jocelyn rocked, silent a moment. "Gram confessed to playing possum at being sick because she liked so much being waited on. But she grew tired of doing nothing, and never mind the guilt that plagued her." Jocelyn laughed with Pete. "From that time on she was a help, cooking and all."

"And you got to do the outside work. You liked that, even though it was hard?" Admiration gleamed in his eyes.

"Yes, and no. I took us to the farm to escape the torture that was my lot in the city. It was a place to hide. Any bright morning would find me up at dawn, tending to my garden, feeding my chickens and gathering eggs, milking the cow; it was a new life that I treasured. I hadn't counted on neighbors being so close, and traveling salesmen coming by . . . . I'm glad of that now, because that's how I got news that there was a way to fix my cleft lip."

"We were all happy for you about that."

She spoke slowly. "I'm not sure I can explain how I felt after the surgery, but it was sort of like being a caged bird suddenly freed, I suppose. The first twelve years of my life was like being locked in a closet. Then with the repair of my mouth, it was walking into a room — a world — flooded with sunshine. Open. Free. No need to hide my face anymore or avoid people. I'll always be grateful to the doctors who helped me."

"It's all fine now, though, Jocelyn; no worries — you're pretty as a peach."

"Yes, all fine." Except when she wondered about having a baby of her own someday. Would the tiny thing be born with an affliction like hers? She'd not want her child to go through the torment like she'd experienced as a child. She could choose to not get married, to not have children, but she wanted so much the opposite. Was it true, she wondered, that soon such surgical repair would take place just days after the infant was born? Leaving a barely visible scar? Not that she wouldn't love her child dearly, regardless.

A deep silence followed, save the rhythmic clank of the windmill up by the corrals.

"Jocelyn." The way Pete said her name, she knew something was about to happen, and she turned slowly to look at him. He left his rocker swinging and came to kneel before her. "I thought about doing this when I was fifteen years old. You don't mind, do you?" Taking her face gently in both work-roughened hands, he kissed the old scar on her mouth, leaned back, and grinned at her.

Jocelyn's face flooded; her throat filled. *Mind?* Few things in her life had *felt so good,* his lips on hers. But nice manners wouldn't allow her to say it.

What in the name of old Hannah would Pete think if he knew he was the first man to kiss her, a woman twenty-four years old and practically an old maid? It was all she could do not to cry. Her back stiffened, and she swallowed her secret.

When she didn't reply, his smile wavered, and his brows pulled in. He stood. "Reckon it's time I headed back to the 7Cs." He slapped his hat against his thigh, then put it on. "I sure don't like leaving you alone, though. You'll be careful?"

"I always am, Pete."

He moved to the edge of the porch and took a step down, then turned. "Keep a gun close, and don't let anybody you *don't know* on the place."

"I know what to do; don't worry." She left her chair and watched him go, thinking that she'd had a good lesson from the old woman who'd threatened her back on the river trail. *Blast away with the shotgun, and put the fear of death into the marauder. Aim deadly if the matter called for it. Simple.*

Chapter Twelve

Pete continued to drop by every now and then, turning his hand to whatever chore he found her doing, because she was "like family." Or they'd sit at the kitchen table chatting over coffee, if they weren't in the front porch rockers, she puzzling with Gram's crocheting in hand, Pete half asleep after a hard day.

She treasured his friendship, decidedly, but the more he came to see her, the more she *foolishly* could see what good husband material he was, something that surprised her but began after that blessed kiss he'd given her.

Useless mooning it was, because Pete wanted no dallying toward marriage; he'd made that clear. What was it he'd told her late one evening? *"I've liked a few gals but not enough to marry any of them and change my way of living. I'm no different from most cowboys, drifters, with no ties. My itchy feet haven't been to all the places my boots intend to take me. I expect to have an exciting adventure or two, maybe three, before I settle into harness with a wife — if I ever do. A forty-dollar-a-month cowboy can't hardly support a wife and children, anyhow."*

To her consternation, the more she tried *not* to think about them as a couple, the more she daydreamed of them together. Making a life such as she'd longed for, for years now; having children, being a family. She felt so possessed by such thoughts about Pete, as she went about her work, that she was tempted to duck her head under water in the corral trough and hold it there until her brain cleared and common sense returned.

Enough was enough. Pete was not going to be the one if she ever did marry. She could count herself fortunate for his friendship and quit the dreamy nonsense. Be satisfied that there were other friends in her life nowadays. Neighbors who hadn't forgotten Rufe Tuttle and his attack on her dropped by as often as they could.

When it came to worrying about her welfare, Mrs. Goody was as good at it as Pete. She showed up one morning when Jocelyn had barely finished her breakfast and was having a last cup of coffee. She poured a cup for her friend and passed her the canned milk and sugar.

"I had to come see you, Jocelyn. I've something I have to tell you. How are you?" Her voice was stern, her brow furrowed as she dropped into a chair. "Has anyone bothered you lately? I can't forget what happened to you and neither can Lyman." She stirred a tablespoon of sugar into her cup and added milk. "My cousin, Louise, come to visit the other day and told me the most awful story. About the things outlaws do, you know? You can't be too careful, is what I'm saying."

"All right. But no one else like that scum, Tuttle, has been here. I'm doing fine, though I surely wish my boss was here. Otherwise, I've had no trouble."

Mrs. Goody looked like she might go into apoplexy getting through to Jocelyn. "Dear, just listen to me, please. You might think things are hunky-dory, but you can't ever, ever be too careful. I was telling Louise about your predicament," she said with a shudder, "and she told me about Ladore."

"What happened to . . . to Ladore? Was the woman, or girl, hurt or something?"

"Ladore is a *town* down in Neosho county, or used to be. It's practically a ghost town, these days, but the place was real enough when Louise's friend was a little girl. You see, this band of seven desperadoes rode into town about noon one day." She hesitated, thinking of something. "Ladore was already a wild town, but it was about to get worse, I tell you! The outlaws proceeded to fill up on whiskey. By night time they'd took over the town, beating up folks, robbing them, committing holy hell to tell the truth. They beat the local boarding house keeper over the head and took his two daughters and a hired girl and kept them with them all night." She waited to see if Jocelyn understood the implications of that. She picked up her cup of coffee, then set it back on the table without drinking.

Jocelyn, fingers pressed to her lips, nodded for Mrs. Goody to continue.

"About dawn citizens organized to capture the devils. Two was caught in a drunken sleep on the floor of the saloon. Another was captured in the timber with one of the girls. The head of the gang and two others were captured on the way to Osage Mission."

"What happened then?" Jocelyn asked through a dry throat. She was beginning to feel cold.

"Those five were locked up in a log barbershop, with guards to keep watch. Each of the five was taken, one at a time, before those poor defiled young girls, ages ten to fourteen, to identify. The men were led to a hackberry tree, where they were strung up on one strong limb. In no time they hung there without a breath of life left in them. Citizens of the town, about three hundred of them, had 'convicted' the five scoundrels for robbery, murder, and their criminal act on those girls."

"What about the other two outlaws?"

"Well, one had been shot to death by another outlaw in a fight over one of the girls. The last one was arrested but later released — nobody's sure of the reason."

"Mrs. Goody, are you sure all this really happened, that it's true?"

"What I'm telling you is fact all right. The story wasn't just written about in Kansas, you know; the *New York Times* and other Eastern newspapers carried it. Louise's friend showed her the local paper they'd kept these years since. The headline said loud and clear: *Five Scoundrels Hung.*" She reached and clasped Jocelyn's hand tight. "You see what I mean, dear? You can't never be too careful."

"Yes," Jocelyn answered, removing her hand to rub the goosebumps on her arms, "I believe I do." Pete could come as often

180

as he wanted. She'd already decided that telling him not to come worked as well as stopping a cattle stampede waving her two arms. Her guns would remain loaded and ready. If a thief attempted to steal her blue-chip band of mules, would she be killed trying to stop them? Could she fire at someone with the intent to kill? She was positive she could, should it become a matter of staying alive.

Summer was a busy season, and Pete came much later than usual one night, wanting to make sure she was okay. She fed him a late supper, then watched him fall asleep in his rocker on the porch. It was good for him, she decided, to get his rest wherever it happened. It was nearly midnight when he finally stirred and headed toward the corrals for his horse.

Jocelyn was about to go in and prepare for bed when she thought she heard an odd noise, a voice, someone talking to Pete. Cold shivers of fear raced over her. She yanked open the back door, grabbed her shotgun, and moved stealthily up the knoll to the corrals. The sounds of grunting and thudding fists came from near the barn. Her eyes strained helplessly to see.

Lips pressed together, staying in the dark,

away from spills of moonlight, she crept that way. Her eyes began to make out two figures on their feet battling with fists. The next moment they wrestled on the ground, only to repeat fighting on their feet, then hitting the ground. One of them was crawling swiftly away toward something shiny on the ground, a gun. On his knees, he fired at the other figure leaping at him, at the same time Jocelyn fired into the air, her shotgun booming.

Things happened so fast after that, it was hard to keep track. There was another gunshot from the writhing figures. One lay still, the other staggered away to a horse tethered in shadows by the barn. He pulled himself into the saddle and rode hard into the night.

She hesitated, all senses tingling until she could stand it no longer. She ran to the unmoving figure on the ground, bracing herself for what she'd find. "Pete?"

"Jocey? B-be careful."

CHAPTER THIRTEEN

"He's gone, whoever it was." Jocelyn knelt on the ground next to Pete, asking with her heart in her throat, "Are you all right?" He was trying to sit up but made whistling sounds through his teeth from pain. Her hand found his shoulder, and she felt the stickiness of blood. "Please lay still." She gently pushed him down. "Put your other hand up here on your shoulder and press hard." She led his hand. "You're bleeding, but maybe that will help slow it down. I'm going to the house for a lantern and to grab what I need. I'll be right back. Don't move."

Still holding his shoulder, he tried again to sit up, to find his feet.

"Pete, please." She caught his arms, his muscles taut beneath her fingers. "Don't make me knock you out." She pushed him gently, and he lay back with a groan.

The house seemed a million miles away as she hesitated, remembered a lantern in the barn, and Sam's room, his bed. A few minutes later, the light from the lantern showed Pete's dirty and bruised face, and blood seeping through his fingers on his shoulder. "I-I can stand," he panted, "if you h-help me. Th-th-think the bugger cracked some of my ribs."

Putting herself under his good arm, her arm around his waist, she helped him toward the barn. Once inside, she got him to lie down, and she covered him with a blanket. She placed her shotgun where he could reach it. "In case he comes back," she said.

Pete breathed hard. "He won't be back — took off like a pepper-shot d-dog. I got in some good licks, t-too. Not sure if he was here for the mules." He spoke through a clenched jaw. "I told him if he was here for Whit Hanley, the owner, he wasn't here and never had been. When he sounded like he might argue, I ordered him off the place."

"What did he say to that?"

"Nothing directly, only that if I didn't own this place, I didn't have any more business here than he did, that he made a long hard ride to be here, and I wasn't going to run him off. He was in a real huff. I threatened to shoot him if he didn't leave right then."

She nodded. "Sounds like he was up to

no good, a thief, coming here at night the way he did. Did you have a good look at him or was it too dark?"

"Too dark, and by then he'd tied into me — and me into him. For a while I was sure one or the other of us was going to end up dead. I determined that it for damn sure wouldn't be m-me."

"For which I'm very thankful." She heaved a sigh. "All right, I'm glad he didn't kill you and that you — we — ran him off. Lay still and be quiet, and I'll be right back."

Jocelyn returned to the barn with the medicine box that came in the supply wagon. Pete's face was drained from shock. She gave him a shot of whiskey, removed his shirt, and washed his shoulder with warm water. The blood from the wound was beginning to coagulate, and that made her feel better. It appeared that the bullet had gone only through muscle, though the bone could have been nicked. No bullet to dig from his flesh, thank Hannah. She pulled the edges of the torn flesh together and applied a plaster. She placed a clean pad of cloth over that and bound his shoulder, using a large dish towel to make a sling for his arm.

Even though he complained, she washed his face and hands and applied ointment to his many bruises, and mustard plaster over his ribs. Finished, she asked if he'd like headache powders to help him sleep. "Another shot of whiskey, or maybe two," he mumbled, and she complied.

"I'm going to see to your horse now," she leaned over him to say. Her hand itched to cup his cheek and kiss him, but instead she hurried from the barn to care for Raven.

A while later, so that she'd be handy if he needed her, Jocelyn made a thick bed of hay near him and curled up in a blanket, fully-dressed. She ached in every bone with fatigue and worry. For the longest while her eyes refused to close, and she lay staring into the dark, listening to Pete's ragged breathing.

Light barely filtered into the barn the next morning when she woke to a rustling sound that turned out to be Pete sitting on the edge of Sam's bed and trying to pull his boots on. "You're trying my patience, Pete Pladson," she said, flinging back her blanket from the hay bed and standing up.

"I have to get on back to the 7Cs and round up some friends to go after the bugger that did this to me."

"You're not going anywhere." She took his boot away. "You're injured, Pete, and not ready to ride. Stay here for a day or two at the least. Let me take care of you."

"I'm not that bad hurt," he mumbled, wincing with each movement as he tried again to stand.

"Oh, no? Gunshot wound. Cracked ribs, at least two or three. Twenty-seven bruises and cuts — I counted. You can't leave. I'll send word to the sheriff by a neighbor. We'll ask for the doctor to come, too. Let me bring you some breakfast. Wait until this afternoon, or tomorrow, and we'll see then how you feel. Please, Pete." Her spine stiffened. "You're always doing for me, for pity sake, now let me do for you."

He frowned at her and, tight-lipped, suppressed a groan as he lay back. "Maybe some bacon, biscuits, and coffee," he said, "then my horse. Don't — don't fight me, Jocey."

She wouldn't. Unless, for his benefit, it was the best thing to do.

On her way to the house, close to where Pete and the intruder had fought, Jocelyn stopped to pick up a piece of newspaper skipping across the barnyard in the wind. She drew a sharp breath, seeing that the torn paper was the article from weeks ago about her and Sam and their mule drive through Council Grove. The photograph was so grainy she hardly recognized herself or Sam. Had the intruder brought this piece of paper with him, intent on stealing — or, she felt a cold river of shock and guilt, wishing to *buy* a mule or two? *Was it possible that Pete had almost killed an innocent man? Or, if pushed further, would she have?*

One thing at a time, she decided. Thank heaven the man was still alive when he rode off — if he was innocent. She reached the house and hurried into the kitchen. Before worrying about anything else, she must fix breakfast for Pete.

He was asleep minutes after he'd eaten. Jocelyn left the barn to do her chores, coming back every now and then to check her patient. She couldn't tie him down, but she really wanted Pete to stay and heal as much as possible before he returned to work at the Carmans' 7Cs Ranch or tried to find the man who'd shot him, whatever was on his crazy mind.

Because his soreness increased to the point he could barely stand and leave the barn even for the privy, she worried about his developing a fever. At her bidding, Mr. Goody rode to the 7Cs home place to tell them what had happened. Pete stayed with her for two more days and three nights, grousing at her by the hour. Nothing could stop him from leaving.

From the back door, furious with him following a huge argument, she watched Pete struggle to saddle his mount up by the corral. Clearly in pain, at last he got a foot into the stirrup and his leg over the saddle. As much as she wanted to help, she knew from living with her father that there were times a man must be allowed to be his own stubborn, prideful self. He didn't look back as he rode off north toward Geary County and his job. *Fool, driving me out of my mind!*

In the house, she threw herself into tidying up the kitchen, slamming pots and pans and sweeping the floor into a whirlwind of dust.

Her feelings were still raw two mornings later when she came out of the house to see Whit Hanley's roan horse in the corral and her dark-haired boss himself shirtless and washing up at the well.

It was all Jocelyn could do not to pick up a rock nearby and heave it at her boss's head. "Where in the blue blazes have you been, Whit Hanley?" She stomped toward him, taking short, fast breaths, her arms sweeping.

"Hey there, Miss Royal. Looks like you've done a good job here." He looked around, nodding. "I'm right pleased." His tone was genial, his smile warm and cheery.

"Rot!" she answered. "Why did you take off without a single word, leaving me and Sam to take care of the mules?" Her heart raced with anger. "Sam's gone, by the way, and I've been here alone for weeks." A soft breeze blew her apron up over her face, and she shoved it down.

"I know. I come across Sam while I was in Missouri, and he told me that he was heading home to his family and that you were doing a fine job here."

She stomped her foot in the dust. "What about my pay?" Expletives she didn't know that she knew were racing around in her head and about to fly from her mouth. She clamped her lips for a second and shook a finger at him. "There's been riff-raff coming around looking for you — to kill you is my guess, for something you've done, or should have done? There've been attempts to steal the mules, and I've been assaulted in the process. A friend of mine who happened to be here was shot and nearly beaten to death. It's only luck that he's still alive. I've had a devil of a time keeping things together while you're off chasing around — I suppose committing more crimes? You owe me answers, Whit Hanley, to six bushels of questions!"

"Yes, I reckon I do," he said, both palms

in the air, "and before you go completely haywire. Can we sit on the porch, or in the house and talk there?" He wasn't really asking; he was only trying to placate her.

"There's coffee made. Go on to the house." Her voice was brittle, and she waved him off. She'd had about all she could take from the men in her life. *Supposedly in her life!*

He took a chair at the kitchen table. She grabbed an enamel cup and poured his coffee. She slammed a sugar bowl and spoon down by his hand, along with a can of evaporated milk. "There," she said, "now talk."

"Where do you want me to start?" He sipped his coffee, setting the sugar and canned milk away.

"Why in the name of Hannah did you leave the drive?" She flung herself into the chair across from him.

"We were being followed." His expression was tight. "I wasn't sure, but I thought it could be three outlaws I once rode with who wanted revenge for something they think I did to them. I didn't want you and Sam involved. And I wanted the mules up here at Skiddy with no trouble from the men after me."

"What about them, the men after you?"

191

"I took care of one, name of Ed Franklin. He's behind bars. I helped put him there, and he thanked me — he was about to decorate a cottonwood tree. Be hanged," he explained. "I believe you dispensed with another of them — I heard in town that Rufe Tuttle got the life kicked out of him by one of our mules."

She sighed and nodded. "That happened. What about the third outlaw? Has he been caught?"

His expression darkened further, and his voice was apologetic. "He's still out there, and I wish to hell that he wasn't; he's the worst of the bunch. That's one of the reasons I'm back, besides preparing the mules for a sale, to warn you . . . to make sure you're not harmed. By the way, I would never have put you in danger if I had known some of the old gang was after me for revenge. I thought all that was past, it was so long ago. I'll see that you won't be bothered again. I've also been in Topeka for a while, visiting my mother, and arranging to have our mules at a sale at the Topeka stockyards. Anything else?"

"You told me once that you paid for the mules, that they aren't stolen. Can I still be sure of that, considering you just said that you rode with outlaws?" Her fist lay clenched on the table; she wanted to slap him.

"I joined an outlaw gang before I was old enough to shave . . . was young and stupid. My attempts at outlawry were pitiful. I was at least smart enough to see that, but not soon enough to escape the law that wanted me behind bars. I served time, paid my debt. And for the last time: yes, I bought the mules. They are legitimately mine. A share, yours."

She nodded, starting to calm. Her fist loosened, and she patted her palm on the table, thinking. "You mentioned your mother; she lives in Topeka?" Strange, but she'd never thought of him having a mother. One of those cabbage-patch births, or something.

"Yes, she and my stepfather live there. They are in financial trouble, and I aim to help them with money from the mule sales. My mother more than deserves my help, after what I put her through growing up."

"Between when you were young and into outlawry, then serving time and now, what were you doing?" Not that it was any of her business, but she felt she was in a position to ask him any darn thing she pleased and receive answers. And she wanted to verify what Sam had told her.

"For one thing, I had a blacksmith shop and saddlery down in the bootheel of Missouri, near Paragould, Arkansas. That was to build a stake so I could become a mule trader."

"Mule trader? This band you have now isn't the end of it?"

"Nothing of the kind," he told her with a pleased grin. "My stepfather made a very good living as a horse breeder and trader, until, due to age, his mind starting skipping out on him. Before that I learned a lot from him, and I intend to make whatever money I can as a mule trader. As soon as this herd is sold, I expect to gather up another bunch. I could use your help, and it'd be a business deal. You'd hold down the ranch and take care of the mules I'd keep here while looking for an upcoming sale. But I can see that's not likely after what's happened. If you don't want anything to do with me, or the job, I can pay you now, and you can go. It'd doubtless be safer for you."

"If anywhere is safe for a woman alone," she muttered to herself. She looked down and smoothed her skirt, then back up at him. "You have the money to pay me now, before the mule sale?"

"Yes, I have money to pay you, as well as enough to ship the mules from Skiddy to

Topeka on the train, quicker and easier this time. I could use your help herding the mules to Skiddy and helping at the auction, later." He explained, "I had short-time jobs in Topeka while visiting my mother." He read suspicion in her face and chuckled. "Honest jobs. One was in a saddlery and another as an express-man delivering mail and packages."

She told him about neighbors Mabel and Lyman Goody paying rent on eighty acres of Nickel Hill land they were grazing cattle on, that they'd like to buy that piece if he was willing to sell.

"I see no reason not to let them rent those eighty acres, or even sell it to them. I may have to sell the entire ranch to help my parents, but I hope I won't have to. I'll need it as a base for the mule business."

If what he said was so, there was a lot of money to be made buying and selling mules, and she could be a part of it. Continuing to work for Whit Hanley could mean she could buy back her old property *sooner,* cash in hand. She liked working with the mules and couldn't imagine what other type work she could find that didn't mean starting over at the bottom. "Let me think about staying on here or not," she told him. "There are chores to do."

He took a last swallow of coffee and stood up. "There are things you probably would like to do here in the house. I'll take care of the chores."

She said quietly, as the door closed behind him, "Thank you." She sat at the table a while longer, drinking coffee and enjoying the brief leisure while she pondered her future with an uplifting of hope.

As she fixed breakfast for her boss — she really should do that if she expected to work for him further — she considered the long list of things needing her attention.

Her bedding needed to be washed, *again,* considering the hot, dusty summer it'd been. The kitchen floor needed sweeping and mopping, and she'd like to make preserves from the gooseberries, plums, and peaches Tarsy Webber had brought her. She'd washed the windows when they'd first come there, but with all the blowing dust when the wind was up — which was most of the time — they needed cleaning again. Possibly there'd be more time to read! Her neighbor, Emma Hunter, who loved books as much as Jocelyn did, had brought her two books on loan, *The House of Seven Gables,* which she'd read once and wouldn't mind reading again, and a book she hadn't heard of before, *Diana of the Crossings.*

In the next days, Jocelyn tackled her tasks with fervor close to enjoyment. Whit Hanley, in addition to taking on the usual chores of the ranch, was preparing the mule herd for the sale. They had wonderful pasturage to graze, but he gave them a bonus of grain and made sure they had whatever amount of clean water they wanted. Unlike horses, mules normally only ate and drank the amount they needed, and there was little concern that they would eat or drink too much and founder. Their small, upright, boxy feet didn't require shoes, but their hooves did benefit from trimming, and Whit spent a great deal of time at that and trimming their manes until they were no more than an inch. One day, Jocelyn was outside ready to clip laundry to the clothesline when she saw Whit with a file inside a mule's mouth. She hurried to stand next to him in the barnyard. "What on earth are you doing to that defenseless mule? Poor Alice!"

"Mules' teeth grow just like horses' do and can wear down from chewing," he explained. "Because they chew from side to side in the same direction, sharp points can happen on the sides of their teeth. I'm filing these points off, because they can cause trouble with eating and digesting their feed, which in turn can cause them to lose weight, or have other problems with digestion." He chuckled. "As you can see, it doesn't hurt the mule, and Alice seems to know it'll help because she's not giving me any trouble."

"I see that. Dinner is about ready. You might want to wash up when you finish there." She hesitated and turned back. "I thought the mules looked fine before, but they're looking so nice it nearly hurts my eyes to look at them." He grinned, nodded, and continued his work.

For the most part, she had stopped asking questions, feeling that Mr. Hanley had told her pretty much all she needed to know, or that he had to say. But the one thing she kept forgetting to ask, of either him or Sam, returned to mind, now. What about the other cowboy who worked for Whit Hanley before she came into the picture? Why did he quit the drive, or if Whit fired him, how come? Wasn't he a friend, not one of the bad guys? Over dinner of steak, potatoes, sliced tomatoes, and fried cabbage, she asked him.

Whit continued to eat, although lines creased his forehead. He sat back and said quietly, "The men who were after me were after him, too. Even more so because he was the younger brother to the head of the outlaws — Carl Bramwell, the hard case I mentioned who is still out there. Rim Bramwell began to worry that his older brother, Carl, and the other two, Rufe Tuttle and Ed Franklin, might catch up to us and make trouble, a notion I didn't put much stock in then. It turned out that he was right, and he had the most to lose."

"How do you mean?"

"Carl Bramwell would kill his own younger brother to keep him from talking, if Rim wouldn't come back into the gang where he could watch his every move. Rim Bramwell's intentions when he parted ways with me and Sam were to go west, to Montana, or Oregon, and lose himself out there. I hope to God he made it. I haven't heard from him. We decided back when he left the drive that it was best to not have any contact from then on. I worry some that the older brother might have caught up with him, returned him to the gang, or killed him."

Jocelyn's hand crept to cover her mouth, and she shook her head. "I have a hard time believing such things happen, but I know that they do." Her stomach roiled, and she pushed her plate away.

After a silence, he said, "Just talking about all this makes me realize the danger I could be putting you in still if you associate with me. Sometimes the skeleton of a past won't stay buried, no matter what a man does to keep it tamped down so he can live a new life. I'm going to pay you for all the work you've done for me, Miss Royal — Jocelyn. Then that's it. You need to leave me in your dust, the sooner the better. Find safer work."

"If I knew what and where that was," she retorted, "I might. If you remember, my choices weren't great when I chose to be your cook on the drive. I've been alone quite a while now and have looked after myself. I want this job, and I want to earn back my farm. It wouldn't be fair of you to cut me loose now. You owe me a chance, Hanley, and you know it." She said then, "Once I'm back on my farm and have a normal life again, I'll be fine. You'll be shut of me for good."

He hated to give in. For a while, from the hard set of his jaw, she thought he wasn't going to, but finally he said, "I don't like it, but . . . all right. Maybe, if we're lucky, we won't have any more trouble. But, just in case, I'm buying you a small gun, a Derringer, you can carry on your person. I'll be giving you advice that I'll damn well expect you to take, to keep you from being hurt." He scowled at her.

"I won't be harmed; I'll make sure of it,"

she said and began clearing their plates from the table. "You probably want to go back to your fine and fancy mules."

"I will, but first I'm going to tell you what got me into trouble with the law at the start. If you're with me, then forewarned is forearmed."

Kind of late, Mr. Hanley! she thought for a second. Then, her curiosity rising beyond all other feelings, Jocelyn put the stack of plates back on the table and took her chair again.

"The plan was to hold up the KATY, the Missouri, Kansas, & Texas train at Calhoun just north of Clinton, Missouri," Whit Hanley told her with a look of embarrassment. He moved his chair away from the table and crossed his legs. "The gang I was riding with, plus me, Sam, and young Rim Bramwell, was all itching for some easy money, a lot of it. We would dynamite the train's mail car, which was said to be carrying a payroll of fifty thousand dollars. I really had to gear up my grit, since my crimes to that time had been penny-ante young'un stuff. This train robbery would be the most ambitious crime of my life, very risky, and somebody could get killed, possibly me."

Jocelyn's eyes had gone wide at the payroll figure, and she realized she was holding her

breath considering the rest. With a flutter of
her hand, she motioned for him to continue.

CHAPTER FOURTEEN

"Trouble was, when me and the bunch arrived at the decided spot close to the town of Calhoun," Whit was saying, "we found that the dynamite and charger we'd tied onto our pack horse had come loose." He cleared his throat. "We'd lost it somewhere on the way."

"Really?" Jocelyn bit her lips to hide a smile. "Lucky for the train."

"An argument exploded that nearly cost me my life," he said in all seriousness. "The bunch of us rode back to where we last remembered the dynamite and charger was secure on the pack horse, and we searched everywhere but found nothing. Sam got the blame; he'd been leading the packhorse, although others loaded the equipment on and fastened it down — not good enough as it turned out. Carl, blood-thirsty leader of the gang and the most hot-headed, was going for his gun to kill Sam Birdwhistle. I drew my own guns a hair faster and said I'd kill him and his two pals, Tuttle and Franklin, if they tried to stop me and my friends, Sam and Rim, from leaving. We'd had enough of their stripe, especially for blaming us for everything that went wrong."

"You got away from them. But how did you end up in prison? The train robbery didn't happen, so it couldn't have been for that."

"We got away, but that wasn't the end of it. Carl Bramwell and his two best buddies weren't about to forget the missed chance to rob that train. They particularly had it in for me, for standing up to them and taking my friends with me, Sam, and Carl's brother, Rim. They'd get their revenge, but first they'd do another, more thorough search for the lost dynamite and plunger." He scratched the back of his hand. "When they located the one who found it, a loner in the woods, he fought them, and they killed him."

Muscles throughout Jocelyn's body went rigid. Whit answered her deep frown with a nod. "They planted my pocket match case, which had my name engraved on it, at the scene so I'd be blamed for the killing. The match case and a compass were gifts from my mother when I turned twelve. The law tracked me down, but I proved where I was when the killing took place and that I couldn't have done it. Now that the law had me in their sights, they sentenced me to two years in jail anyway, for being a known member of that gang, small though my crimes were. Holding the horses, being a lookout, acting tough with a gun though I never shot anybody. I made no argument, just wanted to pay my debt and start over — on the right track."

Jocelyn refilled their tea glasses and motioned for him to continue.

"From what I've learned since, the law has been after the original gang these past years, but Bramwell, Tuttle, and Franklin slipped out of their hands each time the lawmen got close. Carl Bramwell blames me for his trouble, and likely, too, he figures I'd be brought in as a witness if he's ever caught."

"Here in Kansas is the only time you've seen sign, suspicioned, that they were after you?"

"I was shot *at* in Missouri. We all were — me, Sam, and Rim Bramwell — just before we crossed over the line into Kansas with our mule herd. I thought then that it was a couple of thieves after our mules, and that may still be true. We didn't get a close look

205

at the two gunmen who fired on us, but we singed their ears with bullets as they rode off. I considered that they were gutless thieves and that'd be the last we'd see of them."

Jocelyn stood up and took their dirty dishes to the sink. She looked at him over her shoulder. "God willing, the law will catch up with the last one of them, this Carl Bramwell, and you can go on about your business."

"That's what I'm hoping for."

The work Whit had put in grooming the mule herd was complete and clearly worth it. Next came a rush of preparation to drive the mule herd as far as the Skiddy train depot for the journey by rail car the rest of the way to Topeka. Jocelyn marveled at the time they'd save. No less was her excitement at taking the train for the first time. Traveling twenty-five miles an hour, they would arrive in Topeka three and a half *hours* after they boarded. Driving the mules on foot the whole way would take a probable six days!

A list was made of needs for the ranch that could be bought in Topeka and shipped back to Skiddy. Hot summer days made Jocelyn wish to buy an icebox, but she doubted she'd still be at the ranch come winter to cut and store ice from the creek. They would leave the wagon and team in the Skiddy livery, to provide transportation to the ranch on Jocelyn's return. A last objective was to hire someone to keep watch on the ranch and answer questions if anyone came looking to buy mules. Her book friend, Emma Hunter, suggested the Hunters' grown son, Ned, who was recovering from an accidental scything cut to his leg, for the brief job, and the deal was made.

Jocelyn's red shawl served to hold her washed and mended best outfit, which she'd change into in Topeka, a nightgown, and personal items she'd bought on a trip to Skiddy — hair brush, hand mirror, toothbrush, and hair combs and ribbon. Her brogans had finally fallen apart beyond repair. The owner of the Skiddy shoe repair shop had shown her boots they'd repaired and had for sale at a low price. She was quite pleased with her "new" camel-colored ankle boots that had cost thirty cents and fit perfectly. As usual when she went to town, she'd wear the navy-blue straw hat she'd worn near to forever. It was without the veil, which over time had become so tattered she removed it. Depending how successful the mule sale was, she might buy a new hat in Topeka.

Leaving the ranch before dawn and moving the mules along at a good clip, they reached Skiddy by mid-morning and put their herd in one of many holding pens until time to load them. As it turned out, mules weren't the only livestock to be loaded and shipped off on the train. Cattle bawled, probably displeased at being separated from their calves, sheep bleated, and horses whinnied. Jocelyn's mules brayed, no doubt in annoyance at this symphony of complete discord.

Dust floated over the loading pens, the waiting train *chuffed* an oily odor, rail yard helpers hurried here and there, and passengers soon to board were buying food from the vendors outside the station.

Jocelyn's mules were vaguely suspicious of taking the ramp up through wide doors into the louvered car. She led the most trusting of her herd, a pair of greys, offering the two of them a bucket of oats. It took time and patience, and goading from Whit Hanley and rail yard stock handlers, but other mules followed until all were loaded in two cars.

The conductor was calling for passengers to board. Within minutes, Jocelyn sat with her red shawl of belongings in her lap, a food basket beside her, and watched the countryside begin to pass by outside the train window, the view consisting mostly of cattle grazing in endless pastures of blue-stem. Not long after, the small town of Vista came and went. Seeing a pair of cowboys driving a herd of cattle off in the distance, she thought of Pete. How was he? Was the bullet wound in his shoulder healing well, his cracked or bruised ribs on the mend? Was he out of sorts with her still, because of the way they'd parted? Was he — her heart plummeted at the thought — out of her life for good?

From across the aisle, Whit interrupted her thoughts. "Don't know about you, Miss Royal, but I'm starved. What do we have there in the basket?"

She nodded. "I'm hungry, too. Coffee and a biscuit was hardly enough for early breakfast." Lifting the lid of the basket, she removed a bacon sandwich and a second one of butter and plum jam wrapped in used butcher paper and handed them to him. She passed him a jar of lemonade, and an apple, followed by a handful of cookies.

The remainder of the trip was passed in relative quiet, each with their own thoughts. Jocelyn began to read Emma's copy of *Diana of the Crossings*. She was finding it less than enjoyable, the writing showy and stiff about a beautiful British socialite and her marriage troubles with her horrible husband. She did find Diana's headstrong ways something to admire. Still, it wasn't a book for her, and Jocelyn closed it.

A line from the book, however, continued to run through her mind: *"A witty woman is a treasure, a witty beauty is a power."* Maybe that was true in Great Britain. On the Kansas prairie a woman dealing with mules, outlaws, and a man she loved — who had his own headstrong ways and dreams — needed a lot more than wit and beauty. Grit and backbone to start. She closed her eyes and leaned back with a quiet smile.

Feeling rested later, and eager for the venture about to take place, Jocelyn looked out the train window at bustling human activity as they arrived at the Topeka station. She gathered up her things and, Whit Hanley close behind her, made her way from the train to the depot platform. Odors carried on the hot breeze indicated they were very near the stockyards. Blocks away behind them was Topeka's business district, closer at hand the headquarters of the Atchison, Topeka, & Santa Fe Railroad line.

With stockyard helpers, their mule herd was unloaded and penned in a large corral behind the Johnson and Gibb auction barn. With luck, Whit told her, the mules would sell quickly. Paying for the mules' keep at the stock pens could be dear if they were there any length of time, added to the percentage paid from sales to the operators of the auction.

In short order, with Whit Hanley driving a hired hack drawn by a velvet-black mare and Jocelyn beside him, they traveled along Kansas Avenue, the buggy wheels rattling over bumpy brick paving. New business development was evident everywhere one looked, along with ornate, heavy-corniced structures built some twenty years earlier. Older buildings included the Kansas Valley Bank, Welch Land Office, Topeka Drug Store, City Bakery, Barnum and Company Dry Goods, Express Wagon Delivery, and, beyond, a hotel or two. A business to fit every need, Jocelyn was thinking, and this was only part of the town.

Beyond the business district, they turned onto Topeka Boulevard, which Whit referred to as Topeka's "Park Avenue." She could see why. Even with all the books she'd read and pictures she'd seen, she wouldn't have imagined the beautiful mansions that lined each side of the wide brick street. Tall shade trees — elm, maple, and walnut — formed a cool green archway over the thoroughfare. "It's a magnificent neighborhood," Jocelyn said, turning to Whit. "I wouldn't have guessed any street so fine in all of Kansas."

He smiled. "You might find them in other Kansas towns, especially Kansas City and Wichita. Both are larger cities than Topeka, even though this town is the capital."

"I knew that; I just didn't imagine. For now, I'm fine with seeing all this. It's quite a surprise compared with the farm-like area where we left the mules with Johnson and Gibbs . . . almost unbelievable." Moments later, Whit was pulling their horse and buggy up before a stately brick mansion. It was a breathtaking, three-story conglomerate of turrets, towers, cupolas, and wood-lace gingerbread-trimmed porches, behind an intricately designed iron fence and stone wall. Jocelyn took it in and looked at him. "Why are we stopping?"

"To see my mother; this is where you'll be staying while we're in Topeka."

In awe, Jocelyn said, "My goodness! She is very fortunate to be employed here. Is she the housekeeper, or . . . a companion to the lady of the house?"

"She's not an employee. She and my stepfather live here; this is their home."

"But you said —" Jocelyn's face began to

212

warm. "I thought they were . . . poor."

"I did say that she and my stepfather need my help with some steep debt. They do. But Gorham House, as it is known, belongs to them, although they are about to lose it. I'll explain later." He took her hand and helped her from the buggy. "I can't wait for you to meet Mother. You'll love her."

Jocelyn's heart pattered in anxiety, which was relieved the moment the door opened. She had expected a maid to answer the door of this elegant home, but the small woman framed in the arched doorway cried, "Son!" From the look in her eyes, his mother clearly doted on Whit. There was love and respect in the way he drew her into a gentle hug.

He turned to Jocelyn. "Jocelyn, meet my mother, Mrs. Francina Gorham. Mother, this is Miss Jocelyn Royal, for the time being my partner in the mule trading business."

Hearing the word "partner" for the first time, Jocelyn experienced an inner glow but focused on her hostess. "It's nice to meet you, Mrs. Gorham." The lovely older woman couldn't have been more equal to the splendorous setting, Jocelyn thought, as they moved into the stately, marble-floored entry hall. Whit's mother wore a dress of

pale-green voile with the neckline and ballooning upper sleeves trimmed in lace and
citron velvet ribbon. Her steel-grey hair was
waved back into a bun; smile wrinkles at
the corners of her eyes and mouth only
added appeal to her lovely, ivory skin. She
seemed to have trouble moving her left arm,
but both hands managed to grasp Jocelyn's
hands and hold them tightly.

"And I am delighted to meet you, Miss
Royal. Won't you please come in? Come
with me to the parlor; it's a bit cooler there.
We'll have some tea and a nice chat. Whitman told me you'd be staying with us for a
day or two."

CHAPTER FIFTEEN

The entry hall alone was the size of Gram's house in Kansas City, Jocelyn thought, and beautifully furnished with a hall stand to collect canes and umbrellas, velvet benches against the walls, and a table with a silver dish for calling cards. They entered the parlor, comfortably furnished, warm and welcoming. There were three blue velvet settees with polished oak frames, overstuffed chairs to match, tables again of solid, shining oak, and colorful landscape and floral paintings on the maroon painted walls. Enormous windows looked out on a stretch of lawn and profuse gardens of yellow roses.

"As much as I love this house it can be lonely at times, and I am thrilled to have your company," Mrs. Gorham said. She turned to her son. "Whitman, dear, would you take a moment and please find Mrs. Stewart? I believe she's in her room or perhaps outside in the garden. Ask if she'd please fix us tea, while I chat with Miss Royal?"

He agreed and kissed his mother's forehead. "Be right back."

"I must say I've never been in a home so beautiful," Jocelyn commented in awe.

"Thank you, dear. If you like, I'll show you the house after we've had our tea. Perhaps not all twenty-five rooms, but a few," Mrs. Gorham said, with an impish smile touched with guilt. She leaned toward Jocelyn as in conspiracy. "I suppose our home can be considered pretentious, but I've dreamed of living in such a place since I was a little girl." She laughed softly. "A palace, you know, little imaginer that I was. At any rate, I love Gorham House. Frye, my husband, put his heart and soul into building this treasure several years back, and he is enormously proud of it." A momentary shadow crossed her face. "His health of late is fragile. Not for anything would he ever agree to leaving here; it's most important he live his life out in these rooms, however long that might be."

Jocelyn of course had heard from Whit about his parents' financial problems, but for a moment she said nothing. She offered, "I hope both your wish and his happen, as it should be."

Mrs. Gorham nodded. " 'Only feet first,' Frye's always said. 'Carrying me out in my coffin is the only way I'll ever leave Gorham House for good.' " After a moment's reflection, she said, "My husband is a dear, so very good to me, different from my life with Whitman's father. Don't ever fall in love with a bossy, abusive man, Miss Royal. Life can be a living hell. He did this," she lifted her stiff and crooked left arm. "But never mind that now. You'll meet my darling Frye when he wakes from his nap."

"I'm so sorry about your arm, and I promise to be very careful in choosing a husband." *If that opportunity ever comes up.* In the meantime, she admired Francina Gorham speaking so openly, with no pretense, no covering up untidy family secrets. She was who she was, and if relating bad things would help others avoid them, she didn't hesitate. She was wonderful.

Whit returned to the parlor, and, shortly after, a stout woman with a friendly face, perhaps a few years younger than Francina, entered with a tray of moisture-beaded glasses of iced tea, tall teaspoons, a sugar bowl, and a small dish of sliced lemon. Mrs. Gorham introduced her. "Mrs. Stewart has been my best friend for many years, Jocelyn. May I call you by your first name?" When

217

Jocelyn nodded with a smile, she continued, "We've had the best times together, Olympia and I, and she helps me out here at home so much I can never repay her."

The other woman said with a warm smile, "And, along with the good times and helping a trifle now and then, this widow enjoys the privilege of living in this marvelous house with my dearest of friends, Francina and Frye." She took Jocelyn's hand. "It's very nice to meet you, dear."

"Do join us, Mrs. Stewart," Whit said, and his mother echoed the invitation. "Yes, please do, Olympia."

"Thank you, but peonies in the garden are calling for my attention to weed them. Another time, though. And don't scold me, Francina," she said softly and smiled when the other woman looked about to protest, "you know how much I love to be out of doors, and there's much to do, to have the gardens ready for our picnic and rally."

"Oh, my, I suppose so, if you insist. The gardens look beautifully fine to me, but I realize they are your pride and pleasure. Do what you will, Olympia." Whit's mother explained to Jocelyn, "My good friend, Olympia, and I, will hold a Kansas Equal Suffrage Association rally here in a few weeks. We're quite excited to do our part to gain new members and champion the women's cause through KESA."

Jocelyn nodded. "I've heard of such rallies happening in many Kansas towns. It's wonderful of you two, to do this. You must be proud."

"We are. Women's suffrage is a matter dear to Olympia's heart and mine and has been from the time we both were very young women."

Olympia gave up on the peonies briefly, took a chair, and added her voice to the subject. "It has been a long battle that every able woman should take an interest in, I believe. Men, too. Not everyone is aware that back in 1776, women had the vote for a short time. Horrors," her hands flew up and mocked, "women voting? It couldn't be; legislators surely had made a mistake, was the reaction."

"Pure nonsense from those gentlemen and such a pity that state constitutions were immediately rewritten to exclude women from voting." Francina shook her head.

"A pure outrage is what it was! Leave it to *male* legislators to officially outlaw women's suffrage before they'd barely had a chance." Olympia looked around at the others, her voice remaining cool and polite, but her expression of disgust revealing clearly where she stood on the matter. "For too many years, women have been second-class citizens, sentenced to home and hearth, wrongly discouraged against education or obtaining a profession.

"Not very long ago, women didn't have the right to own their own property, keep their own wages, or sign a contract, along with being denied the right to vote. From my first knowledge of what was going on, I've considered all of it outrageously unfair, and my mind hasn't changed."

Having had her own thoughts about the matter, Jocelyn added with a nod, "My Gram told me that when she was young, boys and girls weren't thought of as equal. Little girls could only wish to be as important to their fathers as their brothers were. I didn't experience that myself, since I didn't have brothers, but I would have fought if it had happened, because I also agree about the wrongness, Mrs. Stewart."

"I believe what upset me most," Francina put it, "was the exclusion of women from the dedication ceremonies for the Statue of Liberty in 1886. I lived here in Kansas, nowhere near New York City, but what a proud moment it would have been for women to witness the formal dedication."

Whit had been silent, but from his bemused expression he hadn't missed a word and now defended the male gender. "From what I've learned, many men have supported the suffrage movement. I certainly do. I applaud you ladies in your fight for equal rights. From what I see in the papers, Kansas women are gaining what they've long fought hard for and, in fact, are faring better than women in many other states."

"You're correct, my dear son, and we thank you — thank all men who take up our cause."

Olympia nodded agreement. "Frederick Douglas favored women's rights and signed their bill, at the Seneca Falls convention in 1848. Here in Kansas in 1867, Governor Crawford, Samuel Wood, and others campaigned to convince voters to ratify an amendment that would grant equal suffrage to women and blacks in our state."

She stood, patting her apron pockets. "Time to climb off my soapbox and go back to work. We're succeeding and must never give up." She started for the door, then turned back with more to say. "Kansas women are proud to have had the right for some years to vote in school elections and civic matters. Don't you know that in 1887 we made history when Susanna Madora Salter of Argonia, Kansas, was the first woman in the nation to be elected mayor?"

Jocelyn nodded and smiled. "I was a young girl, but I remember well when that happened. Partly because my Gram was aghast at the idea of a woman for mayor, while I secretly thought it was simply the best thing ever."

Olympia again started for the door, but remembered another thing. "In April elections of that year, women won all five seats on the Syracuse city council. We've far to go to gain full suffrage, the opportunity to vote in national matters. We're working on that all the time, and I vow it will happen, I hope by the next election year." She smiled in Jocelyn's direction. "I'm wondering, Miss Royal, if you'd like to come to our Kansas Equal Suffrage Association rally next month? We'd be privileged to have you join us, and if you have women friends who'd like to come, they would be most welcome."

"I'd dearly love to be there." She hesitated, biting her lip. Topeka was several days' distance to travel by wagon, and taking the train was costly. But somehow, she hoped to join these women in their efforts. She told them hesitantly, "I'm not sure what's ahead for me the next few weeks and may not be able to come to the rally. I know what I could do; if you have KESA literature, I could see that it's passed around in Skiddy, and to my neighbors."

It was agreed, and Jocelyn took a deep breath and relaxed. When she'd left Nickel Hill, she'd had no idea how much she would enjoy this trip to Topeka, that she'd meet like-minded women, older though Francina and Olympia happened to be.

When Olympia had gone, Whit's mother said, "What about the mules? Tell me about them, please."

Whit started to give her facts and figures, but she waved him silent. "No, no, I mean stories about the mules." She spoke to Jocelyn. "My father was a doctor, and our family lived close to downtown Wichita. But when he traveled into the country to treat folks there, he took me with him. I remember the huge wheat, Kaffir corn, and corn fields being worked with mules, and mules helping to build railroads, pulling wagon loads of wheat to the mill. I loved seeing them up close at country fairs, those tall beautiful ears and the long nose. I always thought them interesting creatures, with strong personalities. They know exactly what they want and don't want to do. You've been taking care of Whitman's mule herd, Miss Royal; you must have some stories about mules."

"I — I suppose I do." She told Whit's mother about the wretched woman threatening her with the shotgun, and the poor mules dancing with bees in their ears, and how angry she'd been at the bees and the old woman.

"Oh, my," Mrs. Gorham said, her hand to her mouth. "What nerve of the woman! I suppose, though, to her mind, she was in her rights. But to shoot at you, or at the mules — that is abhorrent."

Jocelyn then told about the escapade in Council Grove, with the mules all over the place, barring the restaurant door, one of them feasting on the courthouse lawn, and another scratching his side against the Post Office Oak.

"Oh, I would have loved to have been there, seen that!" Mrs. Gorham giggled behind her hand. "Aren't I awful to feel that way, but I would have, yes, I would've."

Remembering when the little mule, Rusty, kicked Rufe Tuttle and was at least partially responsible for the outlaw's death, Jocelyn decided not to tell that story. Instead she then told of good things she had learned from mules. "Many people think mules are contrary and stubborn and kick just to be mean. Truthfully, they are very smart, have a good reason for what they do, and if treated right can be gentle, and even seem to have a sense of humor. A mule gives trouble when he doesn't understand, when he loses trust in a person, or when he's been pushed beyond his limit — a lot like human beings."

She ran out of tales at the same time they finished their tea. Mrs. Gorham stood up. "Now let me show you the house and grounds. Come, dear." She took Jocelyn's hand and looped her other arm through Whit's. "And you, too, son. Keep us company."

Jocelyn was enchanted by each room they entered, the arched doorways leading from one room to the next, and the pecan, chestnut, and oak mosaic patterns of the floors. She couldn't help gaping at the white plaster ceiling of fruits and vines in the dining room, as well as the strutting peacock design of the wallpaper. There was a polished table long enough to seat one hundred guests, an immense sideboard with a bouquet of blue hydrangeas on top, and against the opposite wall an enormous hutch filled with light-catching fine china and glassware.

The drawing room had golden-oak walls and furniture, thick, red carpet, and stained-glass windows. Frye used to meet buyers in this room, Whit told her.

On the second floor was the Gorhams' suite, where Mr. Gorham was sleeping. The trio quietly bypassed it and took the grand stairway to the third-floor ballroom, which was complete with a bandstand and billiard room. Mrs. Gorham explained, "Frye's sales of fine horses were by invitation, and people from all over the United States, and from a few other countries, attended. We entertained in this room, with a ball after the important sales."

Outside, they met up again with Olympia Stewart, who was almost hidden in a beautiful forest of pink foxglove and hollyhocks. A wide-brimmed straw hat shaded her face in the hot sun. She had a basket over her arm and was clipping dead blossoms from the shoulder high, leafy plants. For the next half hour, she showed them through flower beds of fragrant yellow four o' clocks, pink cosmos, and deep blue heliotrope. Hydrangeas bloomed in shades of blue and rose around a gazebo. Marble planters were packed and spilling over with portulaca grandiflora, also known as moss rose. Jocelyn's breath caught, and she traced her fingers through the tiny, rainbow-hued flowers. They had been Gram's favorite.

There was a fountain where water trickled down to a concrete statue of a child playing in a pool. Other statuary was prominent here and there among the green lawns and gardens, some whimsical, some formal. Walking through paradise couldn't be much different, Jocelyn thought. She told Whit's mother so, in thanking her.

As they retraced their steps toward the back of the house through the garden, Mrs. Gorham asked Jocelyn, "Has Whitman told you about the Friends of Topeka Government?"

"Mother," Whit interrupted, "do you want to talk about that now?"

"Yes, I do. If you haven't mentioned it to her, I will. After all, it's not every day one's home is in the process of being shanghaied to become a governor's mansion."

Jocelyn almost stumbled into a stone statue of a dog, lean and with a long nose — it was a whippet, Mrs. Stewart had said. "Excuse me?"

"Yes, my dear, a group of rabid, politically-minded citizens of Topeka are on the hunt for a more desirable — let's say more palatial — residence for the governor of Kansas. Their attention is on our house, and one other. The group, being strapped for funds, would prefer for us to donate Gorham House to the cause but have made an offer to buy at a fraction of what it is worth.

If we sold, the pittance would be something to live on for a while, a short while. What bothers me more is that Frye would never want to leave here, nor should he have to, if we can just take care of some problems." She caught Jocelyn's arm and held her to a standstill. "Governor Stanley and his wife, Lenora, are fine folks. But this . . ." she waved an arm, "this is our home!"

Whit rolled his eyes, and his face flushed as his mother poured out the family's personal money problem detail after detail.

Jocelyn, on the other hand, was filled with sympathy. She knew what it was like to lose a home a person loved with their entire soul. Personally, she'd rather have a farm any day than a huge house like this one, but if this, their home, was where Whit Hanley's parents were happy and wanted to stay, so be it; they should be allowed. She believed that to the bottom of her heart.

At dinner, Jocelyn met Whit's elderly stepfather. He was a large, handsome man with a full head of snow-white hair and a thick but tidy moustache. His personality didn't seem to fit his physical size. He was very quiet, behaving almost fearful and shy. He was confused about the use of his eating utensils, passing them to Francina with questioning eyes. Ever patient and sweet, she showed him what to do. He ate very slowly and stared at Jocelyn, his expression confused.

Francina told him, "Jocelyn is our guest, Frye. Remember, I introduced the two of you before we sat down? She's Whitman's friend. They are here in Topeka with a herd of mules to sell."

"Mules? Well, sure," he said, in a moment of clarity, "if there's a sale of importance over at the auction house we should go."

Francina took her husband's hand. "If you're feeling up to it tomorrow, perhaps you can go along with Whitman." She said to Jocelyn, "Besides shopping, we will find some proper ladies' entertainment for the two of us. Livestock sales are no place for women. It's such *male territory* — the haggling, language unfit for ladies' ears, air filled with cigar smoke and animal smells." Her voice lowered. "A body has to take such care where they step."

Jocelyn waited for Whit to speak up, and when he didn't, she said, "I've gone to auctions in the past with my father. I found them exciting, and entertaining." *Besides, I want to be there, with our mules.*

Whit looked relieved. "If it's what you want, I'd like for you to be at the sale." He explained, "There are often buyers who believe an auctioneer's sole purpose is to 'talk' dollars to a mule's price tag. These men prefer to visit the stalls and pens to decide which animals to buy, rather than in the auction barn. Negotiations are quieter, and they can size up the merits of the animal at closer range. For example, a buyer might flip his hat at a mule, and if it cringed or shied, he won't be interested. If the mule does neither, the buyer must then determine if the mule's behavior is because it is hardheaded, lazy, or, as he hopes, calm natured. I'd like you to be near our mules' pens, Jocelyn, sort of a hostess, to answer questions, look after them. You know our mules better than anyone."

"Hostess?" she said quizzically with a half smile of delight while attempting to ignore Mrs. Gorham's look of shock. That could be interesting; whoever heard of a pen of mules requiring someone to be hostess to them?

CHAPTER SIXTEEN

"I think male buyers would find a woman in that role refreshing. I'd like to be inside at the auction, watching the action and talking with other traders." Whit forked a bite of roast stuffed chicken and looked satisfied.

His mother was shaking her head in consternation and scolded, "Whitman, I don't think this is a good idea."

Jocelyn spoke up. "It's all right, Mrs. Gorham. I'd like to do this. I really can't think of any reason why I shouldn't. I intend to be as much help as I can."

The older woman, so dignified and wise, looked as though she could think of at least a dozen reasons, but she stayed silent. She looked at her son and waited.

"I wanted to give a try to your being there, Jocelyn, but I could find someone else to stick with our herd. Mother is right about stock sales being mostly for men."

"I'm glad you agree, Whitman, dear. Those places are so smelly." His mother's glance whipped hopefully in Jocelyn's direction.

She hated to disappoint Whit's adorable mother, but she had to be honest. "It's not as though I'm not used to working closely with livestock." She added, "And I remember that ladies were present at the sales I attended with my father; they provided and served lunch. I wouldn't be the only woman around the auction yard. Won't there be lunch at the sale tomorrow?" she asked Whit.

He agreed that there would be.

His mother read Jocelyn's face, and her thin shoulders dropped in disappointment. She grasped Jocelyn's hand across the table and managed a smile. "I give up. You two win, and Jocelyn, dear, I admire your courage and spirit. I admit that a new day has dawned for women — in many ways that are good and will continue to improve. I'm very much for the right to vote. I strongly support the KESA. But accepting other new and drastic changes is a bit difficult for us older folks. Give us time; we'll be filling elective office beside men in an equal role, owning our own businesses, and who knows — ?" — she smothered a giggle — "playing

232

hostess to a mule herd."

Jocelyn laughed and gently squeezed the small, warm hand grasping hers. She understood Whit's mother's view, that in the end a lady is still a lady in the voting booth, or wherever life takes her. She agreed and believed it possible in all sorts of situations, even those that were dirty and hard. "Thank you, Mrs. Gorham. I really want to do this. It's going to be fine."

She could almost see herself, after the sale, marching into the Council Grove bank and turning over the cash to buy back her farm. And if the mule trade Whit was operating aided his parents in keeping their home, what could be better? Two birds, one stone.

Jocelyn dressed for the mule sale in her second-best outfit, a faded, mended-many-times, blue striped dress with a solid-blue jacket and her poor old navy straw hat. Her mind raced ahead with excitement as well as caution. Francina had been right about one thing: for the most part livestock sales were males' domain, and she — a full-fledged young woman — was charging into it.

Whit's mother, attempting to be more helpful, had offered Jocelyn a bloomer dress that an out-of-town guest at Gorham House had left behind years back. Fortunately, the garment was much too large. Besides which, she wanted to be herself and still look as presentable as possible. She'd earlier spotted Whit talking with his parents, and he was dressed very fine in grey vest and trousers and a white shirt with a knotted black neckerchief. People in the mule trading business, Whit had told Jocelyn, were judged by the appearance of the trader every bit as much as the animals. She could understand why that might be true.

The sale wouldn't start until ten a.m., and although Whit and Jocelyn arrived early, so had many others. Men in farm wagons, others driving fancy black, yellow-wheeled buggies, and riders on horses of every description filled the streets near the Johnson and Gibb stockyard pens and large auction barn. Mules brayed, horses whinnied, and men laughed and talked in loud voices. The climbing temperature indicated that today would be another scorcher.

A few men threw curious glances their way as Whit gave a hand to Jocelyn alighting from the buggy, the handle of her satchel holding paperwork over her arm. A few made teasing remarks, but she pretended not to notice. She was a partner, at least by

Whit's word, in the mule business and was rightly part of these goings-on.

They headed for their pen of mules and found three men already looking them over. To one gentleman's question, Whit answered, "Yes, most of these mules are young and unbroken. I'm aware that's what most buyers want, and that's what I look for when I buy."

"For good reason," a second man said with a nod. "Mules' age is harder to judge than the age of horses. The animal might've been worked hard for years, but that doesn't show in a mule as easy as in a horse. Too often a shady trader fattens an older, broken mule and turns around trying to sell it as a young one."

"Not these," Whit said. "They are exactly what you see: young, bred from fine stock, and left to be broken in a man's own way."

"They are damn fine looking mules," one of the men agreed, hands tucked in his vest and rocking back on his heels. "How you pricing them?"

Jocelyn had to refrain from steadying herself against a corral post when Whit without batting an eye quoted, "ninety to a hundred fifty a head, depending on the animal."

The man nodded. "They could be worth

that. I hope you're figuring in what the buyer can afford when you make a final deal?" He squinted doubtfully at Whit Hanley.

"I would."

"We would," Jocelyn added, but perhaps none of the men heard, since they paid her no heed.

After the men moved on, saying they'd be examining more mules before making a final decision, Whit said to Jocelyn, "Some buyers like to buy in large lots, and, in that case, we could cut the price per animal and give them a better deal. We'll wait and see."

"Good enough." Jocelyn turned to making sure their mules had fresh hay and water while Whit walked away to talk with a couple of farmers. Their mules were a fine lot, she told herself as she cared for them, stopping now and then to stroke and talk to first one then another, and they should bring top prices. As eager as she'd been to sell the herd and be shed of their care, she was going to miss them. It seemed each mule had its own personality and had been such a part of her life for months now. Like Rusty — he was young and feisty but mostly well-behaved. He'd saved her life when he kicked Rufe Tuttle. That was Tuttle's own fault, making the racket he was and paying no attention that he was carrying on right behind Rusty.

Thank heaven, Zenith and Alice wouldn't be sold. She depended on them for so much. She wouldn't be able to do without them when she needed to use the wagon, or a mount to ride, if she stayed on at Nickel Hill. Plus, when Whit brought in a new herd of mules, they would be the teachers, the leaders, Alice in particular.

As the minutes ticked by, Jocelyn realized that the men who came her way were far more interested in her mules than in the fact that a woman was showing them. She was grateful and grew more at ease. Most were gentlemen, even the roughly dressed farmers in homespun shirts, worn boots, and stained and worn old hats.

As ten o'clock approached most men began to leave the outdoor pen area, milling toward the expansive auction barn.

Soon after, male laughter came in loud bursts from the barn, and she knew that the auctioneer was stirring up fun and excitement with his banter. She watched a pair of auction helpers lead a beautiful pair of tall, black mules inside the auction barn and had to quell a feeling of envy. The loud barking chatter of the auctioneer started soon after, and from the shouts of "Yep!" "Yep!" with each rise of the price, she knew things boded well for the owner of the pair.

Their turn would come, though, hers and Whit Hanley's.

When she could stand it no longer, she made sure that her mules in their large pen were content, eating, drinking, or lying down, and that no prospective buyers were near. She scurried across the hard-packed ground toward the auction barn for a quick peek inside.

The inside of the barn was enormous, blue with cigar smoke, and packed to the rafters with men. Centering the room was an arena, and standing on a platform was the auctioneer. He was a short, hefty man in a tan suit and white colonel's hat, and in looks he could have been Teddy Roosevelt's twin. She'd seen several pictures of Theodore Roosevelt, candidate for vice president on William McKinley's Republican ticket, the vote to be settled in November.

The auctioneer was joking with the crowd, waving a cane, saying, "You can't *make* a mule *do* anything, but you can *ask* him, and he'll work for you like a dream. It's important to be polite even with a mule, you see." He added after a moment, "Yelling, hitting, and cursing your mule," he whacked the air with the cane, "will suffer

238

you a swift kick in the derriere." When someone groaned at the humor, he said, "See, that's happened to that feller right over there." He pointed with his cane. "That's how he knows what derriere means; it's still fresh in his memory where he got kicked."

Jocelyn laughed along with the crowd, and she thought again about Rufe Tuttle, who'd assaulted her and likely would have killed her if Rusty hadn't let fly with his hooves.

The auctioneer's staccato bark picked up again in his special high voice, "I'mabid sixtywho'llmakeitseventyIgoteightywho'll gimmeeahundred," as another mule was led into the ring and floor men caught buyers' signals with a "Yep!" "Yep!" "Yep!"

From Jocelyn's observation, there were perhaps fifty or sixty buyers on the floor, and perhaps a hundred and fifty spectators in the stands — a nice size crowd. Out of those, she picked out three women and maybe a fourth, whom she saw one moment but couldn't spot the next. Anyhow, she wasn't the only woman there. Women's rights were gaining ground little by grinding little, and someday it wouldn't be an oddity to see an equal mix of women and men at an event such as this.

She nearly jumped out of her skin at a tap

on her shoulder, instantly thinking *Pete*? Or — she filled with alarm — Carl Bramwell, here looking for Whit? Relief washed over her when she turned to see a middle-aged farmer simply wanting by her through the doorway. "Sorry," she said and stepped aside.

"Beg pardon, m'am," he was saying as he doffed his straw hat to her and went on inside, heading for the crowded stands. She hurried back to her station with the mules, feeling foolish for being so quick to jump to unnecessary conclusions. Pete? He was hardly speaking to her these days, and Carl Bramwell, by God's good grace she hoped he was a long way away from Kansas.

From time to time, a person came from the auction barn to examine mules left in the pens. She waited expectantly when one such fellow, stout and shoulders back, moved in her direction. He was very well dressed, and his gaze was taking in her mules.

His interest seemed to sharpen the closer he came. He stopped, and squinting, chewing on a cigar, he studied the shifting mules in the pen. "Are you in charge here, Miss?" he asked with a wave of his cigar. She nodded, and he said, "That white-legged, sorrel mule there — tell me about him."

She entered the pen and moved, confident but carefully, to the mule. "This fellow is from Missouri, where folks really know their mules. As you can see he's well built and close to eighteen hands high. He'd make a fine draft animal." The mule turned his head her way, and she reached up to stroke his side. "Yes, you're a beautiful mule," she whispered softly. "He's not full broken, but he's been harnessed a few times, and if you'd like to have a closer look, I can bring him out there."

"If you would, Miss, please." He tossed his cigar aside and ground it out with the toe of a fine polished boot, removed his hat, and wiped the sweat from his forehead on his sleeve. Putting his hat back on, he looked the mule over while she stood at the mule's head, speaking to the animal softly while he stood calm and steady. Several minutes later, the gentleman nodded. "I'll take him. Would you put him in that empty pen over there" — he pointed — "while I look over some of the others?"

The process continued for almost an hour. Jocelyn had to ask, "Would you be interested in buying all of the mules we have here in our holding pen? We, my partner and I, could give you a fair deal."

He seemed to be considering her offer,

while she held her breath and waited. The man already had picked a dozen mules that were now penned separate from the rest of her herd. "I expect that you'll give a good deal on these I've picked out, but that's all I'll be taking today. Now, then, what are you asking for them?"

She said as calmly as she could manage, repeating Whit Hanley's price from earlier, "Singly, they would run ninety dollars to one hundred fifty each, depending on the mule. Let's say, a hundred thirty each?"

"That's pretty steep. How about one hundred each?" His eyes locked on hers.

She bit her lip and shook her head. "We can't possibly accept less than fourteen hundred; they are excellent animals."

He shook his head and frowned as though he couldn't possibly give that much, then surprised her and said gruffly, "All right. Do I pay you here? Where is your partner?"

Jocelyn fought a smile about to explode on her face. "It will only take a minute to find him. His name is Whitman Hanley, if you want to go ahead and make out the draft. I'll be right back." She spelled the name for him, while in the back of her mind she was thinking, *The Hanley and Royal Mule Company.* Or *Royal and Hanley, Mule Traders.* Maybe it would be . . . something like that, in time.

At midday, Whit and Jocelyn took purchased ham sandwiches and pie to sawhorse
tables in the shade of a cottonwood grove
several yards from the pens and auction
barn. Jocelyn ate a few bites, drank some
water, and then removed her hat, fanned
with it a moment, then put it aside. Too
excited to finish her food, she related how
the sale she made had come about. Whit
grinned, taking time only between each bite
to tell her how well she'd done, how pleased
he was. When he took out a small tablet and
pencil from inside his vest, recording the
figure they'd earned, Jocelyn sat up straight
and alert, and her skin tingled. She'd
already totted up the figure in her mind,
but seeing it written down, along with the
bank draft Mr. Jennings had given, sent her
mind reeling.

It was an astounding figure, or at least
right smart more than she'd ever dealt with
before. And a share of it was hers — for the
drive, caring for the mules at the ranch, and
helping here at the auction. At one time,
she'd planned to tell Mr. Whit Hanley he
could blamed well pay her double his
original offer, but, after meeting his parents
and learning how much money it would
take to pay their debts and not lose their

243

home, she was having second thoughts. If she settled for his first offer, she'd still have a goodly amount toward buying her farm. Of course, the more money she came by, the more she could stock her farm once she'd bought it back. If Whit wanted to continue this business for another year or so, she'd not hesitate to be part of it.

Whit had shoved the pencil behind his ear and sat looking at his figures. A look of concern had wiped away his earlier broad smiles. "We've done well, no doubt about it, but unfortunately it won't be all profit. Caring for the mules and shipping them to market cost money. Part of that goes to you, of course, and you've more than earned it. Johnson and Gibb charge for the auction services, a dollar and a quarter for each mule sold, plus additional pay for hay, feed, and water while they are penned here."

As she listened, she began to wonder if there would be anything left, and her shoulders sagged. Hanley said, "Mule trading takes a lot of capital. The plan is to make enough from a sale to head out and buy another bunch to sell." He ran his fingers through his hair. "You know I want to help my mother as much as possible out of what we've earned with the debt that's nearly buried them."

"Of course," she said, "you must do that."

Some of the concern left his face, and he looked squarely at her. "I don't want you to worry, though, Jocelyn. You're going to have every penny I promised you and as much of a bonus as I can manage. If that means parting ways now, to use your earnings to locate other work, that's your decision. On the other hand, if mule trading with me is how you want to earn what you need to buy back your farm, then you're welcome to stay on at my Skiddy ranch — take care of the mules I gather, help with the selling of them — a while longer, for a dollar a day and a share of profits. You've proven to be a considerable asset to this business I'm putting together."

Jocelyn fought the impulse to leap into the air and click her heels. She said, as calmly and businesslike as she could, "Thank you, Mr. Hanley. I like our prospects, slim though they may be now. I'm staying on. But first," she gathered up the leavings of their lunch, "we have the rest of this day to sell the mules we have left."

When time came for her herd to be auctioned, Jocelyn brushed aside a young man, an auction helper, who would lead her first mule, a handsome chocolate brown with a white nose, inside. She smiled at the worker.

"I'll be taking this mule in, thank you." He shrugged and sauntered off. She led her mule closer to the door. A man who'd been watching suddenly bellowed, "Who do you think you are, one of them Carrie Nation kinda women, takin' over where you don't belong?"

In sudden surprise, she looked at her accuser, a man in a dusty, black suit, his face bloated and red behind an unkempt beard, bleary eyes trying to focus, smelling strongly of alcohol and in need of a bath. She waved him back. "Excuse me, sir, but you'd best not stand so close behind my mule. I don't want you to get kicked." He ignored her and weaved closer, without a doubt very drunk. She led her mule out of the way. "Go along, sir, please."

CHAPTER SEVENTEEN

"I was down in Kiowa, Kansas, a f-few, few weeks ago," the well-sotted man said, staggering as he spoke, "when that ol' witch, Carrie Nation, she come into the s-saloon where I was drinkin' with my friends," he belched, "at the nice bar with a pretty p-picture of a woman over it. Old lady Nation come in there with a bunch of rocks hidden in pockets under that long, black cape she wears." His hand shook as he lifted his hat and tapped his temple. "One of them rocks bounced and hit me right here, see that? Damned woman ought to be shot, takin' that iron rod of a cane she carries into us men's saloons . . ." He plopped his hat on askew, hesitating to remember what he was saying, ". . . where she don't belong in the first place."

He wagged his head, and his hat fell off. "Damn 'er, she come slashing that thing at glasses, bottles, and the chan— chan—

. . . the lights. At everythin'. Crazy like a tornado. Whackin' ever' whichaway" — he weaved almost off his feet — " 'til good whiskey and beer is spilt all over an' . . ." He was tearful at the loss, wiped at his eyes and red nose, and staggered up to Jocelyn.

One good thing about Papa — and there were many — he might imbibe a little on a holiday, or for medicinal reasons, but he was otherwise not much of a drinker.

Her mule's ears began to twitch. "If you don't stay away from me and my mule, sir," she said more sternly, holding up a hand, "I'll have to ask someone to remove you altogether from the auction yard. You need to find a place to sit down in the fresh air, out at the lunch tables, maybe?" His putrid breath was turning Jocelyn's stomach.

She was not unfamiliar with the name Carrie Nation. Neighbors who subscribed to newspapers often had stories to tell about the speechifying, rock-throwing, cane-wielding woman bent on ridding Kansas saloons of alcohol, from Medicine Lodge, where she'd put saloon keepers out of business, onward. Not a bad plan, if it kept husbands and fathers sober and at home with their wives and children. Many men, however, liked to drink, enjoying the fellowship of a saloon. She doubted prohibition would ever gain much of a foothold in Kansas or anywhere else.

His bloodshot eyes glared at her. "Ya' ain't tellin' me what ta do!" Fury and confusion mixed in his belligerent expression. "They keep throwin' that ol' bat-outta-hell, Carrie Nation, in jail for all the damage she's doin', then she's out. Over and over — in jail, then out, slashin' and wastin' good whiskey, ever' where you look, dammit. They got to prison her for life. *Life.*" He waved a finger in the air and listed to one side. "An' you, young lady, go on home where you belong an' stay the hell there! Gimmee that mule!" He lunged forward and pitched face down on the floor, passed out.

Jocelyn heard her number being called; she had to go. She looked around.

The auction helper sauntered back, standing over the drunkard with hands on his hips. He looked at Jocelyn and shook his head. "You all right, Miss?"

"Fine," she answered, "but I hope that old sop is gone when I come back out here. Could you see to that, please?" At a run, with halter rein in hand and her mule trotting obediently behind, she entered the auction barn and made her way to the center of the show ring. The auctioneer pointed his cane in her direction, a look of surprise briefly on his round, shiny face. He doffed his hat and bowed. "Well, now, see what we have here! A beautiful young lady with one of the finest looking mules I've seen in my time. Let's start the bidding, and be fair to this young lady. Who'llgimmeeightygimme-eightyeightyeightynow ninety . . ."

The day wore on, increasingly hot as Jocelyn led one mule after another into the auction barn. From time to time, she caught Whit Hanley's eye from where he sat in the bleachers. A smile tugged at her lips at his look of satisfaction.

Bids started low, then gradually rose to the auctioneer's chant, the mule eventually selling to the highest bidder. The room was filled heavily with cigar smoke, and the smell of it mingled with the odor of animal offal and sweaty bodies. But Jocelyn was so exhilarated by the proceedings she didn't care. To the last one, their mules sold, and none for less than ninety dollars.

Next morning, feeling proud, hope beginning to deepen as it hadn't for ages, Jocelyn accepted her pay. She tucked it safely into her new reticule, which she'd bought in Skiddy in anticipation of a moment like this.

A flurry of plans for a trip into downtown Topeka followed. Whit had errands to see to at the bank and other places of business. His mother and Jocelyn decided to make the trip with him, devising an agenda to suit them. "I'm happy to keep Frye company," Olympia Stewart said, shooing them on their way. "Off with you and have a good time!"

"Please take us to Mills and McPherson Mercantile, Son," Francina directed Whit, after he had assisted her and then Jocelyn into the buggy. "Jocelyn and I can walk about anywhere we'd like to from there, and you can go on to the hardware stores. We don't intend to spend a lot of money, do we dear?" she patted Jocelyn's hand.

Most certainly we do not, Jocelyn agreed silently. She was determined to save as much of her earnings as possible and to continue adding to the amount.

Mrs. Gorham continued to chat away. "We most of all want to see the sights, the new fashions — whatever is on display in the shop windows. We will pay a call on my dear friend Margaret, and you can come for us there, Whitman. You do remember where Margaret lives?" The horse-drawn buggy rattled into the street. "You do, don't you, Son?" she asked again, reaching forward and grazing his arm with her fingers.

"Yes, Mother, I remember." He looked back and shared a private smile with Jocelyn. Whit Hanley was capable of much more than his mother would ever guess.

Later, as they entered the mercantile, a large building honeycombed with merchandise, Francina said, "It's nice to be out and about for a change, isn't it? Not that I mind tending to the daily care that my darling Frye requires; he's given me so much, including deep love and a new life. I owe him everything and love him endlessly." She took Jocelyn's arm and continued, "I just hope Whitman will be as happy with his Claudia as Frye and I have been with one another."

Jocelyn slowed, feeling a bolt of interest in *Claudia*. This was the first mention of a woman in Whit's life. What was she like? When and where could they have met, considering his past and where he spent it? Her mind itched with curiosity, but Francina was already pulling her toward the store's department that carried a large overhead sign, THE LATEST AND FINEST FABRICS FOR DRESSMAKING.

They'd previously decided that Jocelyn would choose patterns and fabric here in the store and be measured. The seamstress, whose shop was next door, would sew

Jocelyn's choices and send them to the Skiddy post office. It had been a very long time since she'd had a new dress, and Jocelyn intended not to mind turning over a very small portion of her small fortune. She picked lavender gingham for an everyday dress and, to go with it, a white linen pinafore apron to be trimmed with purple rickrack. For dressier occasions, she chose a black, silk foulard skirt to pair with a light-yellow shirtwaist with lace-trimmed collar and leg o' mutton sleeves.

She was feeling horribly extravagant but could not resist a new, broad brimmed yellow hat sweetly trimmed with tiny rose-pink flowers, green leaves, and wide, rose-pink, velvet ribbon. She loved the hat and with great effort convinced herself that it was affordable, and decidedly necessary when compared to the old navy straw.

The shopping excursion over, they walked a few blocks to the elegant home of Francina's good friend Margaret, a slim, silver-haired woman with rouged cheeks and a ready smile. Over tea and cakes in a womanly chat, they discussed a head-spinning variety of subjects, beginning with Jocelyn's unusual partnership with Whit in the mule trade, shocking Margaret a bit. This time it was Francina who defended women's equality, although lightly, looking down and informing Margaret, "Miss Royal is fond of the mules, had cared for them these past few months, and Whitman needed her aid in a sale that was quite successful." She set aside the whole matter with a brush of her hand, her cheeks turning rosier.

Francina was embarrassed about her involvement with the mules! Jocelyn pressed her lips to hold back a laugh and didn't correct her. If all went well the next few months, her affiliation with Whit would be prosperous, and it would be about buying, tending, and selling mules. And she would be as ladylike as such permitted through every moment.

Jocelyn joined in a lengthy discussion of the governor's mansion problem. There was unanimous agreement that Francina and Frye should keep their home.

Once again, Francina proclaimed Governor Stanton "the finest of men." "Heaven knows he has his hands full with that Carrie Nation person and her violent efforts to strike down every saloon in Kansas." She shook her head. "There must be a better way to help men see their importance at home with their families, rather than drinking themselves silly in a saloon for hours on end."

Margaret sipped her tea, the other hand in the air to make her point. "As well, the men's own physical health and esteem are in question. However, I suspect Mrs. Nation, to her dying breath, won't give up her goal."

"It seems that way," Francina agreed with a shake of her head. "She's quite determined."

"The fight for prohibition has been long and hard, but it will be the people's decision whether *no alcohol* will be law in Kansas permanently, or not." Jocelyn thought of telling them about the drunkard who'd accosted her at the sale but decided against it. The other two might, after all, see this as a reason she shouldn't have been there in the first place. She closed her eyes briefly in gratitude when the subject turned to "Whitman and his sweetheart." She so wanted to know more.

"Whitman and Claudia have been smitten with each other since they were very young," Francina was saying. "Beautiful children, absolutely meant for each other."

When Margaret left the room to refresh the pitcher of tea, Francina quietly shared further with Jocelyn. "When Whitman was in his teens, he could stand no more of his father's rages and cruelty, and he ran away.

255

For too long we had no idea where he was, what had happened to my boy. It pained me — I can't describe how much — but I knew *why* he'd left our home. His father, my husband then, and Whitman were at constant odds with each other. Whitman hated how his father treated me, even though he suffered his own abuse at his father's hands just as much."

She sighed and looked about with a watery gaze. Jocelyn reached for her dainty hand and held it. Francina continued in a quivering voice, "Claudia's parents were very much against their daughter's having anything to do with Whitman after he returned, knowing by then about his past — his connection with terrible men, outlaws — even though he was just a boy at the time. But," her lips formed a shaky smile, "Whitman has been showing his true worth for several years now, and Claudia's parents are closer to accepting him. I'm thankful, I must say." She took a tiny hanky from her sleeve and blotted her eyes.

"I'm glad the young woman's parents are coming around," Jocelyn agreed, wanting very much to help this woman through her pain. "He is a fine person, a lucky catch for any woman, and Claudia sounds like an ideal match."

"Yes, she is a lovely girl," Francina's chin lifted, "a wonderful help to her father at his business, his very successful weekly newspaper, which I've been told will soon become a magazine with features and pictures all about Topeka. After that they plan to publish books. Claudia is good to both parents." Francina was recovering; she turned to Jocelyn with a warm smile, although her eyes were still moist. "And you, dear Jocelyn," she squeezed her hand, "do you have a sweetheart you'll someday soon be sharing your life with?"

Jocelyn debated her answer, then admitted with a smile, "I have a friend I care about very much. He's a cowboy and an artist — very independent, but kind. He's near my age. But sweethearts, no." *Not yet, maybe never.*

"*Friend,* my eye! You're completely smitten with the fellow, my dear, and you know it. I see it in your face, hear it in your voice." With a soft smile, she reached to pat Jocelyn's hand. "I am right, aren't I?"

If this woman had any idea about their differences, roadblocks to being more than friends . . . ! "I don't know. Maybe . . . I suppose so, but I have other important concerns — mules and getting my farm back, for instance. Not only that, he may not be in Kansas much longer. He plans to travel, paint landscapes out West and western folks at their occupations." She hesitated, burying a small ache in her heart. "I wouldn't want to be a problem contrary to his dreams. Nor, for the most part, would he, against mine, I'm sure," she added.

By that evening, the air had cooled a trifle, and Jocelyn, Whit, and his mother sat in the Gorham garden, surrounded by fragrant flowers. It came out in conversation that Jocelyn would stay on at Nickel Hill ranch as caretaker, as well as seeing to further mule herds between sales. Francina turned an incredulous stare from Whit to Jocelyn and back again. Whit patiently explained that he'd originally hired Sam Birdwhistle for that job, but he had had to return to Missouri and his family.

"But, Son, surely you can find someone else to do what is man's work! I agree that Jocelyn has a right to take whatever work she chooses. But — but this lovely young woman is suited to — to — Well, I admit there aren't many refined jobs available for women, but she — she could live here at Gorham House with me, as my companion and secretary. Yes!" she beamed, "That's the best answer, until she's ready to marry and have a fine husband to care for her. If not a fellow of her acquaintance already, a young Topeka bachelor; there are many in town. You do agree, don't you, dear?"

Jocelyn was thinking she'd have wonderful company and a beautiful place to live, but Francina's offer would do nothing to help her earn back her farm. *A woman could be "refined" — if that was so important — in whatever her situation, be it seamstress, school teacher, office holder, wife and mother, or mule tender!* As gently as possible, she reminded Francina of the homesteading women who had settled and built up their own farms in the past three or four decades. "Doing a fine job of it, too, those proud, independent women; they made good lives for themselves, their families, and their communities." Not without hardship, back-breaking labor, and endless patience, in some cases losing their minds, but no need to make much of that if she was to win this argument.

"Well," Francina said, "if you put it that way, I can understand. But you'll be out there on the prairie by yourself again, dear. Won't you be lonely?"

"I was a little, at first, but I'm making friends among the neighbors. I'll be fine at Nickel Hill ranch." Feeling confident, she leaned forward with a smile, making eye contact with Francina. "I'll come to see you here in Topeka, if you like, and you and Frye and Olympia are more than welcome to visit me at the ranch."

A tiny frown creased Francina's lovely brow, but she nodded slowly. "Thank you, dear."

Following breakfast early the next morning, Jocelyn chose to tell Frye good-bye first. The old dear seemed to understand, although his eyes watered in sadness when she kissed his forehead. She shook Mrs. Stewart's hand and then hugged Francina, who was still shaking her head, not completely convinced that Jocelyn on the ranch with mules and not charming a young bachelor in the city was the right and proper thing to be happening.

Whit Hanley drove Jocelyn, the new yellow, flower- and ribbon-trimmed hat topping her second-best outfit, to the train depot. "Are you sure about this, Jocelyn? Mother is partly right, you know, and you can still back out. I may be gone a month or even longer. I want the best mules I can find for my money, and it'll take time. When I have them, I hope to speed matters — ship our mules by train when there is money to pay for it."

He hesitated to hand her the large, blue satchel that was a gift from his mother. It contained, courtesy of Mrs. Stewart, a large bundle of KESA flyers, the red shawl holding her personal things, and other small items she'd bought, stuffed inside. "Are you sure?"

Around them was the usual clatter from gathering passengers, noises of the train, the oily smells of the tracks and depot, as well as smoke in the air from nearby industries.

Jocelyn gave him a direct look. "I'll say it again: I want this chance, and I won't be backing out. I'm indebted to you for the opportunity." Working with mules, whenever a comparison came to mind, was plumb high-brow work compared with slaving as a "dove," a saloon girl. Francina's suggestion that she be her secretary and land a young city bachelor had little appeal. She'd much rather marry a farmer or a rancher. She turned to Whit Hanley as she took the last step up to the passenger car. "You can expect everything to be in order when you come back to the ranch. I'll be ready for the next herd of mules."

He reached up and shook her hand. "Good luck, Jocelyn. I'm much obliged to you, for everything."

"The same to you, Mr. Hanley, and . . . be watchful for that outlaw you told me about, Carl Bramwell, if he's still out there. It'd be nice," she added, her jaw firming, "if someone else has already disposed of him."

"I have to agree." He nodded with a faint smile.

CHAPTER EIGHTEEN

"Well, then," Jocelyn concluded, nodding over her shoulder to Whit. Entering the passenger car for her trip back to Skiddy and the ranch, she quickly settled herself on the hard, uncomfortable seat. Beyond the window her boss — her partner — directed the horse and hired buggy away from the depot. He was such a target for the worst. God willing, it wouldn't happen. She liked Whitman Hanley, a lot more than earlier, when trying to get to know him on the drive, or during the months she'd been so angry that he'd left her at tether's end on the ranch. She admired his grit, his decency toward his mother, and his efforts to redeem his past. He was the kind of man who was earning a happy, successful life. He would have it, she believed, with his Claudia. Anyhow, she hoped so, very much.

Outside the train's windows, Topeka began to slide away. To pass the time for the next hour, she entertained herself by privately observing other passengers and guessing their occupation or role in life. Sunburned farmers in straw hat and overalls were easy guesses, as were farm wives in calico with a bonnet tied under the chin. She counted a drummer or two, in rumpled suits, sample cases at their feet. Four or five well-to-do ranchers, most of them in a grey or brown Stetson, western suit, and fancy boots, with their wives in the latest New York or Paris fashion. There were two young mothers with babies. A cowboy slept with his hat down over his eyes. He really didn't need spurs on a train, but there they were, strapped on his boots.

Watching the countryside from the train window, Jocelyn's thoughts moved on to her future. She was excited to be returning to Nickel Hill and the chance to earn money from the mules. Her friendship with Pete floundered, though. Would they part ways for good? Her chest hurt, just imagining it. She loved Pete, a fact she might as well face, little good that it'd do her.

Hours later, in Skiddy, Jocelyn went first to the bank and deposited her earnings. She headed next to the livery for her rig, anxious to be back at the ranch. She stepped into the livery stable's dim, somewhat cooler interior, and there was Pete, handsome and wearing a wide smile as he came toward her. Her heart picked up a familiar happy beat, but she hesitated, wondering where they stood in their friendship. Their unpleasant parting after he'd been hurt saddened her. Flustered, she talked fast, "Pete, I didn't expect to see you here. How are you? How's the shoulder, and your ribs?" Looking at him, Topeka's "fine young bachelors" went up in smoke.

"Doing fine, Jocey." He stopped and gave her a long look. "Bullet wound is healing right up. Ribs still a little sore." He held up a small sack he carried. "Came to town for liniment."

"That should help." She nodded.

He cleared his throat. "I saw your rig here in the livery barn and the hostler said he thought you'd be coming in on the train anytime. He said the owner of the Nickel Hill Ranch is back. You've been to Topeka?"

"Yes, to sell the mules and to do a trifle shopping." She set her new blue satchel at her feet.

"You look good, Jocey; that's a darn pretty hat on you."

"Thank you." A flush warmed her face. After a silence she shrugged and said, "It's time I headed for the ranch; no telling what's happened while I was away."

"Wait, please, just a minute." He removed his hat, showing the white of his forehead above his lower face bronzed from the sun, and bright blue eyes. "I don't think I've thanked you proper for saving my life that night, firing your shotgun and sending that guy hightailing. It took nerve, to come out there where we were about to kill one another. I could've bled to death, too, without you looking after me; I'm obliged for all that."

"You're welcome, Pete. Although, I'm still not convinced that fellow was there to make trouble. Even though it was well after dark when he came, I think he could have been at Nickel Hill to buy a mule, or even a team. But then you two tangled and went to fighting before there was much of a chance for talk." She stood with hands clasped in front her, her reticule dangling from one wrist. "That's how I see it."

"I think you may be right, Jocelyn, and I've got more about that to tell you. I'd like us to have a long palaver, about . . . things. I'd like to ride out with you to the ranch, if that's all right?"

"It'd be my pleasure to have your company." She smiled at him, grabbed her satchel, and hurried to hitch her team. Everything was going to be all right with them, then. Wasn't it? Suddenly she remembered the KESA flyers in her satchel. "I can't leave town just yet, Pete. I have some KESA literature to leave about town."

"Some what?"

Digging into her satchel, Jocelyn explained, "Information about the Kansas Equal Suffrage Association and an invitation to a rally meeting at my friend Francina Gorham's home in Topeka. She and her friend, Olympia Stewart, intend to interest as many women as possible to join the cause. At voting stations in November, they'd like women volunteers from around the state to pass out literature to men and ask for their support in submitting a national women's suffrage amendment. It's very important, Pete. We women here in Kansas now have the right to vote in school and civic affairs, but as much as men, we deserve a say in national matters, too.

"I'd need to study on it more, but if I had the right to vote this coming November, I believe I'd vote incumbent William McKinley for president. He's done a good job already bringing our country out of the depression. And who doesn't love Theodore Roosevelt? He'd make a fine vice president."

Pete looked at her for a long moment, appearing to come to some private conclusion. "Reckon I can help with that." He took a sheaf of papers from her hands. "Where do we start?"

"Main street businesses, first, then homes on the side streets."

"You don't want me to take them to the saloon, do you?"

"My goodness, yes, I want you to; many of the men in there are the sort we have to convince."

They went their separate ways with an agreement to meet back at the livery. More than an hour later she returned to find Pete already there out front, waiting with his horse, Raven, saddled and ready to go, a handful of papers still in hand.

She looked at him, eyebrows raised. "What happened?"

"Managed to give out a few of them. Two women in the hardware store shamed the owner into taking a flyer for his wife. They took several more to pass along to friends. The barber and his two customers each took one."

"We can be glad for that at least, Pete!"

"Yeah, well, but that's about as far as it went. Men in the saloon, including the barkeep, wanted nothing to do with me. The

268

more I tried to persuade them, the more they hurrahed me out the door." He sighed. "Liveryman said he was too busy to hear me out and wasn't interested, anyhow. By then I was riled plenty.

"I said, 'Listen here: women deserve the vote and why not? Most of the time they think smarter than men, are a better judge of human beings, and are more apt to be sober on election day. If that ain't enough, what is?' " He stroked Raven a moment, then told her, "I grabbed me a discarded horseshoe for a hammer, and a horseshoe nail, and I pounded the flyer to the wall by the livery door. The hostler agreed to leave it up there in his barn, when I said I could convince all my friends to go somewhere else for their livery business."

He handed her the remainder of his flyers.

"I appreciate what you were able to do, a lot, Pete. I had excellent luck." She beamed at him. "Mrs. Noack at the general store took most of my stack to keep on her counter and give to women shoppers. Managers at the hotel and café also took some. I walked around the neighborhood, leaving them with housewives who came to the door and listened to my speech. Some folks weren't home, or if they were didn't want to answer my knock. Regardless, I'm satisfied with this first attempt. I'll give the rest to neighbors, or anywhere else a chance pops up." She waved toward the interior of the livery. "I'll bring my team and wagon now."

The miles south from Skiddy passed quickly, and Nickel Hill was just ahead. Pete reined Raven closer to Jocelyn's wagon. "I was down to your place while you were gone, thought I might visit you."

"Was everything all right? Young Ned Hunter was there? I left him in charge, although there wasn't a lot for him to do, no livestock to tend with my mules waiting for me in Skiddy." Zenith and Alice had begun to slow, and she shook the lines and clicked her tongue for them to move faster. "C'mon, you two."

"Ned was there. He said he'd scythed the grass in front of your house for you. He shot a couple prairie chickens and cooked them. He saw a bobcat when he was out roaming the property, in a rocky area north some distance from your home place."

"My goodness! I'm sure he was excited. Eastern Kansas has plenty of bobcats, but we hardly see them. They disappear before a person has a chance to know they are there. A few times, I've come across a den they've left behind in rocks or a hollow log. The nest made mostly of grasses and leaves. Or I've seen tracks. Sounds like Ned kept busy."

"Yep, and mostly everything was jim-dandy. I caught the young feller sparking a neighbor girl who'd come to visit him. They didn't make me feel entirely welcome, and she didn't stay long after I came. Ned told me that they plan to marry sometime next spring." His eyes were lit with good humor. "Poor young swain. He had to watch her ride away all red-faced, on her little pinto pony."

"That'd be Molly Marie Kittredge, Clem Kittredge's granddaughter. She's a sweet girl, a nice girl."

A short while later they reached the home place, where Ned Hunter, a lanky, dark-haired young man, sat at the top of the stone corral and watched them approach. He jumped down into the powdery dust and came forward. "Howdy, Miss Royal." He nodded at Pete. "Howdy, again, Mr. Plad-son."

"Pete, call me Pete. Let me tie my horse, Jocelyn, and then I'll unhitch for you."

She smiled her appreciation and turned to look down at the young man. "Thanks so much, Ned, for taking care of things." She climbed from the wagon and reached back in for her satchel. "No problems while I was gone? Any visitors?" In the back of her mind she was thinking of Carl Bramwell, the outlaw who might still be trying to track down Whit Hanley.

"My sweetheart came by." Color flooded Ned's face. "But she didn't keep me from doing some chores for you. Scythed your front yard." He nodded in that direction. "Cleaned out the barn, although it looks like you do a good job of that regular, so it didn't take much, and Miss Royal, I saw a bobcat!"

"That's fine, Ned, and Pete tells me you have other good news. That you and Molly Marie plan to marry next spring. Congratulations."

"We're thinkin' on it, but her grandpa has dug in his heels against it . . . says we're too young."

Jocelyn gave his shoulder a pat. "Her grandpa will come around, wait and see. Clem Kittredge has a good heart, regardless that he tries to hide that fact. I wouldn't worry."

"I won't. And to answer your other question, there weren't no trouble. Quiet as a graveyard around here, save birdsong, grasshoppers' clacky tune, and a coyote yippin' an' howlin' of an evenin'. A couple men came by, stewin' that there wasn't mules here at Nickel Hill for them to buy. They were mad as he— heck that they hadn't been told about the sale in Topeka but claimed that was too far for them to go, anyhow."

"Maybe they'll come again when we do have mules here to sell." She touched his arm. "I brought you something; wait out here, and I'll go through my things. Be right back."

Moments later, she carried a somewhat battered but handsome brown Stetson to him while he stood transfixed in the yard. "It's yours." Jocelyn handed it to him. "Whit Hanley wanted you to have it for taking care of the ranch while we had to be away." She handed him three dollars as well. "The Stetson isn't exactly new; he won it in a card game and thought you'd like to have it. The story, which may or may not be fact, is that this Stetson once belonged to a famous outlaw, one of the gang of Daltons that caused so much trouble in Kansas and Missouri."

Ned's face lit up, and he gave a sharp whistle. He clapped the hat on his head. "Don't care if that's a windy about a Dalton; the hat fits right fine, Miss Royal!

Thank you, and thank Mr. Hanley."

"You're welcome. We were just happy to have someone we could trust to look out for the place. Glad you were here."

He started to turn away, then whipped back around. "Wait just a second . . . I near forgot somethin'. Mr. and Mrs. Webber come by. They bought an icebox at a farm sale. Since they already have one, Gordon and Tansy wanted you to have it, Miss Royal. We put it up at the house, on the back porch."

Jocelyn clapped her hand over her mouth in excitement and laughed. What an advantage, keeping food cold! *Iced tea.*

When the young man had gone, Jocelyn went up to the corrals to join Pete, with a glass of tea from the jug in the well for each of them. "It's good to be back," she told him as they walked down by the creek. "I don't know where I'd order ice on a hot day like this, but I'll find out where I can find some in the future."

"I can bring you ice," Pete told her. "The Carmans have us cowhands cutting ice half the winter when other work is slow. The 7Cs has a thick-walled icehouse filled with sawdust, where we bury the ice. Most saloons have ice stored in their basement. I'll just have to figure a way to keep it from melting on the way here."

"Don't worry if you can't; I'll manage to find ice someway." In the deepest shade along the creek they found a large, flat rock and sat down. "Pete, in Skiddy you were saying that you know more about that awful night you got beat up and shot. What've you found out?"

"As you know, I was there to make sure everything was all right for you," he said with a sheepish frown, "and, yeah, I fell asleep. But still, I'm glad that I *was* there. It may turn out, though, that I jumped the wrong fellow at the wrong time."

"Go ahead, and don't leave anything out; this does need clearing up."

"All right. Another cowhand who works with me on the 7Cs, Red Miller — you met him the fourth of July — told me that he was spending time in a saloon in White City, down that way visiting folks, when he overheard a man tell a bunch at the bar a story about aiming to buy mules. He'd read an article about them in the Council Grove newspaper. He was saying that it was a long day's ride to the ranch that had the mules so he didn't reach the place until near midnight. He figured it'd not bother anybody if he put up in the barn until daylight — though the folks owning the mules were strangers to him."

So far, Jocelyn had no doubt that Pete's story related to the newspaper article about her and Sam and their drive through Council Grove. "It makes sense to me that he'd want to do that. Sleep in the barn until morning."

Pete's good shoulder lifted in a shrug. "Well, yes, but if he'd bedded down out on the prairie and waited until morning to ride in, the rest likely wouldn't have happened, which of course changes nothing now." He scratched his jaw. "He was telling everybody in the saloon about being beat up, shot at, and having to shoot back for no good reason he could tell, except, by then, to hang onto his life for wanting to buy a mule."

"What did Red do? Did he say he knew all about it?"

"Red didn't say anything. He felt a little suspicious — something about the feller didn't set right; he didn't like his looks to start. When I asked if anyone else had anything to say about the story, he said they didn't. Mostly because a knuckle busting fight broke out with every man in the saloon itching to tangle. The battle started when two hotheaded cowhands argued that Kansas City women were prettier than women in Houston, or Billings, Montana. Doesn't take much for that to happen," Pete said with a sigh.

Seated on the rock, they stared at one another. Whatever the stranger's reason for being there that night, it had gone catawampus, he ending up with bruises and Pete with worse.

Jocelyn rubbed her arms, and her voice trembled slightly. "We're blessed lucky that one of you isn't dead and the other charged with murder. Anyhow, innocent or no, he hasn't come back. And, again, Pete," she struggled for the right words, "there's no need for you to hang around waiting for something terrible to happen." She debated telling him about the small weapon Whit insisted that she carry, then went ahead and told him. "But I doubt I'll ever have to use it, not that I'm not willing and able in a necessary situation."

He was shaking his head, and she stopped him, her chin lifted and giving him a direct look. "Really, Pete, for the most part, I can look out for myself." She shrugged. "I will admit the other possibility. Had 'our visitor' been here to kill somebody, one of us, or both, might not be alive having this talk." Tears welled behind her eyelids. "And Pete, whatever else happens, it does matter to me a lot, that you care the way you do."

"Well, with the mules' pardon, I can be a jackass, sometimes, and a blind fool. I care for you, Jocey . . . I'm finding out just how much . . ." He caught her hand in his.

Encouraged by the sincerity in his voice, and the feeling of her hand in his, she momentarily rested her cheek against his shoulder. *And I care for you, Pete, more than you can imagine.*

They sat in silence a while. Praying that it wouldn't spoil things, but feeling that he should know, the sooner the better, Jocelyn stirred from her comfort and told him about her plans with Whit, how successful the mule sale had been. "I'll stay on here at the ranch while Whit Hanley goes for another gather of mules to sell." Pete made a funny noise in his throat and stared down at her, a deep frown creasing his forehead. She kept her calm. "He considers us business partners; he already has a sweetheart. Her name is Claudia, a nice person he's known for a long time. There's nothing but mule business between the two of us."

"Jocelyn, I don't want to stir things up when we've just made peace, but do you honestly trust this Hanley person?" He was trying to be as careful as she meant to be, and she mentally thanked him for that.

"For a long while I didn't feel easy about

278

him, as I've said before. But that's changed as I've gotten to know more about him." She stood and turned to look at Pete, now sitting on the ground, arms propped back on the rock, legs crossed and looking up at her. She chewed her lip for a second. "His friend, Sam Birdwhistle, told me about when the two of them were younger, in their teens, and got into trouble with the law." She walked away a few steps and came back. "Whit Hanley, himself, told me all about a train robbery that failed, but he was arrested anyway for the attempt and other small crimes. He's spent time in jail." She clutched a fist and very carefully explained there was an outlaw who might still be after Whit Hanley, although two of the old gang had been dispensed with, and more than likely the third had given up the chase, deciding to avoid the same thing happening to him.

Pete's expression was darkening with each word, his mouth a tight line, but he didn't stop her from talking. Just waited.

"All that is over and done and in the past, Pete. Hanley's reformed, a good person, and, yes, I trust him. When we were in Topeka, I met his parents, and, sweet Hannah, but they're wonderful people. Whit got into mule trading to earn money his folks need badly to keep from being evicted from their home. And my working with him is the only chance I have to earn the money for my farm and what it will take to work it — plows, tools, livestock, all of that."

Pete stood up slowly, his voice tightly controlled. "I wish I could agree that it isn't a problem you're in cahoots with Hanley, but I'd be lying, Jocelyn. I've got suspicions that, as hard as he might try otherwise, he could still be putting you in danger. And I don't like it. I'd feel a whole lot better if someone else's skin than yours was threatened. You can hardly blame me for that."

"I don't blame you."

She would have said more, but he held up a hand, his eyes flinty. "It's what you want to do, so I won't fight you about it; I've done enough of that already. I can't deny, either, that the mule trade can be profitable and a godsend for you."

"Thank you, Pete." Relief washed over her, and she hugged him. "Thank you for your trust."

"It does make me feel better that Hanley is off somewhere else most of the time," he admitted, his arms slipping around her, "and not drawing trouble to you here." His gaze on her face grew intense. "I didn't mean this to happen, Jocey, but I more than care; I've fallen in love with you. These things happen to a person, I reckon, and I'm finding out there's no fighting it. Maybe it started way back when I brought you the cow and the fistful of flowers. For sure I know that from the time we met again at the rodeo, I'm thinking about you most of the time." His voice grew husky. "For a while, that scared me. I love you, Jocey; it's that simple. If it turns out Hanley is responsible for any hurt coming to you, *any*, he's going to be one sorry rooster." He gathered her closer in his arms, held her gently, then kissed her.

"Me, too, Pete," she told him quietly, when she could breathe. "I loved you so much for treating me the way you did when we were kids, and it seems I never stopped."

"But it's adult feelings now."

"Yes, we're not children." She grinned, reached up, and placed her arms around his neck. Closing her eyes, her mouth moved firmly to his. A dozen or so yards away, Zenith and then Alice began to bray for attention.

"Reckon my ol' Raven horse is about to come looking for me, too," Pete said. They laughed, moved apart, and walked toward the corrals.

"I'll be back," he said, putting his arm

across her shoulders as they walked, the shadowy figures of their animals taking shape ahead in the dim light, "soon as I can."

"Yes." She hugged him. "I would like that, Pete."

For the next few days, Jocelyn tended to chores on the ranch, cleaning the heat-caused scum from the tank so that Zenith and Alice had fresh water, digging out and burning some poisonous weeds from the pasture, as well as washing clothes and redding up the house with a busy broom.

All the while, thoughts of having her own farm back wouldn't leave her mind. Pete had teased about not wanting to be a farmer, but in time he could change his mind. If they married, they had to start somewhere. A farm, if you bought more and more property around you, could become a ranch and more fitting to his taste.

Decision made, she talked with neighbors, letting them know she was going on a short trip and would be gone for a few days. She'd be driving her wagon with Zenith and Alice, so there'd be no stock to feed and water in her absence. If they wanted to check the place while she was gone and they happened to be in the area, it would be nice, but they were not to feel obligated. And she'd do the same for them any time it became necessary.

There couldn't be a better time, she believed, to visit the bank in Council Grove and have a talk with the banker. She didn't have enough earnings yet to buy back her farm, but maybe she could arrange payments of some sort. She fixed enough food to last for her time on the road, loaded the wagon with extra grain for Zenith and Alice, and packed her things.

CHAPTER NINETEEN

Birds chirped to the breaking dawn when Jocelyn shook the lines over her mules' backs and her wagon rattled down the road away from Nickel Hill. Her excitement that she could ask the Council Grove banker about recovering her farm was almost more than she could contain. She let the mules trot while it was still cool, and she sang her heart out. The miles rolled away south through the Flint Hills, still green in deep summer. Cattle and horses grazed in pastures where tall grass ran away from the wind and occasional windmills churned. As she'd noted months earlier on the drive from Emporia, farmsteads were few — some working, others abandoned by the look of falling down fences and buildings.

As the long hours of the day wore on, the creaking of her wagon wheels, jingle of harness, and the soft plodding of her mules' hooves were the sole sounds accompanying her scattering thoughts. She drove with the lines in her lap, her mind considering that the bank *might* have sold her farm to someone else, or possibly had sold it more than once, other owners having mortgage difficulties and losing the place as happened to her.

It was easier to believe the bank still held the farm, and she hoped that turned out to be true. For most of the past decade, drought had made life difficult across the country. Kansas farmers and ranchers had had to turn to other trades, or their families would starve. She'd seen the evidence on the mule drive up from Emporia, and on the trips to and from Topeka: abandoned fields gone to useless thistle, houses with shutters banging in the wind, roofs partially missing due to violent storms and not replaced for lack of money. Not a soul around. Had that happened to her little farm?

Hour after hour she drove on, her stomach churning from concern as to what might have happened in the two and a half years since she'd had to give it up. There was no other way to find out than to do exactly what she was doing. Thinking that, she felt better.

At White City, she drove about town

distributing the last of her KESA flyers, losing less than a half hour from her trip to do so. Several hours and miles later, she decided it was best to stop for the night. Her mules could use the rest and a chance to graze.

She drove off the road along a grass-grown lane that led to an empty shack in a copse of trees. Meadowlarks sang from nearby bushes as she unhitched Zenith and Alice, and then prepared her supper. She placed a folded blanket on the ground and sat on it with her back against the wagon wheel, eating fried pork and biscuit, and contemplated her farm — how it would be of little account to many people, though not to her. Outbuildings were few and small except for the barn; there wasn't a lot of land, only eighty acres. The creek got low in the heat of late summer, with hardly enough water to keep the garden growing.

Heartened once again, considering the puniness of the property, she was convinced the bank still held it and deserved to be stuck with it! Waiting for her . . .

Crawling into her bed in the wagon, later, she fell asleep under the stars feeling sure it wouldn't be long until the farm was hers and she'd be building it up again.

The next day passed much like the first,

286

and it was hours after the bank had closed when she drove along the main street of Council Grove. Few people were about, with stores closed. The aroma of supper cooking filled the air. She quelled feelings of disappointment that she had to wait until morning to present her plan at the bank. At the far end of town, she left her mules and wagon at the livery stable for a twenty-five-cent charge and walked to the hotel. Fifty cents was a terrible extravagance for a room, and she sweated guilt, even though dinner was included in the hotel price.

Her room was simply furnished but pleasant enough, and she slept comfortably until an argument in the next room exploded in the middle of the night. First a woman's voice screeched that their window had to be closed. A man's voice bellowed in answer that the window would stay open or else. On and on the yelling, stomping, and crashing of furniture continued.

Jocelyn pulled a pillow over her head and kept it there until the argument wore down. It'd been such a racket she couldn't fathom who might have won. She guessed the woman had because that terrible screeching voice would make anyone give in, eventually. Or possibly the couple had been evicted by the hotel manager?

Wide awake by then, she tossed and turned, her mind returning to the reasons she was there. She wanted so much for her errand to end in her favor, easily, quickly.

For a long time, she stood at the window in her nightgown staring down at the dark street below, anxious for her meeting with the banker.

She waited in the early morning sunshine outside the Council Grove bank for an hour and entered the moment the doors were opened.

"Early, aren't you?" the unfamiliar gentleman banker said by way of greeting.

"I suppose I am, but I actually arrived in town last night."

"Important business, then; well, that's what we like." He beamed at her.

She'd hoped to discuss her situation with the grandfatherly but by-the-book banker she'd dealt with before. This man was younger, perhaps in his late forties, stout but handsome with a well-trimmed moustache and beard. He beckoned, and she followed him to his small, cramped office and took the chair he offered. She drew a deep breath and described the location of her farm near Bushong, in the Neosho River Valley, how she'd lost it, and that she wished to possess it again, on special terms if available. Finished, hands clasped tight in her lap, she lifted her chin, feeling hope, and waited.

The banker removed his glasses, rubbed his eyes, and shook his head. "I'm sure I know of the farm. It's southeast of here, a few miles from Bushong? I believe the property has new owners, but let me look it up in the files to be sure."

She waited, her heart pounding in her temples while he pawed through files in a deep drawer of his desk.

"Yes," he said, pulling out a sheaf of papers. "This property was a headache for us for several years, it appears." He shuffled the sheets of paper, his frown turning into a wide smile. "But it sold recently to a couple very interested in salvaging the farm." He slapped the desk with his open palm, his apologetic expression as fake as cardboard passing for oak. "Sorry, Miss, but, just as I thought, that farm isn't available for purchase."

He was waiting for her to leave, but she wasn't ready, not yet. *A headache?* The farm was no such thing to her when they took it from her! She started to speak, to tell him she'd very much like for him to let her know should the property come up for sale in the future, but he seemed to read her mind.

"I doubt there's any chance for that property to come back on the market for years and possibly not for generations. A fine young family bought the place, and, the price being low, they paid in cash. There's no mortgage on the farm. They were delighted to own it."

Jocelyn bit her lip until it hurt, every curse word she'd ever heard boiling for a release that good manners wouldn't allow. She felt her dreams, her plans, disappear like they'd been nothing. Her chest felt tight, and it was almost impossible to speak. Through a dry throat, fighting angry tears and deep disappointment, she asked, "Who bought it? Their name . . . who?"

He smiled genially, and she could have slapped him for his disinterest and uncaring tone. "That's not important, the property is theirs and that's that. I'm sorry, Miss, I really am. Unless you're interested in another property we can help you with, you'll have to excuse me."

She shook her head. "No other property."

His hand signaled her toward the door of the bank as he pushed back his chair and stood up. He turned his back and went to a tall cabinet against the wall.

He looked about as sorry as a hog in a

filled corn bin, Jocelyn thought, fighting the urge to pick up a large crystal paperweight from his desk and throw it at him. She was so outraged by the whole matter that her hair hurt. She hurtled from the bank blindly, untied her team at the rail, and clambered into the wagon. It was another eight miles to her old farm, but blessed if she was going to turn around, tail between her legs, and return to Nickel Hill. *Not yet!* She wanted to see her farm again, wanted to see these undeserving people who had it now. The farm was *hers;* it was always meant to be *hers.*

Her mind was in such a fog, she was barely aware of the passing miles and time — Zenith and Alice choosing their own pace — but she was there. Back on her old home ground, every tree and limestone fencepost, each dip and roll of land deeply familiar.

Jocelyn slowed the team, feeling her heart break as she studied her farm in the distance. She drove a few yards closer and halted her team and wagon. The mules' ears twitched and waited patiently at her quiet command. The entire property, the house and barn, the cows and horses grazing in the pasture, looked well taken care of, when she desperately wanted the opposite. In the yard, a young woman with a crown of blonde braids was hanging clothes to dry on the clothesline. Two towheaded young-sters, a boy about five and a little girl a couple of years younger, played tag nearby. In the barnyard, the wide-open doors of the barn framed a man, likely the woman's husband, shoeing a fine-looking bay horse. Jocelyn swallowed the lump swelling in her throat. They looked like nice folks, good people, happy to be where they were — her farm. Like the banker said, they could be here on her land for generations.

For a second or two, the woman at the clothesline peered back at her. Jocelyn was about to turn her mules and wagon when something about the young woman regis-tered as familiar. The woman had gone back to her work at the clothesline. Jocelyn sat in the wagon and mulled over the details skit-tering at the edge of her mind, remember-ing a pretty girl, blue-eyed, blonde, two years younger than she. *Anne Pladson.* The young woman dried her hands on her apron, lifted the small girl to her hip, and went inside the house, the screen door banging behind her.

There, spread for her to see, was Jocelyn's dream — the farm, the barn and fields, the husband and children. *But belonging to someone else.* To Pete's sister, and he hadn't told her. Through a blur of tears, Jocelyn turned her team and headed back the way she'd come.

Miles passed under the wheels of her wagon before Jocelyn could think rationally, and those thoughts were anything but encouraging. The ranch she headed back to was Whit Hanley's. If the mule trading business didn't turn out as planned, he would have to sell the Nickel Hill property to help his parents. If mule trading did succeed, at some point, he'd likely marry Claudia, and they'd take over the ranch.

She would be left with some money but not near enough to buy a place of her own. As far as possessions, she had a new hat and dresses, a handful of recently purchased personal items, and her red shawl of belongings. Not a whole lot better off than when she started.

Unable to pull her feelings from the mire of dejection in her heart, Jocelyn stared morosely at her mules' rear ends and tall, flopping ears and drove on, mile after mile without end, anger building at Pete. Surely, he knew that his sister, Anne, and her husband now owned the farm. Why hadn't he told her? They had lived there for some time; he must have known. Maybe if he'd told her it wouldn't have changed the way she was feeling now, hollow and lost, but still — a man should not keep such a secret from a close friend, someone he recently claimed to love. It was wrong!

Council Grove came and went. The eerie, green calm of the humid air she attributed to her mood of defeat, until the usual south wind stopped, and she was suddenly damp all over with perspiration. Shortly after came the first peal of thunder. She wiped her forehead on her arm and sat straight, eyes wide as if waking from a dismal dream. Traveling miles, she'd paid no attention to her surroundings, to anything other than the final loss of her farm and disappointment in Pete. In shock, she took in the huge, dark thunderheads towering above the horizon. A flicker of lightning rent the sky, followed by a rumble of thunder. For a second, she remembered Gram telling her, when Jocelyn was a tot, that the sound was a giant in the sky filling his bin of potatoes.

Coming alert, her skin clammy and her stomach tightened from fear, she took heed of nearby surroundings. She must reach shelter for her mules and herself, fast. Lightning killed; she'd heard of it happening to both people and animals too often to take the storm lightly. Up ahead, if she was correct, was the abandoned farm where she'd stayed the first night. She snapped the lines hard over her team's backs and shouted, "Hup, Zenith! Get up there, Alice!" They broke into a fast trot.

Lightning continued to flicker from cloud to cloud, and cloud to ground, followed by the crack of thunder, still some miles away, she thought, although it was hard to tell.

They reached the lane to the old house, and Jocelyn urged her team into a full run while lightning came in brilliant flashes and thunder rumbled louder, closer. "Ho," she said moments later, "easy now. Easy, Alice, easy Zenith. We're here." She drew them to a slowing halt beside the rickety house. A portion of the main wall had been blown away in the past, possibly by just such a storm as this one. Jocelyn jumped to the ground with lines in hand and brought her mules and wagon inside to the furthest depths of the house. After a moment, she grabbed some rotted burlap bags from a corner of a room and rubbed Zenith and Alice down until the bags fell apart in her hands.

Talking to these animals she loved, stroking them, they settled down. She dropped to sit with her back against the wall and wiped her teary eyes and runny nose. Her hands were filthy from the dirty bags; she was sure her face was, too. But at least they were out of the coming storm, somewhat safe, and would wait here until it was over.

Thunder crashed outside; rain sluiced down, making a racket; violent gusts of wind threatened to blow their shelter to smithereens. Hail pounded until Jocelyn was sure what was left of the old house couldn't possibly remain standing. Piling noisily around her were hailstones as large as chicken eggs falling through holes in the roof. After a few minutes, she picked up a hailstone and let it melt on her tongue, then another. "We're fine; we'll be okay," she told the shifting mules. She hummed soft tunes, and it calmed their uneasiness. Briefly she left the safety of her nest and returned from the wagon with handfuls of grain for them.

Although it seemed an eternity passed, as suddenly as it began, the storm ended. Blowing rain tapered to small drops. Rumbles of thunder came less often, quieter, and from farther and farther away. Jocelyn let her animals rest a bit longer, then slowly backed them from their shelter, into the sodden air, onto squishy ground.

It was still a long way back to the ranch, but if it took all night, she wanted to be there. "C'mon, Alice, Zenith — let's take the road."

After the storm, the horizon became beautiful streaks of orange and crimson against the blue and grey, the air was fresh, and the Flint Hills were washed and shining. Jocelyn's thoughts returned to the scene at her old farm. She swiped an arm across her eyes and lifted her chin. Tears were taking her nowhere. She'd figure things out, someway. Maybe she could buy a mule from Whit eventually, buy herself a plow, and hire out as a farm worker. There had to be something . . . somewhere she could put down her red shawl and stay. But how? Where?

CHAPTER TWENTY

After several hours, the moon had climbed high overhead, the night was clear as day, and the road was easy to follow. When it wasn't, she let Zenith and Alice make the judgment while she wearily dozed, the lines wrapped around her wrist.

Jocelyn was barely awake when they arrived at the ranch near dawn, scarcely aware of the shadowy, familiar figure that bolted out of the darkness of her porch to follow her team and wagon up the rise. She drew to a halt between the corral and barn. Every bone in her body ached as she climbed down from the wagon.

"Jocey, in the name of God, have you been driving all night?" Pete's husky, worry-laden voice asked from behind her. "I've been waiting, wondering where I should go looking for you next." He sounded haunted. "I was so afraid something bad had happened to you. Are you all right?" He took her arm.

"I've been to *hell*," she said dully, backing away from him, "and you're partly to blame, Pete Pladson!"

He stopped suddenly. "What'd I do that's got you so sideways?" That he sounded honestly perplexed stirred her anger more. He stared at her in the dim light, hands lifted defensively in the air.

"I'll tell you what you did wrong! You knew that your sister, Anne, and her family had my old place, and you didn't bother to tell me. How could you do that, Pete? Didn't you realize that I'd find out?" She started to unhitch the team; he moved her aside to take over.

He looked at her over his shoulder as he worked. "How could I tell you when you weren't here? You didn't let me know you were going anywhere. I come to see you and was worried sick until your neighbors told me you went off to Council Grove to have a talk at the bank. I didn't know you planned to do that."

"I don't have to tell you everything." She followed in the bleak dawn as he led Zenith and Alice into the corral. "It was my business, and I made the decision to go to Council Grove and the bank pretty sudden, anyhow." She spoke bitingly, "How long have you known that I'd have no chance to buy back my property? You've certainly not said anything about it, and, for all I know, you knew all along."

"I just found out about it! I swear, Jocelyn. I'd written to Mor a couple weeks back to tell her you and I'd met again. And I wrote that I was losing a lot of the itch to head on down the road, follow my dream as an artist — that the idea of making you my wife was topping everything I'd been thinking. I don't write letters, hardly at all, and don't see my family as often as I should, and my mother has a choice opinion about that. Mor wrote back, and in her answer she said that Anne and her husband, Lars, had bought the property that once belonged to you and your Gram. She thought it'd make you happy to know that, but I knew it'd break your heart. I was trying to figure a way to tell you, let you down as easy as possible." He checked to make sure there was water in the tank and tossed hay to the mules.

"Trying to protect me as usual, I suppose? Good job!" She stomped along after him. "Well, I don't need you. Don't need anyone." She stubbornly fought tears that ached behind her eyes.

"Sure, I was hoping to protect you, Jocey. Those times I came to check on you? I finally realized that I also just wanted to be with you. Be with you the rest of my life, I realize now. I love you to pieces and wouldn't hurt you for anything. I know how hard you've worked, how much you wanted your farm back, how much the place will always mean to you."

She stood still, awash in guilt, his words sinking in as the lump swelled in her throat. She'd known even before she'd railed at him that really none of this was his doing. But in her anger and near unbearable, heavy disappointment, it felt so necessary to punish someone, anyone. She told him, honestly, "I'm sorry, Pete, for taking out my misery on you. You do understand?"

"Yes, I do. Now, why don't you come here and let me hold you?"

Faster than lightning she was in his arms. "I was too late, Pete." Her voice caught on a sob. "Too late. I'll never have my farm."

"Honey, oh, honey, I'm sorry." He scooped her up in his arms and carried her down to the house, opened the back door, and carried her inside, holding her tight against him. He kicked the door closed behind him.

In dim moonlight through the kitchen window, Pete scratched a match, lit the lamp on the kitchen table, and moved it closer to where she sat. He removed his blue neckerchief, knelt, and wiped her eyes. "Now, tell me all about it."

In a thickened voice, she choked out what had happened, how angry she was with the banker, who showed no true sympathy when he gave her the bad news. She whispered how beautiful the farm looked with his family there. And, to top it off, the horrible storm coming home, as though even nature had it in for her.

He asked with a twisted grin, squatted on his heels, "Can't do a lot about the storm, it's long over, but would you like me to shoot that cussed banker?"

"I would like it but no, not really." She shook her head and wiped tears from her cheeks with the heel of her palm. "He was doing his job, selling my property." She sighed heavily. "I really can't blame him. This is hard to say, but I'm glad that Anne and her family have the property. I can't hold them at fault, either."

He held her hand. "The last I knew before I got Mor's letter, Anne and Lars and their young'uns were living with the folks. That they'd want a farm of their own isn't a surprise, though. Do you know how long they've had it? My mother didn't say."

"The banker said it'd sold 'recently,' but

by that he could mean months ago, a year or two. The property looked like they'd done a lot to fix it up, plant crops. They have livestock, a couple of horses — maybe more — and cows." She looked aside and said quietly, "I'm happy for them, really."

"To tell the truth, I am, too. Happy for them but sorry as hell it turned out this way for you." He lifted her to her feet and held her for a moment. "I want to take care of you, Jocelyn," he said against her hair.

"I know. And I want to take care of you. Number one, I'd want you to continue painting, whatever else we might do. It'd hurt me as much as you, if you ever gave that up. Art is part of you."

He nestled her chin in his hand, his voice deeply serious as he told her, "The way I love you, Jocey, will last forever, I guarantee you that."

"Exactly how I feel about you, Pete. No one has ever mattered to me as much as you." Her eyes blinked from want of sleep as she rested against him.

"We have to do something about it. Be married."

"Yes, I want to, very much." Then her voice came in soft warning against his chest. "Pete, if we have children, they could turn out to have the same affliction I was born with, my freak mouth. Would you mind, if that happened? There is a chance, I think, that surgery could be done right away."

"Hell, Jocey," he said in a choked voice, "that doesn't matter. You'll have your babies, and, whatever happens, we'll be there together seeing it through . . . loving the dickens out of them. Now then," he kissed her ear, "you need some sleep, and I better head on back to the 7Cs before the sun's full up, or I'm like to be fired." He sighed. "Sure don't want to go, though."

"I know, I don't want you to go, either." Without warning, her mouth suddenly opened in a gaping yawn. Horrified, she clapped a hand over her mouth. "Pardon me, for heaven's sake."

He laughed and kissed her. "It's all right. You have nice, pretty teeth. 'Bye, wife to be. Now go to bed. Any more troubles can wait their turn."

A few days after Jocelyn's return to the ranch, Mrs. Goody came by with a gift of eggs, milk, and a small bottle of vanilla extract. "You make the best custard pies, Jocelyn. Maybe you'll make two, one for me and one for you?"

"Sure, I will. For now, let's sit on the porch. I'll bring some iced tea." She took a moment to show Mrs. Goody her new icebox, complete with a half-melted chunk of ice Pete had brought. She put the eggs and milk on a shelf inside.

"Mercy, me, that's a cryin' shame!" Mrs. Goody said in response to Jocelyn's story about her trip to Council Grove, and then on to her old farm. "Sometimes life is just meaner than a basket of rattlers. Not fair to you, anyhow, Jocelyn. What're you going to do now?"

"Stay on here at Nickel Hill until my boss, Whit Hanley, comes back with another herd of mules to sell. I'm still responsible for the two mules out there in the pasture, and it's my job to take care of this place, besides the fact I promised Mr. Hanley I'd be part of his mule trading business at least for a while. After that, I don't know. I'm guessing he may have to sell Nickel Hill eventually, or, if his business goes well, he may marry and move back here himself. Soon, possibly."

"What about that boy, Pete, been coming around every once in a while? Aren't you two close to marrying and starting a new life together of your own?"

Jocelyn's face warmed. She couldn't help a wide smile. "He's asked, and I told him yes. Although," she held up a hand, "I had

305

to tell Pete the wedding will be after Mr. Hanley and I sell the next batch of mules. I've got a promise to Hanley I intend to keep, and I won't mind having a little more money in my pocket, too."

"Before you put on that white dress and say 'I do,' " Mrs. Goody said, nodding, a cheery smile on her ruddy face.

"Yes."

Jocelyn sat there, remembering Pete's words: *"Right now I'm just a forty-dollar-a-month cowboy, living in a bunkhouse with fifteen other cowhands. But I'm going to find a way to do better than that. I love you way past reason, and I always will. If you were willing, I'd say let's find a preacher to marry us tomorrow, figure out the details of living after that. But I understand why you want to wait until you've finished up your agreement with this Hanley gent, and I figure I'm damn lucky you've gone so far as to say yes to marrying me whenever we can make it happen."*

Thankfully, Pete had accepted her plan and set about one of his own — to find a job as a ranch foreman. Often a ranch foreman's job came with a house, a garden spot, a place to bring up children — plus a chance to raise his own livestock, as well as earn a higher salary. All of which would be a fair life if he found the job. She believed it

306

would happen.

Her mind came back to the present, with the realization that Mrs. Goody was talking about happenings while she'd been away.

". . . Indeedy, it was quite a party over to the Truscott ranch. Oh, the good food, Jocelyn . . . you can't imagine. The lemon meringue pie! I nearly ate myself sick. We had parlor games and, after that, dancing. Neighbors from miles around were there, having a good old time. Visiting, too, because there's so much work to do in summer, we don't have many chances to get together, you know? Everybody was well acquainted with everybody else . . . well, except for one fella, nobody knew who he was. He looked kind of shaggy-no-account, but he didn't do any harm, just seemed to enjoy watching couples dance while he ate a plate of food. By the last dance, he was gone. I looked to see your Pete, there, but he didn't come. Sitting alone up at the 7Cs, pining for your return, I imagine." She giggled.

"Oh, I'm sure of it." Jocelyn chuckled along with her.

Typically, the story of Jocelyn's most recent hardship, loss of the chance to buy her old farm, traveled fast from neighbor to neighbor over many miles, no doubt with

Mrs. Goody's help and maybe Pete's, too. She appreciated the kindness, the sympathy from her neighbors, but she was receiving more company, more invitations to dances and parties than she really needed or wanted. She didn't have the heart to right out refuse invitations, unless she had a good reason like a broken leg, or a sick mule — neither of which took place. The one blessing in those next weeks was that she often found herself dancing in Pete's arms at one gathering or another. Each time they were together, and just as often when they weren't, she was wanting more than dances, more than innocent kisses, impatient for their life together as man and wife to begin.

Pete had a line on an excellent job as foreman on a ranch near the town of Newton. He'd be taking over as soon as the present foreman moved on in a month or two. To celebrate, Pete invited Jocelyn to supper at the 7Cs Ranch.

Adella and Daniel Carman were a middle-aged couple, both tall, angular, sunbaked, and very fond of Pete. "We're going to miss you, Pete, so much," Mrs. Carman said, passing him the platter of steak. "Wish you didn't have to leave us, but we understand. Nice young woman like Miss Royal, you want to give her all you can. I have a good feelin' that the two of you'll do right fine."

Daniel Carman, weathered brown hands taking up knife and fork, agreed. He told Jocelyn, accenting with a shake of the fork, "Pete is one of the best hands we've ever had. We'd make him foreman here on the 7Cs if the job wasn't already filled right capable."

Later, outdoors, Jocelyn was introduced to Pete's friends, a group of cowboys squatting on their heels in the yard out front of the bunkhouse, talking and smoking following their own supper. One of them, named Jim Brown, puffed out his chest, lifted his chin, and grinned at the pair. "You showed that picture to her yet, Pete?"

"Hell's fire, Jim, you're spoilin' the surprise," another cowboy, round-faced, short, and plump, reprimanded. "Ya gotta give Pete a chance, ya know."

"What picture?" Jocelyn turned to Pete, a little surprised to see a flush under his darkly tanned face.

"I'll show you" — he took her elbow — "if these mouthy yayhoos will move out of our way so we can go in the bunkhouse."

Ribald snickers and insinuations followed Pete's words rapid fire, until he glared at each cowboy. "Apologize to the lady," he snapped.

Shamefaced, but still struggling not to laugh or say something that could further offend Pete, each man of them soberly apologized to Jocelyn, tipping their hat again as they'd done when they were introduced. She fought a smile, nodded, and with Pete's hand at the back of her waist, she entered the bunkhouse. It was clearly the domain of males, with rows of cots clumsily made up and odors of sweat and tobacco stale in the air. There were decks of cards on the long table, and, hanging from hooks on the walls, male clothing, rope, bridles, and more.

It was Pete's turn to apologize. "I realize now I shouldn't have brought you in here. Seeing this room through your eyes says for sure it's not a place for a lady. But I wanted to show you something in private." He appeared slightly nervous, not the norm for Pete.

Appearing at the bunkhouse window to the right of them was a grinning freckled face. Pete waved his arm and shouted, "Would you leave us the hell alone, Red!"

"My bunk," he said, motioning to her. "Sit there for a minute." He stooped and pulled a long, flat, wood box out from below the bed. Carefully, he lifted a large envelope from among his belongings and opened it.

"Look here." He handed her a thin magazine. "The cover," he said, pointing.

She stared wide-eyed, her hand going to her heart. "Me, and my mules," she said in wonder. Her breath caught, and she choked out, "For the love of sweet Hannah, Pete! When . . . when did you do this? I didn't know. It's — it's truly wonderful; not me, exactly, but your work, so well done it could be a photograph from a camera." She traced her forefinger lightly over the ranch magazine's cover and repeated, "Me, and my mules." She looked at him as tears spanged into her eyes. She had no more words to explain how happy he made her, how truly good he was as an artist. She threw her arms around him and kissed the daylights out of him. If the cowboys outside wanted to pester, so be it.

Pete was the first to speak minutes later. "I got paid a pretty penny for that cover," he said with a soft, humble cough. "The magazine folks liked it a whole bunch and want more. I see no reason why we can't start planning for our wedding day."

"We can plan, yes." Excitement quickened her heartbeat.

Whit Hanley could show up with more mules tomorrow, maybe, or the day after that. She wondered just how many times

311

she'd had that thought, and then had to wait and wait some more. She crossed her fingers. *Let it be soon.*

"Hello the house? Miss Royal, are you home?" The woman's voice calling from out front of the house wasn't one Jocelyn recognized. She'd been redding up the kitchen and now put aside the broom to hurry to the front door. She walked to the edge of the porch and didn't recognize the young woman. A slender blonde in a green suit climbed from a buggy — which Jocelyn could see had come from the Skiddy livery stable. The young woman stood looking around, a frown on her attractive face.

"I'm Jocelyn Royal. How can I help you?" The wind blew her hair in her face, and she brushed it back.

Her visitor undid the tie-rope from the horse's harness and wrapped it around a porch post. "May I come in? I'm Claudia, Claudia McKnight, a friend of Whitman Hanley's . . . actually, more than a friend — we plan to marry."

CHAPTER TWENTY-ONE

"Of course, please do." Jocelyn motioned for Claudia to come inside. She flushed, suddenly conscious of the spare and rustic furnishings of the front room. This young woman was surely used to something more in the nature of Francina Gorham's mansion. "May I bring you some iced tea?"

"Yes, please." Her voice was strained. "It's been quite a train journey from Topeka, and driving here from Skiddy — goodness, what a name for a small town — to Whit's ranch." After a moment's hesitation, she removed her hat, a wide-brimmed, lavish froth of ivory tulle and tiny blue rosettes. She settled on the buggy-seat sofa with her hat in her lap, her ivory reticule beside her.

Jocelyn returned with the iced tea. Eyes clouded with worry, Claudia looked up and asked, "Is Whit here on the ranch, by any chance? If so, could you call him please, let him know I'm here and must talk to him right away?" She eyed Jocelyn with a look of desperate hope and took a quick sip from her glass.

"I'm sorry, no, he isn't." Jocelyn sat and took up her own tea. "He hasn't been here since we took the first mule herd to the Topeka sale, and he left from there to buy up a second herd. I haven't had any word from him since. Have you?"

Drawing a deep breath, the other young woman said, "I received two brief letters telling me about his buying prospects in Missouri. He was doing well, had found some fine mules at reasonable cost. He was due back a week or so ago, and I'm beginning to worry." Her serious expression deepened. "But that's only one reason why I've come. I have sad news for him from his mother, and I'd hoped to tell him in person." Her hand shook as she put the tea down. "You can't know how much I wanted to find him here."

Uneasiness crept over Jocelyn. She'd lifted her glass but found that she had no interest in her tea. What sad news? She put the glass down on the crate that served as a table. Whit's stepfather was anything but well; had he worsened? Her voice was subdued. "May I ask, is this about Frye, his stepfather?"

Claudia nodded and said quietly, "He's

gone, Miss Royal. The dear soul passed away yesterday afternoon."

Jocelyn pressed her fist against her chest and the gathering sadness there. She'd only just met the Gorhams and now . . . She drew a breath. "I'm so, so sorry for Francina. How is she?" *Whit would want to be with her.*

"For someone as fragile as Francina, she's surprisingly strong when one wouldn't expect it. As she is now." Tears glimmered in Claudia's eyes. "Frye died peacefully in Francina's arms. He was her real love, you know, and of course she'll miss him dearly. At the same time, she's thankful that he died at home, at Gorham House."

"I knew she wanted that very much for him." Jocelyn stated more than questioned, "Frye, Mr. Gorham, was in poor health, wasn't he?"

"Very poor, actually. He'd been bothered with the dementia, but lately he started failing fast, his heart, and kidneys. I suppose you can say that it was his time, and he didn't suffer long." She sighed. "I so wish Whit was here. Mrs. Stewart is a great help, but Francina needs her son. She'd like for Whitman to be at her side at the funeral service."

"Of course . . . I understand. I wish I

knew what was keeping him." Jocelyn's fist clenched as dark thoughts filled her mind. She asked Claudia, softly, "Had he mentioned anything else in his letters? Had anyone made trouble for him about anything other than buying mules?"

There was Carl Bramwell, and his evil intent to destroy Whit. Just bringing to mind what could've happened turned Jocelyn cold, her knees to clabber. How she'd like to make the remaining outlaw disappear, with nobody else hurt, or killed. It was terrible how some people could hold a grudge for a lifetime. This instance unfortunately held terrible danger for Whit, for who knew how long? She doubted that Claudia knew of the matter, but perhaps she did. And should Jocelyn tell her if she didn't know?

Her guest was saying, "Did he mention problems? Not really. Whit had written that he talked to others about the mule trade in Oklahoma, or possibly Texas, but after studying the matter, he learned that folks down that way were more in the market to buy than sell." She chewed her lip and briefly looked away as though seeking answers. "I don't think he'd add more time to this trip without sending me another letter to say where he was going and that it would be longer before he'd return. I pray that he's not laid up somewhere, hurt, and unable to write." She removed a handkerchief from her crocheted reticule and wiped her eyes. "Mother and I are planning the wedding, and I so wish Whit would not be gone for so long. I'd like for him to share in the plans. The two of us should be going to Frye's funeral together and looking after Francina."

For a minute or two, both women were silent. Jocelyn felt desperate to help, without knowing what she could do. "Miss Mc-Knight — Claudia — if there's anything I can help with, I want to know, please. I'm thinking you must be hungry. I can fix you some toast and a boiled egg if you like? Or a slice of raisin cream pie?"

A small whisper of a smile touched her lips. "Thank you, no. I couldn't eat a bite. The tea has been very refreshing, though." She stood up and brought the empty glass to Jocelyn. "What you can do is tell Whit, the minute he arrives here, to hurry on to Topeka and his mother — to me, too, of course, but first to Francina. Tell him, please, about Frye's passing. I'm afraid there's nothing more you can do, Miss Royal — Jocelyn — until Whit shows up."

Recognizing that Claudia was preparing to leave, Jocelyn told her, "Please don't go just yet. Really, Claudia, you could use some rest before making the trip home." She stood and touched her arm. "I'll fix us supper. Please spend the night and leave tomorrow."

Claudia shook her head and surprised Jocelyn with a hug. "You're very kind to offer, Jocelyn. It's nice meeting you, and I hope we meet again. But I must head back to Skiddy now and catch the late afternoon train to Topeka. I work with my father at his publishing business, and I need to be there."

With arms folded, Jocelyn followed Claudia to the door. "Give Francina my sympathy, please, and my love. Tell her I'll send Whit to her the moment he appears. Tell Mrs. Stewart hello for me, too. I'm so glad she's there with Francina." She opened the door and stood with her hand high on the frame.

"They are both strong women." Claudia turned again to Jocelyn. "Their rally, just before Frye's passing, was a whopping success, gaining many new members, and they much appreciated your contribution, Jocelyn. Francina and Whit admire you greatly, for your courage and strength. Taking on the mule drive to earn back the farm you lost, caring for the mules and the ranch."

Jocelyn frowned, embarrassed at the

praise, and shook her head. Her hand dropped from the door frame. "I'm an ordinary woman doing what I have to do, is all. Not near as much as some who've been in worse straits than me. One more thing, though, Claudia: in his letters did Whit mention how he'd make the return trip? Was he going to drive the mule herd back or maybe take the train?"

"I'm fairly certain he was going to drive them. I recall him writing that this time he'd be bringing a smaller herd, maybe only fifteen mules that he could drive without help. He mentioned that a good deal could come up along the way, a chance to sell a mule or two, which wouldn't happen from the train. I understood he would take the same route the two of you and Whitman's friend, Sam, made before."

Jocelyn ticked off the route in her mind: *after the pair crossed the border from Missouri into Kansas they followed the Neosho River northward through the little towns of McCune, Erie, Iola, LeRoy, and Burlington to Emporia, where she had joined them.*

After Emporia, they stayed on the river trail past Americus, Dunlap, Council Grove, White City, and to Nickel Hill ranch northwest of Skiddy. "He would follow that same route, then?" Jocelyn wanted to be sure.

"I'm positive." Claudia hesitated on the porch and caught Jocelyn's hand. "I'm glad we've met, but I'm sorry I had to bring the sad news about Frye Gorham and put more of my worry about Whit on your shoulders. Thank you for the tea. Perhaps on another day you can join me in Topeka, when we're not faced with such worrisome matters."

Jocelyn watched Claudia's buggy heading at a fast, dusty clip back toward Skiddy. She whispered, "You're strong, too, Claudia McKnight, putting up with the likes of Whitman Hanley. But I don't blame you; he's a good man, with admirable intentions toward his mother, plus doing what all he can to compensate for mistakes of his past." They were both lucky women, considering the men who loved them; if there just weren't so many tangles to undo before they could move forward in their lives.

There was one tangle she was about to unravel straight off. She was going to go look for Whit Hanley and his mule herd. He had to be on his way back. There was nothing stopping her from making a search for him — no tasks of great importance for her at Nickel Hill, other than taking care of the house and small chores that could wait. Her two mules would be with her pulling the wagon. She hoped to Hannah she wouldn't have to search all the way into Missouri. Jocelyn began to grab up a few provisions, including a filled water jug and a rolled blanket just in case she'd be bedding down somewhere.

Wherever he was, Whit might need help. He could be close and could use a hand bringing the mules in. Too, this was a different bunch of mules, and she wasn't with him, nor was Sam Birdwhistle. Whit might have been kicked by a mean, contrary-minded mule and was down somewhere along the trail, with a broken leg, or worse. It would be foolish of her to twiddle her thumbs here at Nickel Hill, letting time slip by while her heart chilled with worry.

Jocelyn was well on her way, driving south through White City, when a familiar voice called her name. She whirled to look. In the doorway of a small, blue and white café, with a large sign overhead — All You Can Eat STEAK DINNER Fifty Cents — was Pete. Her heart made a happy leap, quickly quelled by the knowledge that, sure as anything, he would be put out by what she was doing . . . would try to stop her. Red Miller was close on Pete's heels. She drew Zenith and Alice over to the hitch rail planted along the dusty plank sidewalk and pasted on a quick, bright smile. "What are you two doing here?" Beating Pete before he could ask the same of her.

"Our boss sent us down to look at some horses in Lyon County that he might want to buy. Stopped to eat. What brings you this way, Jocelyn?" His sandy-brown eyebrows tented, then smoothed. "Don't you usually do your shopping in Skiddy? 'Course, White City has a few more stores, might have things you can't find in Skiddy?" He waited, grinning. Reflected in his eyes was the joy she was feeling as she ran her eyes over him.

He had to understand. She itched to lie, to tell him that she was here to shop, or was just out for a drive, sightseeing. He'd not believe that windy, so she decided on the truth, keeping it simple. "I'm backtracking the trail Whit Hanley would take bringing mules to Nickel Hill ranch." She took a deep breath. "He should have been back by now, and I'm seeing if he needs my help bringing the mules in."

"That's all there is to it? You're looking a little strange, Jocey. I have a feeling you're suspecting trouble and are heading right on into it. Why don't you wait for him to come on his own?" Her explanation had him scowling suspiciously up at her, hat tipped back and hands on his hips.

"I can't sit by and wait, not this time; it's important I find him." She avoided a direct look at Pete. Not for a second was she going to let him stop her. When she looked at him again, he looked as calm as a shady tree.

"All right then, I'll go with you." He spoke over his shoulder to his friend, Red. "Bring our horses from the livery, will you?" He climbed into the wagon next to Jocelyn. "Now, sweetheart, tell me what all this is about?"

God Bless America but he had the best of her, again.

CHAPTER TWENTY-TWO

Jocelyn's shoulders sagged, and she licked her lips. Lord knew, it was useless to try and fool Pete. On top of that, he deserved to know the importance of her mission. She turned to him on the wagon seat beside her. "Claudia McKnight, the woman Whit is going to marry, came to see me. She had sad news for him, but she's also worried because he's overdue in Topeka for their wedding plans. He should have been back to Nickel Hill with this second roundup of mules, readying them for a sale."

"Maybe business is keeping him longer? Or," Pete's brow furrowed deeper, "it could be this outlaw you told me about has met up with Hanley finally, made trouble?"

Her throat went dry. Pete had hit on her deepest concern. "I think that's one possibility of what could've happened, but I'm hoping that's not the case, that it'll be some problem with the drive itself. I've also wondered if Whit might've been kicked by a mule and is having trouble that way — mules can be cantankerous if something goes sideways to what they want." She wished now that she'd brought the medicine box.

"Yeah, they can be, like when that little sorrel mule kicked Rufe Tuttle's brains out and put an end to his criminal shenanigans, stopped his attempt to kill you."

"You understand then?" Jocelyn asked, feeling anything but sure. They'd made such a beautiful truce, after the fracas over him not telling her that his sister now had her farm. Behind the squint of his blue eyes and set jaw, she could almost see rebellious thoughts tumbling and churning in his mind.

"Yes, I understand why you'd worry. But I don't like the idea of you going on this search, and when I think it over further, I don't see the need of you going at all. Let Red and me take care of this for you. We are going that way, anyhow. We'll keep a lookout for him and the mules, make sure he's okay. You can go on back to Nickel Hill where you'll be safe."

"I can't," she said determinedly, her heartbeat growing louder in her ears, "not until I find him. I have bad news for him, and it's important to me that I tell him in person."

"What's this bad news?" His eyes bored into her. "Does it have to do with the outlaw looking for him?" He shook his head and slapped his hat against his knee, giving her team a start. "For damn sure I'm not letting you go on if that's it."

"No," she shook her head, "that isn't what I have to tell him. Whit Hanley's stepfather has died. Whit's mother needs him, wants him to know about the funeral, and to be there with her."

"I can tell him that, if I run into him." He nodded. "I'll likely recognize him if he's got mules with him."

"I'm telling him myself, when I find him. I owe Whit Hanley that and more." She sat stiffly. "This is not the same as telling somebody a bull jumped a fence and got in with somebody else's cow herd, or that there's a sale on new shirts at the mercantile."

Pete snorted. "Dammit, Jocey, are you going to be this stubborn after we're married?"

"Probably. I wouldn't count on it to be otherwise." *Might as well be truthful, plus she loved the word "married."*

He snugged his arm around her shoulders and kissed her ear. "That does it then; we're all going, Red and me to make sure there's no trouble. You can give this gent the message, and we'll mind your back." Miller had ridden up, slouched in the saddle of his bay horse and leading Pete's black gelding. Pete jumped from the wagon and swung astride Raven.

She put up one last argument. "Blame it, Pete! This could be nothing. You have your own work to do."

He ignored her, rode around the back of the wagon, and reined up beside her. "Let's go."

She wanted to argue further, but his burning eyes said that she'd best keep her mouth shut. Anyhow, it did feel better to have him along.

Driving her wagon and team along the Neosho river cattle trail backward from the time before, Jocelyn saw all the familiar sights. The same copses of trees, pastures of longhorn cattle, windmills turning next to a small ranch house, sometimes a barely visible town in the distance, but no sign of Whit Hanley and a herd of mules.

Guilt sat heavily on her shoulders that this could turn out to be a wild goose chase, taking Pete and his friend from their job, but it was their idea to join her, not hers. If they got fired over it, they could only blame themselves. At times, as they rode some yards away, she could hear their voices in conversation, but couldn't make out what they said. Likely they were jawing about stubborn women, but she didn't care.

That night she pulled her mules and wagon to a halt in a sycamore grove. The two men rode in and staked out their horses. Little was said as they made camp, Red finding an armful of sticks and limbs to make a cook-fire, Pete slicing potatoes to fry in a skillet of sizzling salt pork. Her own provisions consisted of leftover biscuits, cooked side meat, and a handful of plums from a neighbor. The fragrance of frying potatoes and the men's boiling coffee made her mouth water. All told, it was a very good meal, and Jocelyn began to feel better about everything.

Later, she prepared her bed in the wagon. She crept some distance away into some bushes and did her business. When she got back to camp, the two men were sitting by the campfire, talking in low voices. Too restless to sleep, she joined them. Pete poured her a cup of coffee.

"Thank you. Do you mind if I ask what you've been talking about?" Whatever it was would be welcomed, providing it wasn't to make her return to Nickel Hill before she was ready.

"Pondering quite a few things," Pete told her. "Like maybe we aren't going to find a thing, your friend Whit Hanley off safe as a baby in a cradle somewhere."

"I didn't want you to come, Pete. What you say could be true. I understood that he'd be driving the mules the same way we came before. In the end, he may have bought more mules than he expected to and sent the whole batch off to Skiddy on the train, or straight to Topeka for a sale. I don't know." She tossed the remainder of the strong, bitter coffee from her cup into a patch of grass. "Or, he could be waiting out a sale still in Missouri, where he believes he'll buy mules at a bargain price."

"Yep," Red threw in, "it could be any of them things or a half-dozen others." He lay back on his elbows.

"I want to look a bit further," Jocelyn told them. "I'm not going back just yet in any regard."

They grunted without comment, other than to say good night a short while later.

When she was ready to leave camp next morning, they were right beside her. They followed the river for a couple of hours. The air was humid. Buzzing flies and gnats stuck to the backs of their hands and faces and pestered Jocelyn's mules and the men's horses. "I don't think we're going to find anything," Jocelyn said when they halted to talk it over one more time. She wiped an arm across her forehead. "You men should go ahead and check on those horses for sale, like your boss told you to do."

"And you'll go on back to Nickel Hill, then, too, Jocelyn?" Pete's voice was raspy, and a touch sarcastic.

This time she was set to lie and tell him, yes, that was her plan. She'd let them go; she'd drive off toward Skiddy and the ranch. When they were well along on their way, she'd turn around and continue her quest until she found Whit. Or didn't. But she couldn't waste more of Pete and Red's time.

It was in that moment she saw something move down by the river ahead, in a clump of trees. "Wait," she said quietly, "isn't that a mule in those oak trees, down by the river?" She nodded with her head and pointed.

"It's a mule," Pete agreed. "In fact, it is two mules, see, coming out into the clearing."

Jocelyn's heart thundered. She urged her team to follow as Pete and Red set their horses into a trot. When they reached the two mules they'd spotted, there were three more.

"Damn suspicious," Miller said, looking around.

Pete and Jocelyn both nodded agreement. She said, her skin tingling with alarm, "Let's keep looking, this could be Whit's herd, or part of it."

They'd gone a short distance when they rounded a bend in the river. A man in tattered overalls and a boy seven or eight years old and raggedy as the man peered at something on the ground. A few yards away four mules grazed.

The farmer ignored the men and hurried to Jocelyn's wagon, holding up his hand. "Ought to stop right there, Miss."

"What is it?" The knot in Jocelyn's stomach tightened. She began to feel sick.

"A shootout, looks like. Don't think you want to come any closer. When me and my boys heard shots thisaway, we come to see. Hid ourselves a purty long while until we decided the shootin' was for sure over and we wouldn't be the ones kilt." He waved an arm. "One feller is up here on top of the bank, shot dead. Another one is down to the river. Think he's dead, too; at any rate he's been shot up plenty, blood all over him. Must of been a hell of a set-to, grass trampled and blood spattered durn near ever'where you look."

"Jocelyn, stay back!" Pete ordered, his face grim. "Let us take care of this."

She couldn't and followed on foot the minute they dismounted to investigate.

The first body lay facedown, a gun still where he'd dropped it, under the curled fingers of his left hand.

"The other one?" Pete questioned.

In the same moment, a few feet away, Jocelyn, with a shaking hand, picked up Whit's black hat from the trampled, blood-spattered ground.

"Down there by the water." The farmer pointed to the body of a man almost hidden in a tangle of weeds by the river's edge. "Figger he lived a while and crawled down there to drink." He fidgeted, his eyes wide with delayed shock. "I sent my older boy for the county sheriff; he oughtta be here any minute."

Whit lay on his back by the river, his shirt and vest blood soaked where he'd been shot in the chest. "B-boss!" Jocelyn's voice caught. She dropped beside him and felt his bloody throat for a pulse. It seemed she felt something under her fingers; she waited, pressed again, lightly. "He's still alive! I can feel his pulse, but barely." She swallowed hard. "We need a doctor, right away!"

"Doctor'll be comin', too, I reckon." The farmer's voice was shaky and thin. "I told my boy to bring 'em both, in case they both was needed, doctor and sheriff."

"Thank God!" Jocelyn said. She tore off her jacket and gently pillowed it under Whit's head. "What can we do?" she implored Pete. "He's nearly bled to death."

Pete's eyes told her little could be done, but he said grimly, "A sip of whiskey might help with the pain, revive him some. Red, you have a bottle in your saddlebag — bring it, will you?"

Shortly, a half-dozen other men on horseback had joined them, locals brought by the older son's frantic story, along with the unexplainable sight of mules straying into surrounding pastures. One of them led a saddled, riderless blue roan that Jocelyn recognized as Whit's. Heaven only knew where the other man's mount had gotten off to.

Jocelyn moved Whit's head to her lap and touched his lips with the bottle of whiskey, tipped it slightly, and saw the brown liquid trickle away down his jaw and off his chin. He was so still, his face ghostly white under a thick growth of dark whiskers. She handed the bottle to Pete, who squatted next to her, and felt again for Whit's pulse. "I — I can't find it," she choked.

"Let me," Pete said. His tan fingers pressed lightly and stayed there as seconds ticked away like a lifetime. "Jocey, honey, let me take him. Come away. He's dead."

"No!" she cried, when Pete moved Whit's still form away from her. "No, he can't be. We have to do something." On her knees, she whirled on Pete, fists clenched, and rocked back and forth. "Whit didn't deserve to be killed; he was trying so hard to change his life. He was a good man! He was!" Muscles jumped under her skin; she felt cold as ice; her mind screamed for release from all that was wrong. "No!" She struck Pete's chest as he lifted her to her feet. Her legs were water. His arms tightened. "Oh, Pete," her voice caught on a sob as she clutched at him. She buried her face in his shirtfront, sobs tearing her apart.

"You're right, darlin', he didn't deserve this. I'm sorry for you, that it had to happen, and that you had to find him this way."

"His poor mother, Francina," she said, trembling. "She lost her husband, only a few days past, and now her son. So unfair." She mopped her face, looked past Pete's shoulder, and saw what she thought was slight movement from the body higher on the bank. She tore away from Pete and raced to where the man's fingers grasped the gun and lifted it, wobbling, in the air. Jocelyn booted the glinting steel from his hand, sending the gun into the air to land several feet away in the grass.

Fury boiling inside, she had drawn her booted foot back to kick the would-be shooter to bloody pieces when Pete grabbed her. He held her struggling body tight. "Don't, hon. No need. Calm down now. The sheriff's here." His strong arms pulled her away. Red Miller took her other arm.

"Damn," Red said, "she stopped him from killing somebody else. You got a good eye, Miss Royal. And a right smart kick, too."

The gunman who'd killed Whit Hanley had been turned over on his back. His deep chest rose and fell as he took a few final breaths, and stilled. He was a beefy man, stringy hair almost to his shoulders with a tobacco stained beard and thick hair on the backs of his hands.

She stared down at him, rigid with hatred, her fists clenched.

Red Miller, still hanging onto Jocelyn, leaned over the body for a closer look. "I'll be damned, it's *him!*" He released Jocelyn's arm and whirled to face Pete. "Sure wish I'd known it at the time. This lowdown rot-

335

ter is the man I was telling you about!"

"Who do you mean? What man?" Pete, with his arm around her waist, pulled Jocelyn back from the bloody scene, while the sheriff searched the grass and recovered the gun she'd kicked away.

"Hell!" Red barked a hollow, disbelieving laugh. "The one I heard talking in the saloon, his story fittin' yours. You know, about when you tangled in the dark, Pete, at Hanley's ranch. He wounded you. Miss Royal blasted away with a shotgun, and he got out of there, lickety fire."

Jocelyn's knees turned to water, and she couldn't move as Red's words sunk in. Her voice was hoarse. "If this man here is the one you fought off, Pete, then he wasn't somebody come to Nickel Hill to buy mules, as we thought might be."

Carl Bramwell. With that realization, she breathed deep, her body stiffened, and she stood with feet apart, her arms tightly folded over her waist.

Bitterness filled her voice. "That's Carl Bramwell's dead body, unless somebody can show me different. He was at Nickel Hill to kill my boss, Whit Hanley, not for mules."

Goosebumps prickled her arms as her mind ran on. Likely Bramwell had never left the area after the altercation with Pete but was always somewhere close, waiting and watching for an advantage to kill Whit, to silence him as well as have revenge. Once she had a better description of the stranger who came to the dance at Truscott's ranch, when she was down to Council Grove and the bank, she was sure every lick of likeness would fit this bloody scoundrel on the ground. Bramwell no doubt had skulked around Nickel Hill while she was away, in a fury to find no one on the place. Still on a prowl to kill, the coward had likely expected to find Whit at the dance, to shoot him.

Her vision blurred, and her heart beat heavily. Here by the Neosho with his second herd of mules that he'd hoped to sell to help his parents, and no doubt to start married life with Claudia, Whit Hanley's luck had run out. So damnably unfair!

She became aware of the sheriff, talking to them.

"I'll be a son-of-a-gun if you all ain't right!" the sheriff, a gaunt, middle-aged man with a moustache, was saying as he knelt on one knee by the body. He pushed his hat back and looked up at Red, clearing his throat. "A Wanted poster came to the office a short while back, from the law down in Henry County, Missouri. They'd heard Rufe Tuttle had met his maker up here and thought this feller, Carl Bramwell, might show up in Kansas, too. I'll let 'em know we have the body. That'll be good news to them." He spat a brown stream into the grass and wiped his mouth. There was a short silence.

"Bramwell murdered an old hermit in the woods," the sheriff continued, "who'd found dynamite and a charger that Bramwell's gang meant to use in a train robbery. Wasn't long after that he knifed a woman to death for refusing him into her house to cook a meal for him. Her husband survived what Bramwell did to him, but barely. Carl Bramwell was wanted for near a hundred crimes; he was evil."

The sheriff rose and began to take accounts from everyone there, beginning with the farmer and his two boys, though no one had witnessed the actual shooting. Jocelyn moved slowly to her wagon, climbing up to sit and wait her turn. The doctor, also a coroner, had pronounced both men dead and was instructing men to wrap Whitman Hanley's body and take it to the doctor's buggy.

The outlaw's body was loaded into a rancher's wagon, separately, under the sheriff's direction.

Jocelyn, feeling numb, watched Red Miller, Pete, and a group of other men round up the scattered mules. They'd also found a second saddled, riderless horse, likely Bramwell's.

After she'd told the sheriff her story, he found evidence in Whit's things that he owned the mules and she was in his employ. Pete motioned her to slide over so he could take the driver's seat in her wagon. In a swift move he was beside her, palm out for her to give him the lines. He waved at Red, mounted on his horse and leading Raven. He turned to Jocelyn. "Sheriff asked the fellers who came to see what was going on to help us get the mule herd on to the ranch." He nodded toward the riders, led by Red, pushing the mules toward the road. "He said you ought not to be driving alone, and I agreed. I'm taking you home, honey; there's nothing more we can do here."

"But the horses you and Red were to look into — ?"

"That can wait. I'll explain to my boss what happened after I get you back to Nickel Hill. He'll understand."

"I don't know what's going to happen, now, Pete." She'd never felt so haunted, so empty.

"I know, I know." His blue eyes were on her in solemn concern. "But let's worry about that later."

Sitting beside Pete as he clicked and shook the lines over the backs of her mule team, Jocelyn watched the doctor's buggy pull out onto the trail with Whit Hanley's body. "It shouldn't have come to this," she whispered, a roiling pain under her breast. "He helped me so much, and he was good. I wish I'd killed Carl Bramwell myself. I would've killed him twice if I could've."

Pete put an arm around her shoulder and told her quietly, "You helped, Jocey, darlin', pure fact. When you booted that sidewinding scum's gun hand, it almost took his hand off at the wrist. You helped send the sumbitch into the far beyond like he deserved." He kissed the tears from her cheek. "Pardon my swearing."

CHAPTER TWENTY-THREE

"I'm sorry I couldn't be here for Mr. Gorham's service," Jocelyn murmured to Francina. How hard it must be to lose both a husband and a son in such a short space of time. "I would have so liked to have been." They sat together in a front pew along with Olympia Stewart, and Claudia with her parents. Lilies and yellow roses banked Whit's coffin at the front of the church. The heavy fragrance of the flowers mingled with the almost palpable feelings of sadness and pain in the room.

Francina patted Jocelyn's hand and whispered, "You're here now, dear, for Whitman's funeral, and I thank you for that." She added, with a catch in her soft, sad voice, "You were trying to find my son, to help him, at the time of Frye's service, and that means more to me than I can say."

Jocelyn would have told her how much she wished they'd found him sooner, but the organ had stilled, and the preacher was taking his position at the front of the church, candles behind him glowing softly.

"In the Lord's infinite wisdom . . ." the minister began solemnly. And Jocelyn listened with chin up, in her heart saying good-bye to Frye Gorham, but also thinking of her father's passing, her mother's, and Gram's. She wiped at her tears.

Following the minister's lengthy sermon came the singing of several hymns, then a long prayer followed by more singing, and the funeral was over. Person after person came forward, showing their respect for Francina and Frye with kindly words of sympathy and offers to help her in any way she desired.

Jocelyn stayed for a while at the reception in the church's basement, meeting many of Francina and Frye's friends. After quickly downing cake and punch, she prepared to say her good-byes to Francina, Mrs. Stewart, and the McKnights.

Young Ned Hunter was at Nickel Hill looking after the new herd of mules until her return. His father, Jess, who had his own concerns on the Hunter farm, could use his son's help, and she didn't want to keep Ned away any longer than necessary.

Claudia was awash with grief and quiet

tears when Jocelyn hugged her. "I'm so sorry," she told Claudia. "I'd give my soul to have found him in time."

"Y— you did what you could." Claudia wiped her eyes with a delicate handkerchief and shook her head. "You were a good friend to Whitman. He valued the fact that you overlooked his past and trusted him. Not everyone did . . ." She glanced toward her parents, a handsome, friendly-faced couple, and finished, ". . . until they took time to know Whit for who he really is — was."

"You'll come see me again, soon?" Francina said when Jocelyn took the frail little woman into her arms, the two saying good-bye.

"Yes. I'll have the mules ready for the next sale in a few weeks, and I'll be coming to visit you then." Pete and his friend Red Miller would be helping with both the drive to Topeka and the sale. She had taken the train to Topeka to be here in time for Whit's funeral and had hired a rig to drive to the church and back to the train depot for the return trip to Skiddy. It had depleted her cache considerably, but she wouldn't have given a thought to doing otherwise.

Mrs. Stewart had waited her turn to tell Jocelyn good-bye, and now she clutched her

343

to her bosom. "You are a sweet girl, Miss Jocelyn Royal. Francina considers you a dear friend, practically a daughter, and I do, too. Don't be a stranger; come see us any time you're able to be in Topeka."

"Thank you, Olympia, I promise that I will." She couldn't imagine that would be often, other than her trip to sell Whit's last herd of mules, but time and circumstances would tell.

Six weeks later, longer than Jocelyn had intended, she was back in Topeka at Johnson and Gibb's Auction Barn, grateful for Pete and Red Miller's help. Again, she insisted on showing each mule in the auction ring herself. When it was finished, she heaved a deep sigh of relief. She had a very good sum to turn over to Francina and couldn't help feeling proud of the accomplishment, her last task for Whitman Hanley, her onetime boss and friend.

Pete and Red delivered her to Gorham house. Red reckoned he'd stay with the rig, but Pete came inside with her. Jocelyn introduced him first to Olympia Stewart, who came to the door, and minutes later to Francina in a half empty parlor. To Jocelyn's astonishment, Whit's mother was surrounded by packing crates and trunks.

344

After a few words of greeting, she clasped Francina's hands. "You've had to sell Gorham House? You're leaving? I'm so sorry!" She felt sick to her stomach. Poor Francina. *This third enormous loss; how much could she take?!*

"Come sit down, dear, and let me tell you what's come about." Whit's mother led the way to a sofa, one of the few pieces of furniture left in the room.

Jocelyn's heart literally ached for her friend, and she blurted out, more than anxious to share even a trifle of good news, but hating that it hadn't been in time to rescue Gorham House, "We got topnotch prices for the mules today." She fumbled with her bag, took out a thick sheaf of bills, and put them in Francina's hands. "There. I wish it was much more. It's so wrong that you've had to sell to the Friends of Topeka Government so they could hand over your beautiful home to the governor."

Francina smiled. "I didn't sell Gorham House to be the governor's mansion. In fact, the Topeka government group chose the other house they were considering and bought it."

"But how . . . why — ?" Jocelyn looked around at the half empty room. "You still lost your house and must move?" She was so glad she could offer at least the mule money.

"My choice, Jocelyn." Despite the deepened lines of sadness in her face, her eyes showed a brief glimmer. "I sold Gorham House to a nice well-to-do family from Ohio. They paid me sixty thousand dollars, compared to the Friends of Topeka Government's offer of twenty-seven thousand."

Francina chuckled softly when Jocelyn covered her mouth in surprise and added, "I know it's uncouth to discuss money, but isn't it fun?" She counted the bills Jocelyn had given her and handed half of them back to Jocelyn. "This is yours; you were Whitman's partner."

Jocelyn managed to choke out a weak, "Thank you."

"Olympia and I," Francina was saying, "faced the fact that in our autumn years we really don't want all the work it takes to care for Gorham House. We're ready to enjoy a simpler life, and we've found a wonderful, smaller house three streets over near a lovely park and can't wait to start a new adventure."

"I'm glad for that, but if you'd wanted to stay, you could have sold the Nickel Hill ranch." Francina still could, if she didn't like the little house and changed her mind.

"That was Whitman's, and he really didn't care much for the property, it having come to him from a father he — well, whom he hated for his cruelty to me, and to Whitman. I have plans for Nickel Hill, Jocelyn dear — a proposition for you. I'd like for you to stay on there and run the ranch. I'm decently well off at this point, to be honest if not shy about it," she said with a small, quirky smile. "I'd like to stock the ranch with whatever livestock you choose — horses and cattle, or mules. You can pay me a small share of ranch profits if you like, although that's not a condition of my offer."

Jocelyn looked at Pete, who was looking at her trying to appear serious while his mouth twitched with a grin.

Francina caught the exchange and said, "When the two of you marry, you'll be operating the ranch together, and with your children as they arrive."

"This is too good of you, Francina. You don't need to do this —"

"I'm not finished, dear Jocelyn. Whitman was my only child. Now," her lip quivered, "he's gone. I have no one to leave the ranch to, and I want you to have it, when I pass. You've already been written into my will."

Jocelyn stared, disbelief crowding her ears.

"This is all too much, too soon, Mrs. Gorham," she said, finding her voice through a dry throat. "No," she shook her head firmly. "I'm very grateful to you for feeling this way, but you need to give yourself more time to think what you want to do and be sure about your decisions."

Francina held up her hand, "My dear girl, *time* is one thing I don't have a lot of, and I've thought all this out very, very carefully. The ranch doesn't interest me, to tell the truth, and I have no one else to leave it to. I'd give it to Olympia, but she doesn't want it, or need it."

"Claudia? She would have been Whit's wife; shouldn't the ranch be hers?" Jocelyn's heart pounded out of control when Francina shook her head, no. How could any of this be true?

"Claudia's family is quite well to do; she is a popular Topeka 'debutante.' I have no doubt she loved Whitman very much, but when she recovers from this loss, Claudia will be fine."

Olympia, who'd been very quiet from where she sat, finally spoke. "Francina knows exactly what she's doing; I'm witness to that. You can make her happy, Jocelyn, by accepting her offer."

Francina nodded agreement. "This is

what I want more than anything. You will make an old woman happy, won't you, Jocelyn? And you, Mr. Pladson, or should I call you Pete?"

"Pete," he said, "just Pete." He sat back, his eyes on Jocelyn, his open expression clearly leaving the decision to her.

She smiled at him and, after a thoughtful silence, answered Francina's question. "Yes, to our operating the Nickel Hill ranch. Your help in stocking the ranch will be a dream come true, Francina. We will do our best to make it profitable and will insist on your having a share."

"It's settled then." Francina caught Jocelyn in a hug, then went to Pete, on his feet for her hug. She continued, "I know Whitman would have wanted this. Thank you, you two dears, for agreeing. I might add a codicil to my plans, though, to the effect that for the remainder of my years your children will be as my grandchildren."

Of course, Jocelyn thought, happy tears threatening. She swallowed. "It will be our honor, our pleasure, Francina."

As they were leaving, Jocelyn hesitated on the porch, shaking her head. "I feel like I'm in a dream, Pete." She covered her mouth, her eyes going wide as a new thought came to her. She caught his arm. "I'm wearing

349

my new outfit" — she brushed her hand down the light yellow shirtwaist and black silk skirt — "and you are your usual spiffed up self. What do you say to our finding a preacher and tying the knot while we're here in Topeka? Today?" She looked at him, eyes shining, a smile quirking at her mouth.

"Are you serious, Jocey? Do you really want to do that?"

"Absolutely, Pete. We have a ranch to run together; we ought to be married from the start. Can you think of any good reason to put it off longer?"

"Don't you want a fancy wedding with a lot of folderol?" He studied her for a long moment, hands on his hips, and wearing a questioning grin. "You've made so many friends from the ranches around Skiddy."

"So? We'll throw a whopping party for the neighbors later. I do want to do this, very much, Pete."

They caught hands and ran to the waiting rig to tell Red. He war-whooped loud enough to bring Francina's neighbors to their mansions' fine windows on both sides of the tree-lined brick street, and he shouted, "I'm your best man, right, Pete?"

"Hell if you ain't, Red!" he whooped back, with a booming laugh.

Jocelyn was turning back for Gorham

House's front door. "Let's don't leave yet. I want to find out if Francina and Olympia would like to come with us. If they're willing, they can be my attendants." She smiled wide. "Matron of honor and bridesmaid."

ABOUT THE AUTHOR

Irene Bennett Brown is an award-winning author who enjoys using Kansas, where she was born, as background for her historical novels. Previous to her nine novels for adults, Brown authored nine young adult novels. They include *Before the Lark,* winner of the Western Writers of America Spur Award, nomination for the Mark Twain Award, and other honors. *Miss Royal's Mules* is the adult sequel to *Before the Lark.*

She lives with her husband, Bob, a retired research chemist, on two fruitful acres along the Santiam River in Oregon. Visit her website at http://www.irenebennettbrown .net.

The employees of Thorndike Press hope you have enjoyed this Large Print book. All our Thorndike, Wheeler, and Kennebec Large Print titles are designed for easy reading, and all our books are made to last. Other Thorndike Press Large Print books are available at your library, through selected bookstores, or directly from us.

For information about titles, please call:
(800) 223-1244

or visit our Web site at:
http://gale.com/thorndike

To share your comments, please write:
Publisher
Thorndike Press
10 Water St., Suite 310
Waterville, ME 04901